The Heart of the Phoenix

ANNALEE ADAMS

THE HEART OF THE PHOENIX

First edition. October 2022.
Copyright © 2022 Annalee Adams.

The moral rights of the author have been asserted.
Written by Annalee Adams.
This is a work of fiction. Similarities to real people, places, or events are entirely coincidental.
All rights reserved.

No part of this publication may be reproduced, transmitted, or stored in a retrieval system in any form or by any other means, without prior written permission from the author, Annalee Adams. No part of this publication may be circulated in any form of binding or cover than that which it is published in.

ISBN: 979-8-77-3895985

This book has been typeset in Garamond.
www.AnnaleeAdams.biz

For every person seeking the truth,
I see you.

CHAPTER ONE

The first sentence should capture you.

This doesn't. Why the hell am I writing about cupcakes when there's a sadistic serial killer out there?

I slammed the laptop screen down with gritted teeth, spun around on my chair and stared out of the window. Drawing in a slow, steady breath, I eased myself back into the chair. Five floors up, and I could see a good portion of London from here.

I became lost in the beauty of the sunset. Fire danced across the evening sky. The vibrancy of colours blended, like a kaleidoscope of magical realism.

It's getting late. I need to get home at some point today. Huffing, I spun back, opened up the laptop and started again. Before me, the essence of my life was digitised as a blank page; the start, and the end, of an unwritten article.

Cupcakes, captivation and corruption. That was the whole epilogue of the piece. Except there wasn't any corruption. No dire need for a spectacular journalist with a nose for the truth. There was nothing to write about. Only cupcakes, and they were dull at best.

The day had taken its toll. It started great when the alarm didn't go off. I huffed, rolling my eyes. *Okay, so I forgot to set it again.* I missed my shower, the not-so-subtle smell of sweat now infiltrated my blouse. Then Maisy shat all over the kitchen floor, which would put anyone off their breakfast. It's not my fault I forgot her favourite kibbles. I groaned. *So maybe it is.* She was cute, but damn, she was annoying! My tardiness meant I missed my usual subway ride to work, and everything went downhill from there.

I stared at the blank page. I hadn't finished Gerard's article, let alone started it, and I was too damn tired to even see straight. Since when did I believe being an assistant journalist was a good idea?

Drumming my fingertips over the mahogany desk, I groaned; I have no idea how I bagged this job. At twenty-two, I was not long out of university, and I'd scored the job of a lifetime: an assistant journalist. I mean, who does that? At twenty-two? My lips creased. Okay, so it helps that the big boss is friends with my best mates' parents. It's not about how good you are, it's about who you know in this business.

I sat staring at my laptop. The white of the page taunted me. My fingers tensed, gripping the desk. Nope, can't do it. Pushing away, the swivel chair spun me around. I yawned. I need substance. Where's the vending machine around here?

Putting my heels back on, I stood up, catching a flash of my reflection in the floor-to-ceiling windows. Rose red hair, pale skin, and an ass that most would consider an asset. I considered it too big for my body. I found this out last week when I attempted to cycle to work. By some miracle, I didn't swallow the seat on the journey. I smirked.

There's one thing I can say for sure; Lola has excellent taste in clothes. Lola is my number one. My best mate. She picked out most of my wardrobe. Today's ensemble included knitted grey trousers with a cream frill blouse, complementing my stunning hair. I can say it's stunning. As for me, it's the best part about me. I stretched, clearly sat for too long.

Heading out of my office — yes, that's right; I had my own damn office. I mean, eek! — I walked over to Lola's office three doors down. We met at university, roomed together back then too. She was a mean bitch at first, but after a few drunken tantrums and a weekend of bonding, we realised we were both as messed up as each other. Been best mates ever since.

I smiled as I walked in. Lola's office is an oak lover's nightmare. Every aspect of the room had been redesigned in modern plastics and flamboyant coloured glass. She even had room for a ragtag patchwork sofa, similar to the one we'd had back at university. Her head was down as she glided a pen across the graphics tablet. I laughed. She looked so small for such an enormous desk!

She looked up. "What?"

I smirked. "Your desk is way too big for your short arse."

Lola pursed her lips. "Oh, honey, you're just jealous of my greatness."

I chuckled, sitting down on the sofa. Lola was short compared to my 5f-feet 9-inches of greatness.

"So, how's your day going?" she asked.

"Rubbish; I'm stuck and need snacks." She coughed out a laugh. "Where's the vending machines around here?"

She laughed. "Julia Jones, I swear I could hear your stomach rumble before you even entered my office."

"Ha, so funny. So, where are the delicious goodies then?"

"How about we go out for dinner?"

"Err, no I'm good. Your type of dinners involve a tiny salad with a gallon of margaritas."

She smirked. "And the problem is?"

I shrugged and laughed. "Normally I'd be all up for the margaritas, but I can't… I've got to finish that puff piece on the Cupcake Queen."

"The who?"

"Oh, some woman who makes cupcakes." I shrugged. "I bet they're not half as good as what my Aunt Clara used to make."

Lola laughed. "Well, have fun with that… oh, and the vending machines are by Jayden's office."

"Shit. Really?"

She nodded. "Why don't you go say hi while you're there?"

"No, he's an ass."

"He's your boss with a spectacular ass." She smirked.

"Oh fine. I'll wave as I walk by," I groaned.

She waved sarcastically as I walked out, giving her the

middle finger. God, I love that girl.

She was right. Three vending machines were lined up outside Jayden's office. I peeked inside. He was there at his desk, head down. Jayden isn't really my boss, although I'm sure he wants to be. He delights in his seniority as a fully-fledged journalist. Plus, he has Gerrard in his back pocket.

Sneaking past, I faced the first machine with my back to his office. Gerrard is a great boss though; he rarely bothers us, and only ever stresses if we miss a deadline. Besides that, we are free to come and go as we please. I smiled, staring at the yummy goodness inside the machine. Licking my lips, I put in the first coin. The machine rattled and groaned.

Behind me, the office door creaked. I turned as Jayden tapped me on the shoulder.

"Can you do it?" he asked, standing shoulder to shoulder with me. His dark blond hair curtaining his deep brown eyes.

"Yes. I'm good, thanks."

"Okay." He paused. "How's the cupcake article going?"

"Slow," I said. Then winced. I really needed to think before I spoke.

"Why?"

I sighed. "It's boring. It's about cupcakes after all. There's got to be more to London than cupcakes."

He laughed, "Oh there is. The London Butcher for one." I shuddered. Now that really was a story! He stood, watching me. "If you're ready for more, I can ask Gerrard to send him your way." He smirked. My brow furrowed. Was he trying to be nice to me?

"Err, I'd rather not have the Butcher heading my way."

Jayden laughed, then sighed. "He's killed more girls than I can count in the last year."

I nodded, knowing full well how many he murdered. The Butcher was the one piece I'd been secretly working on.

"Well, I believe Gerrard wanted to settle you in slowly."

"Slowly… It's been three months."

He smirked. "Three months of you avoiding me and these machines."

I feigned a smile. "Well, what can I say? I caved today."

He smirked. "I'm glad you did."

He watched as I pressed the buttons on the machine. It started moving, then ground to a halt, my Cheetah bar jammed, trapped behind the coiled mechanism.

"Damn."

He grinned, watching me. "Step back," he said.

I nodded, taking a step backwards.

Jayden jumped forward, knocking the machine back and forth, releasing the Cheetah bar and three other goodies. My eyes widened. "Thanks," I said, smiling.

"No problem." He grinned. Maybe he wasn't as bad as Lola made out. I grabbed the snack food and turned to walk away.

"So, when were you going to show me your research?" he shouted after me.

I stopped dead, face flushed. How did he know?

"How about you turn that research into real journalism?"

I turned to face him. "What?"

"You're working on the Butcher from now on."

"But what about Gerrard?"

"Send him the Cupcake piece, then get to work on catching the killer."

My eyes widened as fear choked me. "I, err, okay," I spluttered.

He smirked. "Good luck, Julia Jones," he said as he walked back into his office. I jumped in glee, fist bumping the air. Then nausea hit. I realised my name would be all over the psycho killers' articles. Would I be a target? I took a deep breath, shaking it off.

Jayden had been at the *Chronicle* for almost seven years, according to Lola. Journalism hadn't been easy on him. He had an avid group of fans on social media, but twice as much hate mail than the average serial killer; apparently reporting the news meant we condoned the violent world we lived in.

I sighed and walked into my office. Even with hate mail, I still feel I will make a difference. Imagine if I can catch him. My eyes sparkled. Imagine if I am the heroine that takes down the villain, saving London from his demonic debauchery. Eek! I sat down before I fell down. But first… I sighed, staring at the blank page before me. Cupcake hell. Yawn. Burgh, I could dream!

One more shitty puff piece and I'll be headlining. I can finally tell the public the truth. Finally take down the notorious London Butcher. Taking a deep breath, I smiled, stretched out my fingers, and began to type. I was made for this.

I took an oath when I started, a personal one, something close to my heart. I vowed to always tell the truth. The public needs to know, and it is my job to tell them. If they believe the truth hurts; it doesn't. Well, not as much as the lies. It's the not-knowing that pains you the most, and I will never wish that upon anyone. I sighed.

Wrapping my arms around myself, I looked at the picture of my mother on my desk. Mum was always my greatest fan. Granted, she wasn't always the best mother in the world. In fact, she was hardly ever home. Her work came first. But I miss her, and I will damn well find out who killed her.

I sighed. Jeez, I am heading down another depressing path of dismay. Food. That'll perk me up. Cheetahs and M&Ms. The rainbow-coloured yummy goodness that could bring a smile to any saddened face. I tucked in, filling myself with the euphoric chocolate taste. Leaning back in the chair, I turned, watching the last of the sunshine turn to darkness. Fiery rainbows cascaded across the sky. That's it. Cupcakes and Cashmere. That moist, fluffy goodness that tantalises your taste buds with every mouth-watering bite.

To be fair, I would write this article easier if I had actually tasted one of her cursed cupcakes. I'm going off of reviews here, and who's saying they were even the slightest bit truthful. I yawned. The epic comedown after a sugar high.

Finishing the article, I sent it to Gerrard, packed up and headed home for the day. Tomorrow, Jayden promised me more than just fluff. Tomorrow, I'd be more than an assistant. I'd be writing the news every journalist dreamed of. I sighed, lost in thought. One can only dream.

CHAPTER TWO

The next day, my research rang true as I received an eyewitness account of the London Butchers' most recent attack. He murdered seven girls in the last fortnight alone. I knew I was right. Jeff's testimony confirmed it, but I needed more. I needed The Butcher. We had to meet, and I knew he wouldn't like that. Jeff had said the man behind the murders was butch, mid-thirties, with an unnatural strength. Even if he was caught, could he be contained? Who or what was he? These were questions left unanswered as I flicked through my crime book, filled with off the book statements and unproven conclusions. The latest epic failure being my inexplicable knack of turning the predator into the prey. I mean, why so many girls? What if the Butcher was being forced to kill for another purpose? It doesn't make sense. A serial killer's high doesn't involve killing a girl every other night. The Butcher's pace gives no time for serious stalking, naff all time for torture, and there were no 'missing items' taken as trophies. The whole thing went against the core rules of serial killing. He had to be working for someone else. But who?

Then there was the discovery of another six girls, all reported missing in the last year, and all found in dirtied cream jumpsuits, wandering the streets with no recollection of where they'd been. Was there a connection? I shrugged.

Jayden tried to get an interview with the fifth girl, but the National Crime Agency had stepped in, and they took her in for questioning. I should have gone. Maybe they would have let me speak to her. But if I had, then I'd be painting yet another target on my back. I sighed. When this information was released, it was going to be a shit storm.

After a strenuous day at the office, I gathered my things together. Stretching, I spun around on my chair, stopping to gaze out at the beauty of the sun as it set through a mirage of colours. It was time for home. Lola had already left. The floor was empty, well, except for me and...

"Heading out so soon?" Jayden asked as he caught me in the corridor.

"Yeah, it's time I put this lot to rest," I said, tapping the top of my crime book.

"That's some research you've got there!"

I laughed and nodded.

"Well, if you want a hand pinning the Butcher down, make sure you give me a holla."

I smiled. "I will, thanks Jayden. Night."

Jayden smiled and headed back to his office.

Walking down five flights of stairs, I huffed. Fitness wasn't my forte, and my curvy figure delighted in my love of cake. Grinning, I headed out into the world.

"Bye, Miss Jones," Dennis said as I left. I smiled and waved goodbye. Dennis had been a security guard at *The London Chronicle* since way before my time; an avid part of the furniture.

Leaving under the veil of moonlight, I glanced down at the puddles beneath my feet. I groaned, splashing myself. Buttoning my coat up, I began the long walk to the subway station. It was bloody cold tonight. Winter finally set in, with darkened nights and frosty mornings, and these LED street lamps were bloody useless. I sighed. No female should walk these streets alone. Especially with the Butcher out there. I would have called an Uber, but I was poor until payday next week. Shit. I had a death wish; I hadn't even thought about how I was going to get home. Research had occupied my mind, and I'd lost track of time. I shook my head and carried on walking. Considering the fact that my workload involves horrific stories of murderers and rapists, you'd think I'd be more careful. I pushed my hand in my pocket and gripped my door keys, ready to strike.

Hunched shoulders, coat pulled high, I shivered. It was dark, cold, and miserable. The last of the traffic sped past. "Watch it!" I yelled, stepping away from the edge. Absolute morons, don't they realise how dangerous that was? Must have been over the speed limit. I groaned. I sounded like an old lady tutting at townsfolk, but I had reason to fear the road.

After they killed Mum, I'd tried everything to find her murderer. I believed in bringing criminals to justice; even considered joining the force; until I found out they were even more corrupt than the criminals they arrested. Mum's file had gone missing, evidence astray. There was nothing but my eyewitness account to say they had even killed her that day. Well, that and her death certificate. I don't think they bothered looking into who drove the black Mercedes, or why she was so upset beforehand. The whole thing smelled wrong, and one day I'll find out.

People needed the truth. It's how we moved on. I gulped, looked both ways, and crossed the road quickly.

Skeletal trees wavered in the dim light of the moon. I was alone. It was blustery cold tonight; I pulled my briefcase tight against my chest and picked up my pace, my stomach rumbling, ready for dinner. I'd not eaten since lunch, completely bypassing my usual three pm coffee and cake. No wonder I was hungry. But looking at the pot belly I had developed, it'd probably do me good.

I headed over the road and into Harp Alley. Soft footsteps caught my attention from behind. Shivering, I held my coat closed and headed over to Lydia's coffee shop to dry off. Three doors down and a slithering of fingertips crept across my backbone.

"Who's there?" I yelled, turning around.

No one. I laughed as my nerves cried out for comfort. I was tired… that had to be it. My mind wandered to Dalen Frost, the last bad boy I'd encountered one lonely night in London's suburbs. I shuddered, my hand pushing against the scar on my thigh. I'd been at university investigating the real world for the next big story. I needed it to get in. No paper would employ me without it. But damn, this job needs hazard pay. I gulped, back straight, head held high. I carried on.

Three doors to go. Footsteps mimicked my own. I gulped, panicked, and quickened my pace. The silence of his strike was deadening, protruding from the dark like a feather floating to the floor. My insignificant life became a tally on his list of recent targets. Big brutish hands gagged me. Intoxicating my mind with a cloth filled with some kind of sedative. Mouth held shut, the sweetness of its vapor numbed my senses. I gasped, panting for air. Eyes bulged. Body limp. A single tear fell as my last thought was that tonight I would be his next victim.

Ears ringing, head heavy, I eased my eyes open. Darkness obscured my vision as the midnight sky clouded above me. I stretched out, shaking from the icy blasts of winter's reign. Where am I? My neck strained, sore and stiff. What happened? Gagging, I coughed, choking for breath. My heart pounded as I reached around in the dark.

Blinking to focus, the dark skin of a man came into view. I moved, pushing myself backwards, hands scraping against the wet concrete. He leapt forward with an unnatural agility, his long brown hair matting in the wind. My frame shook, jaw dropped as I shifted to get away. High-pitched screams silenced when he landed on me. Choking out a gasp, my ribs shattered under his weight. Numb to the touch, I remained there, a warm fluid flowing freely from my mouth. The shock of his impact caused my body to go into shock. Adrenaline surged, salty tears streamed freely.

Hitting out, I lunged forward, too weak to overcome him. Gloved hands rose, and he slammed a fist into my cheek, knocking my jaw sideways. Bloody saliva spat out of me as he held my neck in place. Something pierced my skin. Wide eyed and screaming, my head felt severed, slammed on a sharp pike. Yet still attached as my fingers clambered upwards, shaking over my collarbone. Blood trickled warmth over my frame as I became paralysed for a moment. With my nerves igniting, he released a thick silver needle. My body trembled through chemical reaction, eyelids flickered, muscles seized. *Something's wrong!* With my brow furrowed, mouth agape, I screamed, kicking out at him, thrashing at his darkened figure.

Death coiled across my throat. Snippets of shadows corrupt the air. I choked out a strangled gasp, pleading for release. His fists tightened, nails gripped, curled around my throat. With my chest pumping, a heart wrenching panic engulfed me. Wide eyed, silently screaming, my broken nails scratched at his gloved fingers.

Help!

Acid erupted from my gut. Body tense, I lay there, dazed by fear. The sharpness of his gaze severed my grasp on reality. Night-time demons danced through the gloom as my lungs burned in anguish. I kicked out for freedom on the hard, damp concrete, screaming inside, crying hard. He gripped tighter, taking away any chance of survival.

I gave one last push, one more feeble fight for my life. Adrenaline surged. I slapped and kicked, twisting under his restraint, knocking him sideways. Small, ragged breaths escaped as he fell away from me. I used my final breath to scream. A blood-curdling, heart wrenching scream.

Heavy hands pressed down as he heaved his weight on top of me again, his hands squeezing my neck. I clawed at his arms; nails dug in. Blood emerged, trickling down his arm. He yelped, angered, as I shoved him backwards, clambering to be released. I wailed, yet no sound escaped me. With bulging eyes, I pleaded with him, fearful of my impending doom. Cyanosed lips spluttered. Sodden cheeks stung from the salty tears that fell.

This was it. I was the martyr I'd written about. Front page of tomorrow's news. Blasted across social media, broadcast over all the channels. Another victim, a new number on an ever-growing case file. It made little sense… they'd investigated it, reported the facts. I wasn't his normal type, a rich, blond city girl high on drugs. Was it even the Butcher, after all?

As my strength failed me, my heavy arms sank down to the ground, legs silenced and still. A solemn sky hazed over, and speckles of stars danced in the moonlight. With energy waning, I settled into death. Brightness faded as his face flickered from view. I shivered, stripped bare under his gaze. His dark brown eyes cut through me. Thick, brutish arms remained straight, gripping harder, tighter.

The evening sky dimmed as beads of rain soothed my battered face. Sluggish eyelids dwindled, battling to stay open. Peace warmed through me, releasing the agony of electrifying nerve ends that fired, hoping for a reaction, pleading for me to resist. But there was no fight left anymore. He was too strong, too agile, too fast. Did my curiosity kill me this time? Had I gotten too close? Was he the Butcher? The reason I'd be severed from the world I once knew?

In the quiet of death, the howl of a beast angered, thickening through the airwaves. Footsteps pounded over the ground I lay on, splashing through the puddles as a deep voice shouted out to assist. Crushed limbs inhaled as my attacker was pulled off and flung to the side. A fight broke out, sirens blasted through blackened raindrops, help was close by. Roars of anguish screamed as my murderer's blood painted my cold, dying body.

My voice shouted out, empty, shattered, and croaky, too pained to speak. Heavy black boots gritted the pavement, knees hit the ground. The musky scent of leather snuffled my sinuses. The chiselled face of a young man with a trimmed beard and soft brown hair filled my view. Kind brown eyes stared, and I lost myself within them. He lowered his arms, lifting my frail figure from the puddled alleyway. Reaching up, my hand shook. "It's okay," he said. "I won't hurt you."

My body ached as he carried me away. The fluorescent lights of the city blurred into my eyes. My neck faltered as I turned away from them, eyes puffy and swollen.

Caressing my fingertips up and over his chin, I could feel thick hair. Bristles moved as I felt further up. Each hair thinned, ran across my fingertips, and shortened. In its place remained the softness of a neatly trimmed beard, delicately protecting his lips, deep lips with a wide mouth. A mouth that moulded back to its human form before my eyes. Leaving me with the enchantment of his face; his smile.

Cars littered the street as my unearthly saviour stopped. The solemn face that saved me, set me free. He laid me on a stretcher, the cushioned surface cradling my frame. Lights flickered with obscurity, hues of red and blue flashed overhead. My saviour stood silent and still, pausing, listening to my ragged breaths. My eyelids flickered, and I croaked out a thank you as he left me in the ambulance crew's care.

Strapped to monitors and fastened onto the stretcher, my pulse rate rose. Something had hold of me again. I thrashed out to release myself. I was stuck. Trapped. Help! Panic rushed through me as I searched for escape.

"It's okay!" a female voice soothed.

Her bright blond hair lit up against the fluorescent lighting. She wiped my mouth and stroked my forehead. With wide eyes, I pulled at the seatbelt. "You need to leave that on," she said, placing her hand on my arm. "You're safe now." The paramedic smiled, concern echoing in her eyes.

I inhaled, taking a moment to breathe. Safe, she said as I exhaled out the suffering, anxiety easing as they shut the doors. I closed my eyes, my mind stripped of rhyme or reason.

Safe.

CHAPTER THREE

The soft hue of buttercup yellow greeted me as I roused, opening my eyes. A mirage of pastel colours entwined into an accord of delicate delight. Walls guarded me, softening as I looked over them, creating an awareness of my surroundings.

"Doctor, she's awake," a female voice spoke. I watched as the woman in blue scrubs left the room. Two men in white coats walked in, standing at the foot of the bed. One was tall with carrot red hair and a mass of spots covering his forehead. The other was average height, much older, with glasses and greying hair.

"I'm Doctor Johnson," he said in a curt tone.

"And, I'm Roger, Doctor Johnson's trainee," the younger, spotty man said.

I stretched out my arms, pushed up on the bed and sat upright, battling against the aches and pains that accompanied the move. Groaning, I forced a half-smile, wincing at the fat lip I appeared to have.

"Do you know where you are?" the doctor said, staring down at his clipboard.

I nodded, croaking out the word, "hospital." The bed and pastel décor was a dead giveaway.

"Yes… go ahead Roger," he said, turning to the trainee.

The trainee stepped forward, picked up the chart at the end of my bed, and looked through the notes.

"This is Julia Jones, twenty-two years of age, brought in last night with two lacerations to her clavicle, a crushed trachea, signs of petechial haemorrhage and bruising to her laryngeal prominence. She was kept overnight for observation and to run a set of neurological tests, all of which appear fine."

"Good," the doctor said. "Continue neurological observations overnight and review for discharge in the morning." He turned and walked out of the room.

Roger nodded, smiled, and walked out of the room after him.

Moments later, a nurse came in, singing away to herself. She filled up my water jug and wrote down my vitals from the monitor. Two people appeared outside the room. She went outside, spoke to them, then came back in. "Julia, there are two detectives here to talk to you. Is that okay?"

I nodded.

The nurse left and two middle-aged detectives walked in, one overly large-bellied male with brown hair and the other a female with black hair. "Julia, I'm Detective Monroe and this is my partner, Detective Melissa Lee."

I attempted a smile.

Monroe stepped forward to sit beside me. I edged back

in my bed. He stopped, paused, and stepped back again. Melissa looked at him, smiled and stepped towards me. "Can I sit here?" she asked, pulling a chair over. I nodded, "Julia, I'm Melissa. We're here to find out what happened to you last night."

"Okay," I croaked.

"Do you remember what happened?"

I winced, nodding. Monroe pulled out a notebook and began taking notes.

My eyes welled with tears as I gulped back the bile that retched in my throat. Heat rose through my body, surging to protect me. I pulled up the sheet, sat back in the bed, legs up, arms cradling myself, recalling the events of the horrifying night.

"Can you tell me what you remember?"

I bit down on my lip, wincing in pain. Tears fell, absorbing into the sheets as I recounted the ordeal. Throughout, Melissa nodded, listening attentively, while Monroe made notes, looking up from time to time.

Melissa took a deep breath in, then exhaled slowly. "Okay," she sighed. "And when you say you saw a needle, did you see what was in it?"

I shook my head. "All I know is it burned when he injected me."

"Hmm... would it be okay if we requested a blood test to identify the substance?" I nodded.

"And when you said you heard a... roar, was it?"

"No, it wasn't a roar, it was more of a howling sound that happened just before someone pulled him off of me. But... the howl could have been the wind."

Monroe looked up. "It wasn't windy last night."

I gulped.

"So, what happened after the howl?"

"I, I'm not sure. I couldn't see very well. All I heard was his screams." Shuddering, I clung to myself for comfort.

"Do you know how you ended up covered in blood?"

"No, something warm and wet splashed over me when he was screaming. Was that his blood?" I retched, swallowing back bile, grabbing a tissue from the side table. "Sorry," I said.

"It's okay. I know it's a lot to go through. Take your time." She smiled.

I cleaned my mouth, wincing as I drank a sip of water.

"Can you remember anything about the person who pulled the attacker off you?"

"Yes… he had a kind face and brown eyes."

Melissa smiled. "Do you know why anyone would want to hurt you?" I shook my head.

Monroe looked up. "Aren't you a reporter?"

"Yes… well, an assistant journalist."

He shrugged his shoulders, rolling his eyes as he looked down. I scowled.

"What are you working on at the minute?" Melissa asked.

"A new piece about the London Butcher."

"What about him?"

"I have got nothing concrete yet… but I received a testimony from an eyewitness," I said, probing for more information.

She nodded, smiling. "Okay, is there anything else you can remember?"

"No, but could my attacker be the Butcher? He's murdered seven already!"

"That we know of," Monroe mumbled, taking notes.

Melissa looked over at him and shook her head. "We don't know… but why do you ask?"

"Because that's the story I am working on."

"Hmm… it is a coincidence. We will ensure we look into it."

"It's not him," Monroe said.

"Who? The Butcher? Are you so sure?" I asked.

"Because you're not his type." I frowned.

Monroe looked up "No, he doesn't use chloroform or needles, he butchers his victims then leaves them in pieces all over the city." I gulped.

Melissa gave Monroe a disgusted look. "Monroe means he removes any form of identification."

"Yeah, their teeth and fingers are always missing," he said. I shuddered, holding the sheets tighter.

Melissa shook her head. "Well, I think we have everything we need for now. Here's my card. Contact me if you remember anything else."

I nodded, taking the card, placing it on the side table. They left, closed the door, and stood outside, discussing my case with the nurse.

My body hurt, throat tender. Every muscle ached as I leant back into the pillow. What time was it? It didn't matter anyway; I was exhausted. I shuffled down the bed, rested my head and closed my eyes, relaxing into the sound of a dreamless sleep as I drifted away.

Darkness protruded through the ward. I turned on my light. Gargled noises echoed three doors down as suction tubes freed patients from drowning in their own bodily fluids. I awoke sodden from sweat. How long had I slept? My head pounded as I turned to see the drip stand refreshed. I must be low on fluids. Sitting upright, I stretched, pushing and pulling at my limbs to ease out the tension. Dangling my legs over the side, my feet touched the cold bare floor. Tanned legs reminded me of my trip to Florida a few months back. My best friend Lola and I stayed in an all-inclusive resort, spending most of our time by the pool bar or delighting in sensual massages under the sun. I sighed. I wish I were there!

Both of us were singletons, both engaged to our professions. I was the wannabe journalist; she was the graphic designer. We'd been friends since university, roomed together for all but one semester. After graduation, she moved back home, missed her folks too much. But when her mother pulled some strings, and a job came up at the *Chronicle*, she jumped at the chance, clearly loving city life. A year later and we're both still single, living off holiday romances and weekend cocktail parties.

Testing the floor with my feet, I leant forward. My legs wobbled as I swayed to gain balance. Vision blurred, head pounding, I stood still, holding onto the drip stand until everything settled down. Heavy limbs trudged forward, taking one step at a time. I made my way over to the bathroom. My hospital gown flapped open at the back as I reached for the door handle. I groaned, clambering around to find the light switch. Squinting, I turned the light on; the glare pierced my retina like a needle to the skin. My hand soothed my neck, my skin felt rough, dry almost. It still burned from the attack. I could remember his thick, brutish hands curled around my throat… and how he squeezed, with his eyes piercing daggers into mine. No matter how hard I punched, how much I kicked, I was no match for him. If it weren't for the stranger in the street, I'd be dead.

Gripping the sink, I fell forward, my heart thumping, chest heavy. I inhaled like my life depended on it. Eyes wide with fright, I looked in the mirror, searching for some resemblance to my former self. Bloody lips, a swollen eye socket, and huge, blackened bruises covered my neck. Even my olive-green eyes were bloodshot, well, the one you could still see was.

Salty tears streamed down my face as I gulped back a wail. I can't do this. Can't let him win! Turning on the tap, I splashed cold water over my face, awakening my senses to the reality of the situation. I'd nearly died. He'd almost killed me. My legs gave way as I crumbled into a heap on the floor, sobbing atop the linoleum tiles. The bandage on my collarbone was hanging off. I pulled it away and threw it to the side. Through all the cries, one thing remained, I was alive. I survived, and I wouldn't let the memories of him beat me down.

Letting out a heart-wrenching wail, I cradled my body, crying into my knees. This was the next stage, relief, as I grieved my life before me. A wave of heat engulfed my interior. I'd survived. Tears fell, turning to steam, dissipating in the air. My breathing slowed, my heart calmed to a steady beat. I took a long, sharp breath in, then exhaled the pain and panic out.

Wiping my eyes, I pushed myself up onto my feet. Hanging onto the drip stand, I looked in the mirror, my face blotchy from crying. I paused, staring at myself. Brows furrowed; lips pursed. It made little sense. I'd changed. Splashing my face with water, I could wash off the dried blood encrusted on the surface of my lower lip. It was clear, perfect, and healed. The lacerations on my neck were next. Water soothed away the residue, leaving a curve of soft skin, radiant and warm. The only evidence my neck wore were age old bruises, healing at a rapid rate. My eye remained encased in black, but nowhere near as bad as before. But how? A fresher face stared back at me. I looked human again. Perhaps I always had. Maybe my negativity had taken over and seen things worse than they were.

The longer I stood there staring, the hotter my skin became. Temperature rising, hands hot and clammy. Have I got a fever? It must be all the stress of my body healing its wounds. I was exhausted. I wretched as nausea took over, leaning over and vomiting into the toilet. It was all too much. Heading back to bed, I settled in for the night, closed my eyes and drifted off to sleep.

CHAPTER FOUR

"Morning Julia," a chirpy voice said, snapping me out of dreamland. Bright light bled through my eyelids. I yawned, squinting, opening my eyes to the vibrancy of the room. A redhead in a blue nurse's uniform stood with a big smile at the foot of my bed. "How are you feeling today?" she asked.

"Better," I said, stretching my arms and sitting upright.

"That's great news." She smiled, moving towards the drip stand and disconnecting it.

"How are you feeling on a scale of one to ten?"

"About a three."

She nodded. "Would you like any paracetamol?"

"No thanks."

She nodded, took my vitals, and said, "The doctor will be around shortly." I thanked her as she left.

Moving my head from side to side, I stretched my neck. It felt stiff, but better, less painful, in fact. As I pulled myself upright, I groaned. Everything still hurt, granted not as much, but it felt like I climbed a mountain or two. I swung my feet over the edge of the bed; the floor was cold underfoot, and I walked across to the bathroom. Opening the door, I faced reality, hair a mess, no make-up and bugger all facilities. I took a deep breath. I needed to go home. Cleaning myself up, I headed back and sat out in the chair, staring out of the window. I must have been four floors up, by the looks of it. You could see for miles. I bet if I looked closely, I'd be able to see Lola's apartment from here.

Just then my mobile phone rang. Lola! "Hi Julia, how are you feeling?"

"Better, thanks. I should be home today!"

"Oh, honey, that's great, I'll come meet you. Do you want anything picked up?"

"Please, can you bring me a change of clothes? Oh, and how's Maisy doing?"

"She's fine, the little kitty scratched me earlier though."

I laughed. "Thanks for feeding her."

"No problem."

"Oh, and my toothbrush, can you bring that too? My mouth tastes vile."

She laughed. "No probs, I'll be there in an hour."

Putting the phone down, I smiled. Home time! They had better be discharging me today, otherwise I'm walking out. There's only so much work you can do on a mobile phone.

I sat, mesmerised by the rays of sunlight hitting the treetops below. Glistening with last night's raindrops, their vibrancy exceeded expectations. Stretching out into the comfort of the armchair, I relaxed. Cushions moulded into my back, taking the strain off. Whatever he injected into me damned well hurt. The fever and aches have got to be the aftermath of it. I jumped, heart racing. What if it was a virus of some sort? A pathogen designed to wipe out humanity. Damn, I'd watched way too many episodes of *The Walking Dead*. If it were a virus, I'd be showing signs by now. It's been over forty-eight hours. If I remember right, it starts with a fever. I had one of those. I gulped; hands clammy. Jeez, sit back and calm down. If I were a zombie, I'd be wanting raw meat by now. I gagged at the thought of it.

"Julia," a sharp tone said.

"Shit!" I jumped. "Yes, sorry," I said when I saw the doctor walk in. His trainee followed. I pulled the sheet from the bed to cover myself over better. The hospital gown didn't provide the best coverage.

"Go ahead, Roger," the doctor said, looking at his junior.

Roger smiled, picking up my hospital file. "This is Julia Jones, twenty-two years old and brought in because of a recent assault."

"Yes, yes, we know all that," the doctor interrupted.

"Okay, skipping ahead," Roger said, brow furrowed, "Julia, how are you feeling today?"

"Much better, and I'd like to go home please." I smiled.

He pulled out a small pen torch, walked over and shined it in both of my eyes. The light was enough to give anyone a migraine, let alone the concussion he was looking for.

"All fine," he looked at the file. "Well, we ran your bloods twice. They appear fine. In fact," he paused. "That's astounding... your levels are perfect." He looked at the doctor, puzzled.

The doctor grabbed the file from him. He squinted, brow furrowed. "Hmm... you appear to be the healthiest patient I have ever had." He paused, scratching his head. Then shoved the file back into Roger's hands. "Send her home," he said, and walked out of the room.

"Okay," Roger said, "well it looks like you have your wish. I'll send through the paperwork, and you can get ready for discharge early this afternoon."

I smiled. "Thank you!"

He nodded, smiling as he left the room.

I closed my eyes, took a deep breath in, counted to five and exhaled. What day is it? Err... I left work Tuesday after the meeting, discussing my crime book with Jayden. I stopped. Jaw dropped. Shit! Where was it? I searched through my things. There was nothing. My briefcase was empty. Shit. Shit. Shitty Shit! Damn it! Where was it? He wouldn't have taken it... would he? Then again, why wouldn't he? It's an in-depth expose on all things Butcher related. Bloody hell. I huffed, sitting back on the bed.

Anyway, I couldn't do bugger-all about it now. Tapping my fingers on the rail I thought... so if the 'thing' happened Tuesday night and I've been here two nights', then today's Thursday. Damn it, my piece is supposed to be finished for tomorrow's edition. Shit.

I picked up my mobile and dialled Gerrard.

"Yes, Gerrard speaking."

"Gerrard, it's me Julia."

"Julia," he said, his old voice croaker than ever. "How are you feeling?"

"Good, I'm good. I'm phoning about the piece on the Butcher,"

"One second, Julia," he said, muting the conversation. I sat in silence, awaiting his return. Gerrard had been with the company since before I could remember… probably since before I was born. I remember him saying he'd risen in the ranks from a newsroom clerk, delivering mail, to editor-in-chief of *The London Chronicle*, Martha Danes.

"Sorry, yes you were saying," he said when he came back on.

"The London Butcher, I have new information."

"Okay, it'll have to wait."

"Have you held the spot for it?"

"No, Julia, you're in hospital. You should rest!" he said in a stern tone.

"Yes… well, I'm being discharged today. Lola's picking me up"

"That's great news. Will you be back next week?"

"Yes, of course, but…"

"Perfect," he interrupted. "I'll get Jayden to release what we have. That'll buy you time to recover. It can wait another week."

"But the public needs to know he's out there."

"They will, don't worry, take care of you." He paused, sighing. "Anyway, did they find out who it was?"

"Who what was?"

"Who the attacker was, Julia. Was it the Butcher?"

"No, I don't think so, they haven't told me yet."

"Perhaps you should look into that. He targeted you for

a reason. You need to be careful."

"Yes... I guess so," I said, gulping. I thanked him and said goodbye. My hands were sweating as I ended the call.

He was right. Eyes wide, I took a deep breath. My stomach churned, muscles tense. Wiping my hands on the sheet, I stood up. I needed to know more. Biting down on my lower lip, I headed out of the room to find the nurse. I need to know what he injected me with and why? Was it to do with the Butcher article? Did I dig too deep?

Walking down the corridor, I came to the nurse's station. Two women in grey uniforms sat down, typing on the computer. A box of chocolates with a thank-you card sat on the desk.

"Well, hello, Julia," the chirpy redhead in blue said as she walked out of the back room. I smiled. "Everything alright?" she asked.

I nodded, "Yes, but I have a few questions."

"Okay, let's head back to your room and we can talk there." She smiled, ushering me back.

When we reached the room, I perched on the bed. She entered, closing the door behind her. "Mind if I take a seat?" she asked.

"No, of course not," I said.

"Thanks, I've been on my feet all morning." She smiled, sitting down with a sigh of relief. "So, how can I help?"

"Well, I guess you've read my file," I said, pointing to it.

"Yes, we discussed you in handover this morning."

"Okay," I nodded. "Well... I wondered if you could help me work out what happened."

"Oh, honey, that's something you need to work out."

"Yes, but do you know what he injected into me?"

"No... Well, let me have a look." She picked up the file and sat back down, looking through it. "Okay, well, according to the results, there isn't anything unusual. So, my guess is he injected you with saline."

"What's that?"

"Saltwater, it's what you've been hooked up to since you came here."

"Oh, but why would he do that?"

"Oh, honey, I don't know. You need to ask the police that question. Have you seen them?"

"Yes, they were here yesterday."

"Why don't you call them, see if they have any news," she said as she stood up, opening the door.

"Yes, thanks, I will... Thank you for your help."

"Anytime," she said as she stepped out of the room.

"Oh, wait!" I called. She turned back and smiled. "Do you know where he is now?"

Her brow furrowed; mouth pursed. She stepped back in the room and closed the door to. "I'm not supposed to tell you."

"Please, I need to know what happened."

"He's in intensive care. He was cut up pretty badly according to the paramedics." She paused. "Claw marks, apparently." She shrugged. I shuddered.

"Thank you," I said as she smiled and walked out.

Damn. He's in the same hospital. I need to know what happened and if he has my book. The redhead said he was cut up...who did that? The man who saved me didn't have any weapons; he couldn't have hurt him…so who did?

I sighed. What else could I do from here? There must have been a reason he targeted me. I scratched my head, pushing on my temple to ease my impending headache. So, if it isn't the same killer as the blond rich girls…then is there a new killer in town? Was I his first? Could it have been a gang initiation? That mark on his wrist certainly suggested so. I recalled the black dagger tattoo. What did it mean? There was only one way I would know for sure. Ask him.

I knew he'd be in police custody right now, handcuffed to the bed rails. I'd be safe. Those brutish hands couldn't come anywhere near me. But how could I get there?

"Are you ready for home, honey?" a familiar voice asked. Lola walked in with her long blond hair swishing to the side. Bright eyes sparkled, as eyelashes fluttered.

"Who are you calling honey, short stack?"

"Ouch! Harsh." She laughed, jumping up to give me a hug. "If you weren't so tall, I wouldn't have to jump."

"If you weren't so short, you mean," I said, laughing.

"So, what did Doctor Death say?" She grinned.

"Who, Doctor Johnson?" She nodded, smirking. "He said they couldn't find anything wrong with my blood… apparently I'm one of the healthiest patients they have."

"Err, do they know what you eat?"

I laughed. "Well, something's not right, as Doctor Grimshaw at my local surgery said I had anaemia, so that should have shown up."

"Hmm… Are we thinking conspiracy? Oooh or maybe Doctor Death wants you to go home so he can have you all to himself and eat your brains… you know, like that Lecter guy."

"Shit, you're evil."

"Hey, you started it with the short stack comment."

I pursed my lips. "Truce?"

She squinted; brow furrowed. "Fine, but you're staying at mine tonight just in case," she said, punching my shoulder.

"Oww!"

Her face dropped, mouth agape. "Crap, sorry. Was that where he hurt you?"

I removed my hair scarf from my neck, showing the remaining bruises.

"Shit... what happened?"

"It's a long story."

"A long story that wine and Chinese takeout can fix?"

"Not quite, but it'd help." I smiled, hugging her.

She held me tight. "You had me worried, you know."

I pulled back. "I know." I sighed. "Come on, the sooner I'm out of this place the better." She nodded. "But I have to make a quick stop along the way."

"Hmm, where?"

"I need to go to intensive care."

"Err... why?"

"To ask my attacker why he tried to kill me."

Her eyes bulged, face paled. "Are you mad?"

"He's in police custody. They handcuffed him to the bed rails."

Frowning, she paused. "Are you sure you're ready for this?"

I nodded, teeth gritted.

She took a deep breath. "Fine. But if he Hulks out and kills us, I'll be angry with you."

I smiled. "That's the spirit."

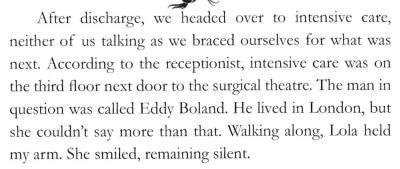

After discharge, we headed over to intensive care, neither of us talking as we braced ourselves for what was next. According to the receptionist, intensive care was on the third floor next door to the surgical theatre. The man in question was called Eddy Boland. He lived in London, but she couldn't say more than that. Walking along, Lola held my arm. She smiled, remaining silent.

I shuddered, body tense, hands clammy. *Am I ready for this?* I could picture him, his piercing brown eyes, matted hair, an aged face with the lines of a fearful past. *What reason did he have to want me dead?* Every part of me ached as I walked on.

I'd told Lola there was nothing to fear, but right now fear crept up my backbone. My heart was pumping, mind on high alert. He would have handcuffs on, wouldn't he? I hoped so! He'd committed attempted murder... *What's the penalty for that nowadays?* I scratched my head. *How many years would he get for trying to kill me?*

Reaching the end of the corridor, we walked past the entrance to the emergency theatre and stood outside the door for intensive care. We'd arrived. This was it. Time to face the man of my future nightmares.

"Are you sure you want to do this?" Lola asked.

I nodded, gulped, and marched forward. If there was any way I could get over what happened to me, then it would be by hearing the truth.

"Do you want me to come in with you?" Lola looked concerned.

"No," I said, taking a deep breath. "I need to do this alone."

She nodded, hugged me, and stepped back to let me go.

I peered around the corner. According to the receptionist, his room should be four doors down. Outside, a male police officer was sitting guarding his room. *Shit. He'll never let me in. What should I do?*

Lola saw me pause. "What's wrong?" she asked.

I pointed down the corridor. She smiled. "Ah, leave this to me." Lola walked down the corridor swaying her hips. She stopped in front of the officer to use the drinks machine. "Oh no, it's swallowed my money," she said as she bent over to check the hatch.

Lola turned around to see the police officer wide eyed and staring at her. "Excuse me, Officer, would you be so kind as to have a look at the machine?" she asked, fluttering her eyelashes.

He stood up, brushed his hair back, and walked over to help her. The officer pushed the machine backwards. "Oh my, you're very strong," she exclaimed, giggling. He smiled. Lola faked a dizzy spell.

"Are you alright, madam?" the officer asked.

"No, I think I need to sit down," she said. "Could you help me?"

He steadied her towards the seats on the far side of the corridor. I slipped into my attacker's room, listening to Lola thank the officer as I left.

As I entered the room, I closed the door behind me,

paused, and braced myself to look. Could I do this? I had little choice left now. Heart pumping, breathing faster, I gasped. Where is he? The bed was empty. The name above said 'Eddy'. This was his room. I thought they would handcuff him, but the restraints were dangling down the side of the bed. He should be here somewhere! Body tense, eyes wide, I panicked. What if he's hiding, ready to jump out and finish me?

In the bathroom beside me, the toilet flushed. I panicked, jumped, and darted behind the curtain. How can he still walk? I thought patients in intensive care were at death's door. It makes little sense. The bathroom door opened, and I heard footsteps trudging across the floor. Holding my breath, I remained as still as a statue. The sound of weight pushing down on the bed enabled me to breathe again. Relief flooded over me.

The door opened. "Right, we best get these back on you," a female voice said. "Don't you go telling that nice officer I took them off!"

"Aww, I won't, Aggie," my attacker said. His voice was kind, yet poignant.

"You be good now." The door closed behind her.

Peeking from behind the curtain, my heart raced. "I know you're there," he said. I gasped. "Better come out now," he chuckled. I remained still. "Oh, Julia, you must come out sometime."

Shit. He knew my name. How did he know my name? Heat rising, I gulped, hands clammy, eyes wide. He must have targeted me; it was a planned attack! Adrenaline surged; anger reigned through me. With gritted teeth, I pulled back the curtain, coming face to face with my attacker. Dark eyes bored into me. Inhaling a deep breath, I marched over to the foot of his bed. He won't destroy me again!

"How dare you laugh? Do you think it's funny to hurt someone?" He laughed again.

"Why would you do that? Why would you hurt me? You don't even know me!" Anger boiled, adrenaline surged. He laughed harder. I clenched fists, slamming them down on the bed frame. "Answer me, dammit!"

A spark of light surged around me. Flames ignited before my eyes. Heat consumed my body as he laughed even more. *How dare he?* Exhaling out a scream, I gripped the bed frame, white knuckles bared, teeth gritted. Black smoke rose beneath my fingertips as the stench of noxious, molten plastic engulfed my senses. Flames exploded out of my hands, ravaging his bedspread. *What's happening?* I backed away, leaving molten handprints behind.

His piercing brown eyes widened as he shrieked, "IT WORKS!"

Alarms sounded as callous cackles broke through his composure. "IT WORKS!" he screamed, his legs burning beneath the flaming sheets.

I backed into the wall. Mouth agape. What was happening? I looked at my hands. Nothing. They looked normal. Yet, he remained in a stance of sheer horror and rabid laughter, insanity welling in the pit of his soul.

"IT WORKS!" he screamed, kicking at the bedspread.

The stench of molten flesh engulfed the room as the skin on his legs boiled and blistered. Eyes wide, I trembled. Panic surged as the room turned into an inferno. I fled, barging into a team of nurses as they ran in to save him.

Entering the corridor, I banged into a man in a leather jacket. I tripped, and he caught me as I fell. He smiled; soft brown eyes calmed me. His fingertips curled through my hair as he held me. "Your hair, it's beautiful, so… Red," he said. His voice was smoky and delicious.

For a second, I studied him, a neatly trimmed beard, curls of wavy brown hair. His chiselled face came into view as he stood me upright, our bodies still so close.

"Thank you," I said. He was familiar. Did I know him? Without thinking I reached over, touched his neatly trimmed beard, then pulled back again, my face heating up. "I, err… sorry!"

He grinned. "You can feel my beard anytime Red." My face flushed even more. He smiled again and continued to walk past me. As he left, his leathery aroma caressed my senses. *It is him! The man who saved me!* I stopped and turned back, but he was gone.

Lola jumped up from the officer's lap. "Call me," she said, as she blew him a kiss.

I ran down the corridor, into the lift, and out of the building. I needed to calm down, to think. Lola followed. What the hell just happened?

"Let's get you home, honey," she said as she caught up with me. "We can talk about it all over coffee and biscuits. I think you need to rest."

I must have looked like a hysterical mess. Smiling, she interlinked her arm with mine. Taking a deep breath, I smiled, putting my head on hers, and we hailed a cab back to her apartment.

CHAPTER FIVE

Lola's apartment was on the other side of the city. It overlooked the river Thames with the iconic Saint Paul's Cathedral to the East. We were realistically within walking distance from the hospital, but a cab ride saved my weary legs.

As we walked up the path to the front door, I noticed a host of potted conifers. I eyed Lola. "Mum," she said. I nodded, smirking. Her mum was always trying to make her place more of a home. It was bound to be some deal she'd seen on a shopping channel or something.

"Don't the other tenants mind?"

She laughed. "No, they encourage her. Old lady Joan swapped numbers with her last time she visited. Now the old woman won't leave me alone. She's always listening in, checking up on me and reporting back home." She grimaced.

I laughed. "You can tell you're an only child."

She nodded, unlocking the door to her apartment.

"As you know, my home is your home."

"Actually, it's your parents'."

"Oh hush, if I didn't let them pay for it, they'd develop a hernia."

I grinned.

"Now sit your bum down here and I'll put the kettle on," she said, patting the sofa.

I made my way over to her four-seater and sat back, snuggled in comfort. Kicking off my shoes, I sat staring out of her floor to ceiling windows overlooking the city; the landscape was glorious, even on a cloudy day like today. Lola's apartment was on the third floor. You could see past the rooftops all the way to the cathedral and beyond.

Beneath the skyline, my eyes darted to the street. Something was amiss. A black Mercedes parked three doors down. What's that doing there? To be fair, I had an obvious fear of that type of car. After all, it was the weapon the murderer used to mow down my mother seven years ago. I picked up my phone and walked out of the apartment.

"Back in a minute," I yelled as I headed downstairs.

Just as I opened the front door, the black Mercedes sped off. Memorising the plate, I jotted it down on a scrap piece of paper. It couldn't be. Could it? The last part of the plate was the same as the one that hit Mum. But why was it here? Could it be a coincidence? It's been seven years. It's highly possible the driver sold it on by now. Maybe it's nothing.

Lola greeted me at the door. "Everything okay?"

"Yes." I shook my head. "I just thought I saw

something."

She shrugged, and we headed back to the apartment.

Beside the sofa was an oak coffee table to match the flooring. The TV was voice activated, as were most of the appliances in the apartment. Her Dad was a tech nerd. He set up everything to work off the newest assistant technology. To the right were the bathroom, master bedroom and spare room. Then, to the left, beside me, was an open kitchen that stepped down into the lounge area. Her place was stunning, a real eye opener. I always wondered why she worked full time. It's not like she needed the money. After her parents sold the farming land up North, they invested their wealth in shares in a new company, which tripled in value within six months. Self-made millionaires, I believe you call it.

Lola walked over with two mugs of coffee, popped them on the table and followed through with a plate of biscuits. "You can't have a coffee without a custard cream or two," she announced, sitting beside me, dipping a biscuit in her coffee.

I smiled.

"So, do I have to ask?" she asked.

"I don't know what happened in there. One minute I'm hiding behind a curtain, then…" I took a deep breath. "He called me out. He used my bloody name. "

"Shit!"

"Yeah, he knew me."

"That means he targeted you…" She grimaced. "But why?"

"I don't know, he just kept laughing," I said, eyes wide, brow furrowed.

"What… why?"

"I have no clue. He was nuts. Completely hysterical with laughter."

"Shit. Did he say anything?"

I pursed my lips, brow furrowed. "Yeah, actually he did, he kept saying… it works."

"Err... he's crazy, honey, well and truly psychotic."

"Yeah, that's what worries me." I bit my lip. "Did you see the smoke?"

"What smoke?" she asked, looking around the room.

"His bedsheets caught fire."

"What! When?"

"When I was there… they just set alight."

"How?"

"I don't know, it was horrible."

"What did you do?"

"I, err… ran," I said, looking down at the floor.

"Oh, honey," she said, leaning over and holding me in her arms. Tears welled as I held on tight. My body trembled, breathing rapidly, throat tightening. Why was this happening to me? Sobbing, I shook. Salty tears caressed my lips as cries of pain fled my body.

Lola held me close. "It'll be okay," she said as she stroked my hair. "Let it out."

I cried harder. My mind was full of dread. If he were after me, could there be others? Fear burrowed deep until I reminded myself he was locked up in hospital. There couldn't be anyone else. They'd have taken me out when I was unconscious that night, finished the job. This was just some maniac stalker that took his messed-up reality one step too far. My breathing eased, and I took control again. Coughing and spluttering, I sat up.

Lola passed me a tissue, her face full of sympathy and worry. She sat for a moment, allowing me to wipe away the tears, blow my nose and compose myself. "What happened that night, Julia?" she asked, her face riddled with concern.

"I… I was walking home from work; I'd stayed out late working on the Butcher article." She nodded. "The roads were quiet, just the odd car or passer-by, nothing unusual."

"Okay." She nodded.

"Then I passed the alleyway… I should've listened to my instincts, as that's when I heard it."

"What?"

"The footsteps, they came quickly, then he grabbed me and put a cloth over my mouth."

"Shit," she said, mouth agape, eyes wide.

I gulped. "I woke up in the alleyway, head pounding." Taking a deep breath, I continued, "That's when he was on top of me. I hardly had any time to think. He brought out a big needle and injected me with something." I paused, body rigid. "He was so strong, really heavy… he pushed me down… I tried to fight him. He grabbed my neck, tried to kill me!" I said, eyes wide, heart racing.

Lola was crying, tears streaming down her face. She took my hand.

I nodded and carried on, "I was almost unconscious when a man pulled him off me. If it wasn't for him…" I gulped, sniffling, tears threatening to spill again.

"Oh honey." She cried, wiping her tears, swallowing

them back. "You're safe now. He'll be locked up. No one can hurt you anymore."

I nodded, my bottom lip trembling.

Sitting upright, she asked, "Who was the guy that saved you?"

"I don't know. He didn't say anything."

She frowned. "Strange."

"Yeah."

"Plus, I'm sure I saw him at the hospital."

"Huh. When?"

"When I left that room."

She paused, thought for a moment. "Oh, I don't know honey, why would he be there?" I shrugged. "Maybe it's your mind playing tricks on you. There's no reason he'd be outside that monster's room. After all, the police want to question him, don't they?"

I nodded, wiping my tears.

The phone rang. It was Detective Lee. I showed Lola. She nodded, picking up the cups and heading over to the kitchen. "Hello," I said, answering the call.

"Julia, this is Detective Melissa Lee. We would like you to come into the station and identify your attacker in a line-up."

"Okay. When will it be?"

Melissa sighed. "With it being the Christmas holidays next week, we're short on staff. So, it will have to be after then."

"Okay."

"But in the meantime, if you remember anything else,

please ensure you contact me."

"Yes, I will. I'll see you there." I thanked the detective and said goodbye, ending the call.

Placing the phone down, I relaxed back into the sofa, staring out across the city. It was getting dark, and the reflection of the room shone in the window frame.

Lola walked over. "Everything alright?" she asked.

"Yes, I've got to go and identify him."

"When?"

"I don't know yet. They're short staffed. But she said it'll be after Christmas Day."

"I'll come with you."

"No, you have work!"

"Gerrard will give me the day off; I just rang him. He's fine and said if there is anything you need, he will try to help."

"What... really?"

"Yeah, you're not doing this alone. I'm here to help." I smiled. "Speaking of help, have you spoken to Aunt Lydia?" she asked.

"No, I didn't want to worry her."

"She'll be pissed, if you don't tell her."

"I know. I'll see her tomorrow. Hopefully, these bruises will have gone down by then."

"Fingers crossed," she said.

"Right, who's up for wine and Chinese?"

I smiled. "You know I am!"

"Want me to call the girls?"

"No, don't worry about them. Plus, I don't think Matty

will enjoy being called a girl."

"Ha, he loves it, really. I told him he's one of the girls, with locks like his."

I laughed. "Maybe tomorrow, I really just fancy food and bed tonight."

"Of course, I'll order, you put your feet up," she said as she threw me the TV remote. "Check what's on TV, I could use a good film."

"Sure." I smiled, flicking through the channels.

Sitting down to take out Chinese, a bottle of wine and a cheesy old romance movie was all I needed after the day I had. Tomorrow would be another day, a day of piecing together the puzzle that was my life.

Could I face my messed-up maniac next week at the station? I had to. I'd be behind glass anyway; he wouldn't see me. I took a deep breath. I had to keep going, not let this nightmare bring me down. I was lucky. I'd survived. Few people lived to tell that tale. So, I'd make damned sure I kept on living and find out whatever the hell happened to me that night.

"Morning, beautiful," Lola said, striding into the bedroom, holding a cup of coffee.

I groaned. I'll never be a morning person. "What time is it?"

"11:00, you needed the sleep."

I nodded, yawning. She perched on the edge of the bed as I sat up, stretching. "Here, have a sip, it'll help." She smiled.

"You're way too energetic," I said. Smiling, I took the coffee. The warmth of the cup comforted my icy hands. Even with the heating on, it was still bloody freezing this time of year.

"Fancy lunch out today? We'd better see your Aunt Lydia." I sighed. "It's best she hears it from you rather than on the grapevine."

I grimaced. "I know, it's just, I know how worried she'll be."

"Yes, and she should be. You're bloody lucky to be alive, honey."

I nodded, gritting my teeth.

"Come on, take a shower, get ready and we'll get this over and done with." She stood up and walked out of the room. "Oh, and don't forget... drinks tonight with the girls," she yelled behind her.

I groaned, fell back into bed, and hid under the duvet.

The walk to Lydia's coffee shop was refreshing. Damp pavements splashed underfoot as we skipped across Mable bridge to Forks Lane. The park here was glorious, always a favourite picnic spot of ours during the summer months. Damn, I miss the heat. Bikini tops, prosecco and hors d'oeuvres. It was what summers were made of. That and Matty setting his hair alight trying to work the BBQ last August. I smiled, lost in memories.

"What?" Lola asked, jabbing me in the rib, interlocking her arm in mine.

I laughed. "I was thinking about our picnics last summer

and Matty's hair catastrophe."

She chuckled. "Yeah... It never grew back the same, did it?"

I shook my head, grinning.

"We'll have to do it again soon." I nodded. "Speaking of good times... What are you wearing tonight?"

"Shit. I didn't think of that. I'll have to nip home."

"No, how about we stop by Fifth Avenue after Lydia's, they're bound to have something there."

"Oh, I don't know." I frowned. Could I really afford to splurge right now?

"What's not to know? It's my treat."

I smiled. "Lola, you've done enough; I should treat you."

"Honey, it's great just having you at home so I can keep an eye on you."

"Okay, but can we head to Dames and Dancers instead? It's quieter over that way, and they have some great outfits for half the price."

"Deal," she said, smiling.

Turning the corner, we stood before the entrance to Lydia's. "You ready?" she asked.

I took a deep breath, shook out the stress, and pushed open the wooden glass door.

The bell dinged. Aunt Lydia looked up from behind the counter. Her grey hair tied in a bun on top of her head, with two pencils sticking out either side. I chuckled. She always said she could never find them.

"Girls! Girls!" she exclaimed, racing over to hold us.

"Lola! You look like you need to gain a few pounds. Have you been eating?" she asked.

I smiled.

"Yes, Mum," Lola joked.

"Here, come sit down. I'll fetch you some lunch," she said, patting me on the back.

"Lydia, I need to tell you something," I said.

"Yes, yes. Lunch first and we can all share all the stories." She grinned. "I want to tell you all about Dennis."

"Dennis?... Our Dennis?" I asked. She nodded.

"Lydia, you minx," Lola chuckled. I laughed.

Dennis was a lovely old chap. He'd been the security guard at the newspaper for over 10 years. Always smiling, always friendly. He'd be good for her. Lydia was beaming, telling the tale known to a thousand love stories. He bought her flowers, serenaded her by the docks. Then took her out to see a show, finalising the weekend with a good old romp in the bed. Clearly, this was too much information, but Lydia never held back. I smiled, watching her beam from ear to ear. She reminded me of Alice's Cheshire Cat, laid back, mischievous and full of flair.

My eyes wandered, peering out of the window. The solemn winter weather had calmed for the afternoon. The tail end of Storm Diane was on course, stirring up a flurry of emotion as Jack Frost rebelled, bleaching the sidewalk. Give it a few hours and the pavement would resemble an ice rink, old ladies skating down, breaking their brittle bones. Young children high on ice, swirling and twirling under the blanket of a heavy, snow-filled skyline.

Besides the cold, winter used to be one of my favourite

times of the year. Mum decorating the Christmas tree, Uncle Joe hanging the decorations. The entire house was alight with festive galore. I smiled. Even Christmas carolling was a triumphant time. Aunt Clara with her radiant smile and her god-awful voice. She had the highest pitch I'd ever heard, and it wasn't a pleasant one at that. I wonder whatever happened to her. I know she moved after Mum died, but I never heard from her again. Then again, Mum and Clara were always close, grew up together, only a few years apart. Clara used to be a midwife. They were both in the healthcare industry; trained together, too. I smiled as heat radiated through my chest. They were happy times. Aunt Clara used to watch me as a child, while Mum worked the late shift. The cakes she bought were scrumptious, always in several flavours.

Aunt Lydia said my mum and Clara had fallen out just before Mum died. She never found out what about, but whatever it was, it drove my mum to tears that day. Uncle Joe on the other hand, left and shacked up with a floozy near Brighton, never to be seen again.

The police labelled her death, an accident, a hit and run. They never caught the driver of the black Mercedes. I'll always remember the last part of the number plate. L, zero, L. L0L. Like it was mocking me. I tensed up. I always hated how he got to live a normal life after he murdered my mother, ploughing her down in the middle of the road like she was nobody. I sighed. That's when I discovered life wasn't fair. Shit happens, and the truth is never told. That's why I became a reporter, to let the truth shine free. Every person deserves to live a life without manipulation, lies, or distrust.

"Julia, are you in there?" Lola said, snapping her fingers in front of my face.

"Yes, sorry," I said, smiling.

She smiled and nodded.

Henry, Lydia's server, walked over with a tray of food. Cheeseburger and chips, my favourite. We thanked him and tucked in as Lydia left us to it while we finished our meals.

"Are you going to tell her?" Lola asked.

I wiped my mouth with a napkin, finishing my mouthful. "Yes... I plan to. I just worry about upsetting her. She's in such a good place right now."

"She is, but you still have to tell her."

"I know," I said, sighing.

I took a sip of coffee, swallowed, and coughed, clearing my throat. My hand gripped my neck. It still ached, even though there was no bruising left anymore.

"All finished?" Lydia asked as she walked over.

"Yes, it was delicious as always," Lola said.

I nodded in thanks. Taking a sip of coffee, I eased my dry throat, took a deep breath, and asked, "Can you sit for a minute?" Lydia smiled. My heart pounded; clammy hands gripped one another as sweat beaded on my skin.

Lydia sat down. "What's wrong, my sweet?" she asked, hesitating.

I cleared my throat and rubbed the back of my neck. "I, erm... something happened to me a few nights ago."

"What? Are you okay?" she asked, her brow furrowed, eyes sunken.

"Yes, don't worry. I'm fine now."

She sat forward in her chair. "What happened?"

I bit my lower lip, swallowed, and said, "I was attacked on the way home."

Lydia's eyes widened and her mouth fell open. She reached out, clasping her hand over mine.

Tears welled in my eyes as I tried to talk. But nothing would come out. Lola reached out, clasping her hand on ours. She took over, telling the tale of the tragic event that befell me. Tears streamed down my face. Lydia's sodden cheeks matched my own, but she stayed silent, listening intently to Lola's tale. After she had finished, she sat frozen to the spot, blinking slowly.

Pulling me towards her, she flung her arms around me. The table next to ours went silent. A mother and two children stared with curiosity. The entire coffee shop silenced its chatter, listening in to what was being said.

After a few minutes, Lydia pulled away and inspected my neck. I sniffled as she wiped the tears from my cheeks.

"I'm okay," I said. "It was just… a shock."

"You're bloody lucky, that's what you are. If that man hadn't come along when he did, God damn, you wouldn't be sitting here right now," she said, her face as pale as the frosted glass that covered the window.

"I know," I said, taking a deep breath.

"Do you know who he was?" I shook my head. "Okay, but they caught the guy, didn't they?" I nodded.

"She went to see him," Lola said. I frowned at her. She winced, mouthing the word *sorry*.

Lydia's eyes widened. "What? Why on earth would you do that?"

"I needed to know why he attacked me."

She sighed, shaking her head. "I understand... but, don't EVER do that again!" She pulled me in close, held me tight, stroking my hair. I coughed and she let go. Her face lightened. "What did he say?"

"Nothing much, he laughed at me and repeated the words, it works."

"God damn, he belongs in the looney bin."

I nodded.

"So… you were just in the wrong place at the wrong time my sweet?" She sighed. "That's good to know."

I frowned, lips pursed.

"Actually..." Lola said.

"What?"

"He knew her name."

Lydia's eyes bulged; mouth fell open. "Is he locked up?"

I nodded. "Yes, I've got to go identify him next week."

"Damn," she said. "I'll close up, I'll come with you."

"No, no, it will be fine. Lola's taking me."

She sighed, squeezing my arm. "Phone me afterwards!"

"I will."

"And any news you get, you let me know."

"I will, I promise."

"We've got to go, honey," Lola said. I nodded, standing up.

Lydia stood up and hugged me. Holding tight as though her life depended on it. "Promise me you'll be safe."

"I promise." I smiled, holding her tight.

"I'll keep her safe, Lydia. She'll be with me all weekend,"

Lola said.

Lydia nodded, feigned a smile, and walked away, wiping her eyes.

As we left, I waved. She nodded, blew me a kiss, and we got into the taxi that waited for us.

CHAPTER SIX

"Shit!" Lola yelled, making me jump. She tapped the taxi driver on the shoulder. "We need to go to Dames and Dancers."

Crap, I'd totally forgot. Then again, it wasn't like I wanted to go shopping right now.

Lola seemed to read my expression. "Half an hour, tops," she said.

I nodded. I was tired, gazing out of the window as the world passed by.

Nodding off, I rested my head against the cold window frame. Heavy eyes dozed as I slipped into a land of nightmarish dreams and delicious desire. The man who saved me appeared before my eyes; his delicate gaze softened my body into a state of ultimate relaxation. There was something about him. His supple figure calmed the nerves that twisted within my soul. Detective Melissa said he was the reason my attacker was in the hospital. I was thankful he dealt the payback that I couldn't. My saviour, who was he? I hoped I would see him again. Something about him called me closer.

The car jolted to a stop. "Honey, we're here," Lola said, shaking my arm. "Did you fall asleep?" she asked, smirking.

"I may have done." I smiled, wiping the drool from my chin.

"There will be time for a kip when we get back. Come on, let's get you a dress for tonight."

We paid the driver and stepped out into the freezing cold street. Snowflakes were falling, black ice threatened to topple us over. "Shit, it's cold," I said, wrapping myself in my deep red coat.

"Oh, quit whining, we've only got to walk across the street." She grinned, punching my arm.

"Ow." I winced, pushing her back.

Laughing, we walked towards the shop; the bell rang as we entered. Dames and Dancers was an old favourite of mine. It'd been here for decades. A family run business passed down from generation to generation. They stocked the largest variety of unique clothing, from old and vintage to modern and futuristic. There was something for everyone.

"So, what are we thinking for tonight? A kinky mini, or a classy fishtail?"

"Err... How about neither," I said, smiling, heading over to the vintage section.

"Oh, so it's old and musty we're after." She grinned.

I smirked. "Also known as vintage, my dear."

Thumbing through the rails of clothing, I spotted a

mid-sleeve, knee-length number. The top half was a deep burgundy, with a patterned skirt that complemented the design.

"Wow, that's stunning, go try it on."

I smiled, heading over to the changing area with Lola in tow.

Stepping into the cubicle, I pulled the curtain across, removing my cream sweater and jeans; my body aching. Staring at my reflection, I smiled; I had grown to love the body I was blessed with. Well, all except the three-inch scar on my right thigh. I felt the bump and shuddered. Granted, I would never be as skinny as Lola, but damn I had the curvature to die for.

Slipping on the dress, it skirted over my body, caressing my curves, and defining my silhouette. I grinned, looking in the mirror. I loved it.

"You ready?" Lola asked, growing impatient.

"Yeah, I'll be right out."

Pulling back the curtain, Lola gasped. "It's like it was made for you," she said.

I grinned from ear to ear. My bosom was ample, shown off by the low-cut V-neck. My waist was taut, pulled in to reveal my curvy hips and long legs. It was beautiful, heck, I was beautiful... and it felt good to say that.

I hadn't always had the best relationship with my body. Fad diets and binge eating hadn't helped. Then there was the gym membership that lasted all of two months. I'd given up and grown to accept who I was and how I looked... and damn, I looked good today.

"That's the one," I said, smiling.

Lola clapped as I disappeared behind the curtain and changed back into reality.

After we paid, we made our way back to Lola's apartment. She cracked open a bottle of bubbly, turned on the Friday night tunes, and we got ready for the night ahead.

"Come on, honey, drink up, there's plenty more where that came from."

"That's if you don't drink it all first," I said, laughing.

"Oi, oi," she said, grinning, holding the bottle and dancing around the living room to the latest clubbing tunes.

I sat in front of the mirror, applying tinted moisturiser and apple blossom lipstick. My pale face warmed with the luscious decadence of subtle cream, and a tint of rose to accentuate the cheekbones. Now the eyes, sad and lonely eyes. The sparkle had been lost in them lately. It'd take a miracle to rescue them. Thankfully, the black eye had healed. I went for a palette of reddish browns to match my dress. It worked well with a winged look and deep black eyeliner. Finally, I was ready. Lola looked like she'd been taking one too many trips on a merry-go-round, her swaying figure clearly inebriated by the bottle she clung to.

"Ready!" I said, standing up and twirling. She clapped, whistling, running over for a selfie. Social media was a Lola special, every thought, every action documented for the world to see. She had thousands of followers, perverted ones at that. The amount of dick pictures she received were unreal. People obsessed over her too much. If only they knew she bit her toenails and spat them all over the apartment. Burgh, I shuddered. I'd dare her to put a picture of that on Instagram! I chuckled under my breath, posing for another selfie. Apparently, the lighting on the first one wasn't adequate enough. Jeez! I smirked, chuckling under my breath. Faults and all, this vile girl was my best friend.

"Where we off to then?" I asked, quizzing her as we skipped down the stairs and out the front door. A taxi was already waiting. The door opened as we reached it and Fiona jumped out, grabbing me.

"Julia Jones!" she exclaimed rather loudly in my ear. "I've bloody missed you!" She squeezed my arse.

"Oi, hands off the merchandise," Matty said, hugging us all.

I laughed. "Hot damn Fi, you look gorgeous tonight!" I said, stepping back and taking in the sight. Pastel pink hair swirled up into a bun, winged eyeliner, and hot red lipstick. She looked stunning!

"Oh, girl, I know, I've been at this face all day long." She winked. "Oh my, look at that dress," she said, forcing me to spin around. "Where, oh where, did you buy that little number from?"

"Dames and Dancers, isn't it just gorgeous?" Lola piped in.

I smiled as Matty pulled me close again and stroked my back. "Don't you ever go get yourself hurt again, love," he said. "We were all so worried." He squeezed me tighter.

"I know, it was horrible," I said, tearing up.

"Damn it, don't make her cry," Lola said. "She'll ruin her makeup." She laughed.

I nodded, smiling, waving my hand before my eyes. "Okay, okay, I'm good." I smirked. "So, where we off to?"

"Oh, you're going to love it!" Matty exclaimed.

We piled in the taxi, Matty in the front, us three in the back, heading off into the city for a wild night ahead of us.

According to Fi, the Southern end of London was full of drunken hen and stag groups, inflatable penises, and ride on traffic cones; they'd driven through it all. It sounded a little out of my league. Well, not sober anyway!

"We're here!" Matty exclaimed, jumped out and opened the door for us

Stepping out, I could see a dark painted brick wall, black panelled doorway and two security guards standing in shadow. Now these security guards weren't just any type of guard. These were muscle men on steroids. How the hell the human body could sustain arms that big, I've no idea. The first was as pale as the first flakes of snow, whereas the second was as dark as a midnight sky, with its stars twinkling through his eyes.

Matty ran up to the paler bulkier guy, put his arm around the guard, and ruffled his hair. I stiffened up. *What the hell is he thinking?*

"Matty, my main man," the guard hollered. "Oi, Kenny, this is Matty, the man that saved my lard arse from that fire last Tuesday."

Jeez, he knows them. Thank God! We walked over to join them.

"Matty!" Kenny exclaimed, squeezing him tight until his head went purple.

"Err… he can't breathe," Fi said, tapping Kenny on the shoulder.

"Shit, yeah… I forget my own strength." He laughed.

"How could you forget that?" Lola said, placing her

hands around his biceps.

Kenny grinned. "And who might you be?" he asked, smiling.

"Oh my," she gulped. "I'm Lola," she said, fluttering her eyelashes and twirling in her gold sequined mini.

"Well, hello there, Lola," Kenny said, grinning. "Would you care for a drink?"

"I would love a drink," she said, smiling, taking his arm.

"Oi, John, watch the door, mate. Matty's here,"

"Matty!" he yelled as a large headed muscular man bounded through the door. He picked Matty up and squeezed him tight.

"Enough, John, the kid can't breathe," Kenny said, laughing.

Matty coughed, gasping for air. "You're the kid that saved my man Derek from the fire on Rosen Way," he stated. "You're welcome 'ere anytime, mate!"

"Thanks man," Matty said.

"Yeah, go on, Kenny, I'll watch the door. You and Derek go have a drink to celebrate."

"Thanks, mate," Derek said, wrapping his bulky arm around Matty's shoulder. "Come on mate, I owe you a whisky or two!" He grinned, waltzing him through the door. Matty grabbed my hand and pulled me along.

"Come on Julia," Matty said, leading the way. I took Fi's hand, and Lola and Kenny followed behind.

Entering the club was like entering a haunted mansion. It was dark, lit by lanterns and disco beams, a gothic misprint of a nightmarish landscape. The subtle smell of sweat sat at the back of my throat as I tasted the youth in the air tonight.

It felt wrong in there, a mixture of hormones mangled together, kids pretending to be adults, adults believing they were kids. Kenny and Lola disappeared, headed over to a private bar. She seemed to be having fun. Whereas I… I wasn't so sure. I shuddered as an uneasy feeling crept beneath my skin. Lavish purple walls embarked a miscreant of luminescent pictures, depicting an array of mythological beings. Out of four paintings hung along the corridor in the entranceway, one stood out in particular. It reminded me of a biblical painting we'd studied back in high school by a painter named Hans Memling. It was a fifteenth century depiction of the afterlife. A tragic portrayal of mortality embracing immortality through the marriage of sexualised erotica. In the centre of the image, the horned beast was sat defiling the remains of an enchanting woman. Her dead body lay bare, taken by the beast for his own sexual satisfaction. It was dark, a twist of nightshade noir, rose red and defiant dark browns. I shuddered. Darkness lived in that painting; I could feel it calling out to me. It lived in this bar too.

After downing a few shots, we were woozy enough to start the night ahead. It wasn't busy in here, but we seemed to be the main lively crowd that everyone watched in awe. Who were they? The regulars? The girl behind the bar with the wild pink hair seemed to know everyone's name and what they were drinking before they even asked for it.

A couple of cocktails down and the wild pink barkeep was chatting to Fi about the delight of the Unicorn Spectacular… apparently a cocktail named after a real-life unicorn who lived in the New Forest. She believed it too, the barkeep, I mean. She was deadly serious. Fi, of course, was having none of it but continued to entertain her as she clearly had the hots for the barkeep by the name of Kat.

This was it… I was a drunken victim alone in the world. Jeez, give me a bucket so I can hurl. I patted Fi's shoulder and headed off to find the bathroom. The place spun like a carousel with a manic number of nutters on board. Why was everyone staring? What the heck did they know that I didn't? Great, the paranoia stage. Just what I loved. Why had I drunk so much? Burgh.

I turned the corner, staggering to the side. The wall, however, was further away than I'd originally planned it to be. I reached out, clambering as I fell, unearthing my drunken body to see a dark pair of black biker boots. *Oooh, shiny!* I reached out to touch them. The boots buckled as two knees bent down and masculine hands gripped my waistline, pulling me up from the floor. I couldn't see who it was, but accepted the help. He walked me into a bathroom and held my hair away from my face. Jeez, the embarrassment of it. I hurled right down into the white porcelain toilet, wiping my mouth, and clambering around for the handle to flush it.

Too late. My mystery man flushed it for me, lifted me up as though I was as light as a feather, and walked me straight over to the sink. Splashing cold water over my face, he held my waist as I bent down, rinsing my mouth. Standing up, I straightened my hair in the funhouse mirror before me, then turned to face him. He held me with one arm, using the other to grip my chin, staring into my eyes.

Soft brown eyes stared back at me. Kind, sweet, caring browns. His face, although blurred, was familiar. He didn't say a word as he lifted me up into his arms and carried me out of the bathroom. The disco lights in the club blared through my retinas. Squeezing my eyes shut, I turned to hide in his chest. A leathery aroma tickled my nostrils. Familiarity struck again. *I've been here before.* The softness of his skin, the safety net of his grip. It was all too familiar. Clarity struck. I gasped. *Is this the man that saved me?* Had he saved me from Eddy's wrath as his twisted fingers clawed at my neck. My hand reached up, soothing over the remains of the bruising as I leant back into his chest. *Where is he taking me?*

We stepped through a heavy door onto the roof of the building. The cool air hit me. Bending down, he helped me to stand, steadying me as I swayed, and wrapping his leather jacket around my shoulders.

All around us, fairy lights twinkled under the stars of the night sky. A glass pergola shrouded an old settee from the snowflakes that fell, delighting my rose-coloured cheeks with the crisp nature of winter's reign. Falling into a heap on the settee, I lay staring up at the starry sky. Lights danced before my eyes, establishing themselves as a force against the darkness, twirling and swirling in a rhythmic dance of delight.

It was cold out here, but the warmth of his jacket cradled my body, soothing away the shivers of the frosted landscape surrounding me.

My mystery man's body silhouetted against the stars, blocking their delicacy from sight. He bent down before me, leaned in, and took my hand, staring into my eyes.

Finally, he spoke. "How are you feeling?" he asked, brow furrowed.

I knew his voice, the recognition of his soft tone reverberated through me. It had to be him. He had to be the one that saved me.

Adrenaline pumping, hands clammy. I sat upright, squinting to define his face. One shot too many and I couldn't see for shit. A chiselled face, with a trimmed brown beard warming his square jawline. With his pale complexion, soft brown eyes stared back, while wavy brown hair caressed his cheekbones, as the wind took flight around us.

It's him. It has to be! "Do I know you?" I asked, stammering.

He shook his head.

"It's just, you look like someone that helped me."

He smiled; a mesmerising upturning of his lips soothed my soul. Is it him? "You look so familiar! Were you there?"

"Where's there?" he asked. I frowned.

"In the alleyway, you saved me."

"Did I?"

I rubbed my head. Had I banged it again? "I think so... didn't you?"

"Possibly. Have you sobered up yet?" His eyes softened as his lips curled at the edges.

"I, erm... yes... well, I'm getting there," I said, with the world spinning around me.

"That's great!" Smiling, he stared out into the night sky. "I've never had a girl throw herself at my feet before." He grinned, raising his eyebrows.

I laughed. "Oh hush, I was clearly drunk."

"And I believe you still are." He winked.

I paused, staring at him. "Why did you help me?" I

asked, frowning.

"Why wouldn't anyone help you?" he said, smiling.

I smiled. "Not many people would stop and help."

"That's rather sad."

I nodded. "So, how did you help? He was very strong."

He smiled. "Don't you think I look strong enough?" he asked, pretending to flex his muscles. I smirked, sitting back on the sofa. He sat beside me. "I was crossing over the street when I saw you. Then he attacked you."

His eyes softened as he gazed over at me.

I shivered. The cold was working its way through my body, tormenting every part of me.

He watched as I pulled his jacket tighter to my chest. "How about we go back inside, get you a coffee?"

"That sounds good," I smiled. He helped me up, steadying me as we walked back through the door and down the staircase to the bar. The lights were blinding. Music thumped and my head pounded. Damn, it was loud in here. My mystery man nodded to the girl behind the bar, and two coffees appeared. "Thank you," I said, smiling. I winced at the strength of the music as we sat beside the bar.

He lifted his hand, touching my forearm. "How about we head over there? That booth is the quietest in the club."

I nodded, following him over to the furthest booth away from the dance floor. "Do you come here often?" I asked.

He laughed. "Kind of."

My face flushed, and I bit my lip, wincing at how stupid I'd sounded. "You seem to know a lot about the place." He nodded, smiling. "So, is this where you normally sit?"

He nodded again, taking a sip of coffee. I matched him, sipping at my own. A double espresso. How did he know? "Is it good?" he asked.

"Yes, thanks."

"No, thank you… it's nice to share a coffee with someone."

"Ah… so you're the mysterious lonely type then?" I asked, smirking.

"It would appear so." He grinned.

Sweat beaded on the top of my lip as I removed the jacket to cool down. The smell of leather soothed through me as I handed it back. "Thank you," I said, "it's hot in here."

"Ah… that'll be your body coming down from the alcoholic revolt you put it through." He laughed. "The heat's got nothing to do with it."

I bit my lower lip, then smiled. "Well, maybe."

"So, what bike do you own?" I asked, nodding towards the jacket.

"Ah, that would be Gladys, my closest friend."

I laughed. "You named your bike Gladys?" He nodded, feigning offence. I laughed again. "So, what model is it?"

"It's a little before your time." He smiled. "But Gladys is a Black Lightning Vincent."

I nodded. "So… your bike is a model with a manly name, called Vincent, and you called it Gladys."

"Yes, that would be correct."

We both burst out laughing.

"Can I ask why?" I asked.

"Because the lady that sold her to me was called Gladys."

"You're not very original are you?" I smirked.

"It would appear not," he said. I chuckled.

Taking the last sip of coffee, I sat back, staring into my empty cup. My mind wandered to the night of the attack. My neck ached, so I sat upright, bringing my hand up to soothe it.

"Does it still hurt?" he asked.

"Yes, but it'll ease soon."

He nodded.

"Thank you," I said. He smiled. "No really, thank you… without you I wouldn't be sitting here." My eyes welled with tears. Breathing heavy, chest tight, hands clammy.

He gave a clenched half-smile. "It's okay," he said, reaching out to rest his hand on my own. "You're safe here."

I nodded, pursing my lips. "I know, I'm sorry for being so emotional… a lot has happened over the past few days."

He nodded. "Well, I'm always here if you want to talk about any of it."

"Thank you," I said, standing up. "But I think I need to sober up first. Thanks for the coffee." I smiled. He stood up, took my hand as I turned to leave, kissed it, then smiled.

The warmth of his kiss left me as I turned to walk away. His delicate lips left an imprint on my hand, soothing the skin with his touch. I brought my hand up to my heart, smiling as the sensation of butterflies fluttered inside my stomach, then headed off to find my friends.

CHAPTER SEVEN

The weekend. The sun rose, my head throbbed, bleaching my retinas as it blasted its way through the gap in the curtains. "Damn," I said, rolling over. *How much did I have to drink last night?* Half the night was a blur. *How the hell did we get home?*

I looked under the covers. I was changed and in pyjamas. Burgh, my head pounded. Taking my time, I sat upright. The room span. *Shit! I'm going to hurl!* Stopping dead still, I breathed, steady and slow. *No. I'm good.* Pushing my aching body forwards, I clambered off the bed. My mouth tasted like something had shat in it. Pulling open the bedroom door, I staggered across to the bathroom and tried the door. *Locked. Damn it.* I knocked. "Lola… I need a wee," I said, jigging about, crossing my legs.

The door opened and one huge bulky bouncer stood half naked in front of me. A mere hand towel covered his manhood. "Excuse me," he said.

Eyebrows raised, I smirked, took a step back, and let him pass. His naked butt continued into Lola's room as he shut the door behind him.

Okay, well, that was a sight! I walked into the bathroom, locked the door, and emptied my bladder for what felt like forever. *Why is it that the morning wee lasts ages, yet when you want the toilet in the day, it's urgent and hardly anything comes out?* I puzzled.

I cleaned up and flushed. Staring into the mirror, I looked like someone had pushed me down the stairs, then thrown me through a hedge backwards. My neck was still sore, and my face looked like a tire iron squashed it. What the hell had I slept on? I had lines imprinted up one side. No wonder big, bulky Kenny stared at me strangely. Jeez, this would take more than foundation to fix. *How long before I de-line?*

I spent the next half an hour cleaning, toning, and moisturising myself into the average human being when the door knocked and Lola walked in. Damn, I forgot to lock it. "You made me jump," I said.

"Not as half as you made Kenny jump!" she laughed.

I scowled. "Yes, I know, I look like shit… I'm working on it." I smirked.

"Work harder, damn you," she said, laughing. "I'll go fetch us a coffee."

"Where's lover boy?"

"Kenny?"

"Yes, unless you have another one in there?"

She smirked. "He's gone. He had to head back to the club," she said, shrugging her shoulders.

"Aww, okay… did you guys have fun?"

"Yeah," she said, squirming and smiling from ear to ear.

"Anyway… who was that hot guy that gave you his jacket last night?"

"Oh, so that happened?" She nodded.

"That was…" Crap what was his name? "I don't have a clue! I never asked his name." My jaw dropped as I raised my hand to catch it.

Lola laughed, "Nathaniel,"

"Huh?"

"His name was Nathaniel Night… he owns the place."

"Ah…." I nodded, "Well that makes sense." Lola smirked and walked out. "Oh… and did you know?" I shouted.

"Know what?" she yelled from the kitchen.

"He's the guy that saved me."

Silence. Then the thudding of footsteps as she ran into the room. "WHAT?"

I nodded, pursing my lips. "Yeah."

"Shit, that's a coincidence," she said.

"Just a bit!"

"He's your very own sexy saviour." She grinned.

I laughed as she walked out again to make a coffee.

We spent the rest of the afternoon relaxing in the apartment, a pyjama party involving old movies, soft drinks and eating our weight in popcorn. It was like being back in the dorm room again.

Saturday came and went as Sunday ended with a day of romantic comedies, more popcorn, and furry pyjamas. Perfect.

Monday morning rose as the sun cast a misty veil over

the river Thames. Lola's apartment was dark and cold. I yawned, stretching. Today I planned to head into the office. I had too much work to do and a ton of paperwork to look through. I had to meet Jeff Walters, the eyewitness from Philippa Langdale's murder, and I needed to let the public know about the London Butcher. I still believed it was Eddy Boland, but there was no evidence. I had to find something, anything, to tie him to the other murders.

I washed, dressed, and applied my make-up, finishing it with my favourite apple lip balm. Lola had lent me one of her work skirts and chiffon blouses, but it felt a little tight for my liking. I made a mental note to keep some clothes here for times like these.

Walking into the kitchen, I turned the coffeemaker on. Lola's door jarred as she trudged out of her bedroom, yawning. "What time is it?"

"About seven."

She straightened up. "Shit, I'm going to be late!"

"You've plenty of time, Lola. Here, have a coffee, it'll wake you up."

She walked over, taking a sip. "I suppose Gerrard won't mind on our first day back."

I smiled. "It'll be fine." I watched her for a moment. No banging headache, no nausea. She was positively gleaming. Good. "How are you doing?"

"I'm fine. You?" She smiled.

"Same," I said, surprised.

An hour later, we were both ready and leaving for the office. The walk across Mable Bridge was a cold one. Mushed leaves squelched under foot as we peered down at the frozen river below.

"Jeez, hurry Lola, it's freezing!"

Lola was too busy taking a selfie on the bridge to notice the clouds threatening a downpour above.

"It's going to rain!" I said, pulling her by the arm.

"Oooh, honey, that won't do my hairstyle any good. Let's get a move on!" I sighed, and she laughed at me.

"Look, we're nearly there," she said as Lydia met us at the door to her coffee shop with two coffees to go.

"Be safe out there, girls," she said.

I thanked her, kissed her cheek and took the coffee, heading up Bride Street.

The clouds drizzled as we both picked up pace. *The London Chronicle* was just past the consulate. I shuddered as I walked through Harp alley. Lola grabbed my hand, smiled, and pulled me through.

Past the alley, the *Chronicle* stood tall, towering above the consulate as we headed over to the mirrored building. It was iconic in the centre of London, a monument to our duty of candour. Many newspapers were gossip mongers, but for us, the truth stood before all else, and it was our duty to tell it. I smiled as Dennis held open the door. Thanked him and headed up to the fifth floor.

"See you later, short stack," I said heading to my office.

At the office, I settled in my chair, staring out at the cityscape before me.

"Coffee?" Selene asked as she bounded into the room. Selene was the saviour here at the *Chronicle*. She kept everyone hydrated, booked meetings, organised galas and even picked up your dry cleaning... not that I ever did any.

I smiled, shaking my coffee cup and nodding. I needed all the coffee I could get if I was going to get through the Butcher piece today.

"Thanks, Selene, that would be great." I smiled.

She turned to walk out of the room. Stopped and turned back. "How are you doing?" she asked, her hand to her chest.

"I'm good." Pursing my lips, I smiled. "Surprisingly good." She smiled and turned away.

"Oh, and thanks for feeding Maisy!" I shouted as she left. She waved as she walked off.

I turned my laptop on, stretched out my arms, and kicked off my boots. I was going to be here for a while.

Selene bounded back into my office with a black coffee in one hand and a bouquet in another. "These came for you," she said. "No name on the card though." She smiled and placed the vase of flowers on my desk.

I grinned. "Thanks, Selene." She smiled and walked off, closing the door behind her.

The flowers smelled beautiful. I read the card. *"I saw these and thought of you."* No signature, just a sideway number eight. The infinity symbol. Infinite Encounters. It had to be Nathaniel. I melted, picturing his gorgeous brown eyes. Beside the card was a description. *'Belle in Black. Ecuadorian Da Vanda Black Orchids, magnificent Maurv Memory Roses, Black and Sunset Calla Lilies, Scottish Eryngium Thistle, Copper Ruscus and Pistacia enhanced with gold wire and finished in a black vase.'*

The door opened and Gerrard walked in. His hair a mop of brown, brown eyes, chiselled face, thick-framed glasses to suit. He huffed as he entered, out of breath from the ascent of five flights of stairs. "You ought to take the lift, Gerrard," I laughed, as he sat down to catch his breath.

"No, I'm determined to lose the gut." He smiled, shaking his belly with his hands.

"Less cheese might help!" I grinned. He loved cheese!

He frowned. "Never going to happen." He sighed, then raised his eyebrows. "But I have joined the gym downstairs."

"Brilliant! Susan will be pleased."

He scoffed. "Hopefully, she'll stop packing me wheat grass for lunch then!" I laughed.

"Anyway, how are you doing?" he asked, staring at me.

My hand clasped it. The bruising had almost gone now. "I'm feeling a lot better. Plus, they caught the guy."

"Eddy Boland, wasn't it?"

I nodded. Of course he knew all about it.

"So, can you pull together a story on him, or would you rather I ask Jayden… if it's too close to home."

"No, I'll do it. I want to know more about him, anyway."

He nodded. "I thought you'd say that. I'll ask Jimmy to go photograph the scene."

"Okay." I smiled. He stood up, taped me on the shoulder and walked out of the room.

I took a deep breath, flexed my fingers, and typed, or at least tried to. How the heck was I going to report on either of these incidents? I sat back, drumming my fingers on the arm of the chair. I mean, how would I write about Nathaniel saving me and a howling beast that ripped up Eddy Boland? Then there was Eddy setting on fire in hospital and coming out unscathed. Where the heck do I start?

Well, as with any good story, it needs a beginning. A transcendent tale of the perpetrator's past, his criminal activity, and where he comes from. Then bring in the victim. Why did he choose her, what made her worth him being caught and locked up for? With Eddy, he didn't appear to have any motive. That's the strangest thing about it. I frowned, pursing my lips. I rolled my chair back to the desk, sat up and typed out the sequence of events, shuddering at certain moments as I relived the horrendous experience.

Selene popped in with another coffee in hand. "I've organised your meeting with Jeff for tomorrow."

I nodded. "Thanks Selene. I don't know what I'd do without you!" She walked out, smiling.

So, who was Eddy Boland?

I logged on and searched for any information on Eddy Boland in London. Nothing. Zero search results. How is that even possible? Okay, so I needed something more. He looked in his mid to late thirties and was extremely strong for his appearance. I had nothing. There was no reason to target me. We had no history. The only way I could learn about why he wanted to hurt me was from Eddy himself, and I certainly didn't fancy that again. Perhaps Gerrard was right. Maybe I was too close to this. I sighed, locking my laptop, and standing upright. I stretched and walked out and into Jayden's office. Piles of folders littered his desk. Portrait photographs of the lost and found.

He glanced up from his laptop. His deep brown eyes studied me, then he frowned. "What?" he asked. I took a step back. My eyes widened. I guess Lola was right after all.

"Have you found anything yet?" I asked, nodding over

at the files.

"No, and there's two more reported missing this week."

"Could they be runaways?"

"No, these were from well-established families. There's no reason they would up and leave."

I paused, thinking. "I wonder if it's connected."

"What?"

"If it's connected to the Butcher."

"He murders his victims, and they're all blond-haired city girls. These were brunettes."

"Hmm... still it's worth considering." *Especially as I'm a redhead and Boland might be the Butcher.*

He looked up from his laptop. "Aren't you working on the Butcher?"

"Yeah."

"So why you here then?"

Wow, he really is an ass!

"I need help on the Boland case. Have you found anything?"

"What case? The guy that attacked you?" I nodded. "Why are we reporting on that? It's open and shut."

I shrugged. He has a point. The police already had him. "Gerrard asked me to. But honestly, Jayden, I think there's more to it."

"You would say that. He attacked you, didn't he?" I nodded. "Well then, why did he? Do you know him?"

"No, that's the thing. I don't know why."

"Did you write anything about him lately?" I shook my head. "Okay, well there has to be some connection."

"I don't know. There's nothing on the search engines."

He frowned. "Seriously?"

"Yeah." He sat upright and scratched his head.

"Wait, remind me, what's his info?"

"Eddy Boland. Mid-thirties, brown hair, brown eyes."

He started tapping away on his laptop. I waited, walked in further and took a seat. He frowned, tapped away again, then frowned again. "Weird!"

"Yeah, I know. I couldn't find a thing on him either."

He nodded. "Okay, I'll see what my contacts at the police station can find out."

I smiled. "Thanks." He was a jackass but a jackass with a father in the force.

He grimaced and rubbed his chin. "You sure you've not written anything?"

"No, I've only been working on the Butcher," I puzzled, brow furrowed.

"When did he get arrested?"

"Last week, straight after it happened."

"And there's been no killings since?"

"No, which is strange as the Butcher was killing one, sometimes two women a week."

"There's your connection."

"You think?" My lips pursed. "I considered it, but like the detectives said. I'm not the Butcher's usual MO."

"It's strange." His eyes widened. "Could it all be connected? Could you have survived the Butcher?" He rubbed his hands together. I shuddered. "Leave it with me, Julia, I'll let you know what I find."

"Thanks." I smiled, stood up and walked away. I paused, remembered, and turned back. "Wait," I said, taking a deep breath. *Do I ask him?* I walked back to the desk and pulled out a piece of paper from my pocket, placing it on his desk.

"What's that?"

"It's the number plate from a black Mercedes. I think it might be connected somehow."

He nodded. "I'll check it out. Leave it there," he said. I nodded and left the room.

After leaving his room, I walked over to Lola's office. I was still in two minds whether he was a jackass after all.

"Fancy a late lunch later?" I asked, peering through Lola's door. She was busy sketching something on her graphics tablet.

"Sure, can we stay local, though? I've got a ton of work to do."

I smiled. "Of course, the canteen it is."

"Oh God no, how about Nero's?"

"Nero's it is, I'll text Fi and Matty to meet us… about 2pm?"

"Yep," she said, smiled and blew me a kiss as I left.

Back in my office, I texted Fi and Matty and booked a table at Nero's.

Over the next few hours, I tidied up a few other outstanding articles, answered emails, and rang Detective Melissa Lee.

"Hi Detective, it's Julia Jones."

"Hello Julia, what can I do for you?"

"I was phoning for an update on Eddy Boland. Is he

still in custody?"

"Yes," she sighed, "but we're struggling to put the evidence together. He was clean and didn't have a spec of your DNA on him."

"What about his wounds? Didn't you get anything from the swabs?"

"No. They were unidentifiable."

"What do you mean?"

"The samples from Eddy Boland's wounds could not be identified. They are not from anything.... err... normal."

"Huh?"

"I mean, we don't know what it is, so we can't use it as evidence."

I sighed. "Okay, but what about the scrapings you took from under my nails?"

"They came up as inconclusive."

"Damn, so what now?"

"For now, we've charged him, but will continue to work to gather as much evidence as possible. The last thing we want is for the case to be thrown out of court."

"What about bail?"

"The lawyers are still pushing for bail; the preliminary hearing is next week."

"Do you need me to attend?"

"No, we have your statement. We just need you to identify him at the line-up."

I gulped. "Okay, I'll be bringing a friend though."

"That's fine," she said.

"Okay, well, I have one more question."

"Yes, of course. What is it?"

"Do you know why he targeted me?" The phone went silent. "Melissa?"

"I, erm, no. We haven't found a connection yet."

"But who did he work for?"

She went silent for a moment. "Why do you think he worked for someone?"

"It's just, the Butcher has killed no one in a week, and I thought, well, perhaps as Eddy is in jail, perhaps he's the Butcher."

"Hmm…"

"It would make sense, considering I have an eyewitness coming in to give me their testimony. He said he'd already been to see you and Monroe."

"Yes, I know who you mean, Monroe took his statement."

"So have you considered it?"

"Yes, we have. But your attack was quite different to the Butcher's."

"Maybe, but if you consider all those missing girls, perhaps it's similar. Perhaps the Butcher took them too?"

"I don't think so, Julia. It isn't normal for a serial killer to let some of his victims go."

"But what if they escaped?"

"They don't remember that, though. It just doesn't fit. Monroe looked into it."

"Okay, well, if you have any new leads, can you contact me, please?"

"Of course."

"Thanks Melissa."

"No problem, speak later."

"Bye." I ended the call, tapping my fingers on the desk, lips pursed. At least she's going to consider the possibility, no matter how ludicrous it may seem. But the fact that the Butcher had not killed another girl since they arrested Eddy spoke volumes.

The door opened. Lola walked in. "Come on, honey, finish up. It's lunchtime."

I smiled, closed down the laptop and headed out for lunch with the girls… and Matty.

Nero's was just a few doors down from the *Chronicle*. It was a favourite of Lola's, and mine, to be fair. They offered more of an Italian menu with their pastas and pizzas. Ham and cheese tagliatelle were my favourite from their menu, and just what I was going to choose today.

As we entered, Fi and Matty were already there. They were both deep in conversation. Matty had his firefighters' uniform on. His rich, dark brown skin lit up under the light free flowing from the window beside us. He would make a good living as a model if you ignored his foul eating habits and dirty mind. But he didn't care. Firefighting was his life.

Fi, well, she looked as glamorous as ever. A chic cream outfit, showing off her tanned complexion and modern jewellery. She had styled her hair to sophistication, matching this season's newest trends. Looking at it pastel pinks were back in fashion. It helped as she worked as a top stylist for London's celebrity scene. They both stood up and hugged us. The server came, pulled out our chairs and seated us at the round table. He tried to hand out menus, but we refused; we knew it off by heart. After taking our orders, he disappeared into the kitchen.

"So, how's it hanging, ladies?" Matty asked, smirking.

"Matty, you sound like a pubescent teenager," Lola said, laughing.

I smirked. "It's all good," I replied, smiling.

"So, who's this Nathaniel I've heard mentioned?" Matty inquired.

Lola grinned. "He's Julia's very own sexy saviour!"

"Oh, I need more!" Fi said, shuffling in closer.

I laughed. "He's the owner of Infinite Encounters."

"Ooo," Matty said. "So, when'd he save you?"

"The other night, from Eddy Boland."

Fi shuddered, took a deep breath, and pulled back. "Girl, the fact that he walks this Earth scares the shit out of me." She paused, concentrating on her breathing. "But with people like your Nathaniel out there, well, it eases my palpitations a little!" she said, hand to her chest.

I nodded. She smiled. "Plus, he is kinda cute… if you're into guys, that is." She laughed.

Matty shoulder bumped her, smirking. "Oh Matty," she said, fluttering her eyelashes. "If I enjoyed the male penis as much as you do, you'd be my number one any day."

Laughter echoed in the room as I hushed them, feeling all eyes staring at us. "Oh girl, lighten up. They wouldn't know what to do with Matty's penis, anyway." She smirked. Matty's face reddened as he feigned a laugh.

An older lady at another table tutted and turned back to her conversation with her husband. He shook his head.

I smirked, laughter escaping me.

"So, tell me about the woman behind the bar?" I asked Fi. "She seemed interested."

"Oh, you think?" I nodded. "Well, she was beautiful."

The server arrived with our drinks, placing each of them down in front of us. I had to delve into a medium glass of Sauvignon Blanc. I needed it after the last twenty-four hours. Lola had gone for her pink gin and lemonade, whereas Fi was on the whisky. Matty, however, was relegated to cola, considering he was still on duty.

"So, are you going to see her again?" Lola asked, taking a sip of her gin.

"Oh, I do hope so," Fi smiled. She paused, taking a sip. "Perhaps we should all go... "it appears there's a temptation for each of us at that club... wouldn't you say?"

I smirked, eyeing up Lola and her girl crush on Kenny.

"What about me?" Matty said.

"You're bisexual, you sweet thing. You can have the pick of anyone in the entire club." Matty's eyes widened.

"Good point." He smirked. "I'm in. When we going?"

We compared calendars. With Christmas Day being next week, and Matty on shift, things were tight.

"New Year's Eve it is then," I said. They nodded, tapping it into their mobile phone calendars.

Food arrived. Ham and cheese tagliatelle. It was as scrumptious as ever. We finished up our drinks, hugged, and headed back to the office. It was already nearly four in the afternoon. The time had flown by with laughs, taunting, and plenty of giggles. I waved goodbye and headed home to feed Maisy.

CHAPTER EIGHT

The shrill sound of my alarm clock echoed through the room as I fumbled around for my phone, quieting the disturbing noise. Sunlight streamed through the window. I shuddered from a blast of icy winds, pulling the duvet up to my neck. Why was it so cold in here?

Maisy must have heard my alarm as she jumped on the bed and purred, plopping herself down on my chest, her tail curled around her tiny body.

"Yes. Yes, I know. I'll feed you in a minute," I said, mid-yawn. I blinked a few times, wiped my eyes, staring up at the ceiling. "Come on Maisy," I said as I lifted her off my chest, sitting myself upright and fumbling down the side of my bed for my dressing gown. "Let's turn the heating up." Pulling the gown around me, I found my slippers and stood up to face the reality of the day. The bedroom door was wide open, my lips pursed. It must have been Maisy. I gazed down at her as she wrapped herself around my ankles, determined to trip me over. I smiled, bent down, and picked her up. "What have you been up to?" I asked, tickling her white tummy. She purred, lifted her paw to my face. "Come on then," I said, walking towards the door.

On the shelf, right there out in the open, was my crime book, albeit a dirtied, ripped version of it. But still my crime book. My brow furrowed. How the hell did that get there? I picked it up, walked downstairs through the living room, placing it on the side table. Did Lola drop it off? I shrugged, then wandered into the kitchen to get a coffee.

The back door was wide open. I stopped. My brow creased, eyes wide. How did that happen? Looking around, nothing appeared to be missing. Placing Maisy on the work surface, I walked over and closed the door. No wonder it was cold. I shook my head. Did I forget to lock it? Even if I did, it wouldn't have come open on its own. Fear crept up my backbone as I stepped back into the living room. What if there was still someone here? I looked around. The boxes of mum's old things still sat piled up in the corner of the room, untouched. I shook my head again. Lips pursed. It must have been the wind? Shrugging, I turned on the electric fire and went back to feed Maisy. It was going to be one of those days. I could feel it.

An hour later, I had showered, dressed, and was ready for work. Maisy had already disappeared out of the cat flap, and the house was as snug and warm as it could ever be. I looked at the kitchen clock, eight-thirty, time to head out to meet Jeff Walters, eyewitness to Philippa Langdale's murder.

Jeff hadn't wanted to meet at the office, nor did he want to meet at a public place like Lydia's coffee shop. Instead, he'd wanted to sit out in the freezing cold in the middle of St. James Park. Granted, it was as public as public could get.

But with the storm en route, we'd be icicles by the end of the day.

I checked my bag. Notepad, pen, digital recorder with a full battery and my mobile phone. I was ready to go. Heading out of the door, I wrapped my red coat around me, fitted my long boots over my jeans and adorned gloves and a scarf; it was going to be a cold one today. I smiled, looking in the mirror. I was ready for the arctic, let alone a clandestine meeting in the park.

I wasn't wrong either. As soon as I left the house, the wind rushed past me, hair flying everywhere and sticking to my apple lip gloss like glue. Damn it. I pulled it back, took a scrunchy out of my bag, and tied it back out of sight.

The walk to the park was eye-watering, hail battered at my body and rough winds encircled it. There was no point in using an umbrella, it wouldn't have lasted five minutes. I passed the local primary school, crossed over the road, and opened the creaky gate to the park. Old iron railings encased St. James. It was an enormous park with a children's play area on one side, a bridge over the lake near the centre and an old bandstand to the right. Jeff wanted to meet at the bandstand. I sighed in relief, at least it had a roof over it. As I walked over, I could see a guy in his mid to late twenties in dark clothing and as skinny as a rake. That must be him.

I entered the bandstand, shook off my coat, and sat beside him. "Jeff, I presume?" He nodded. "I hear you can help me learn more about what happened to Philippa Langdale?"

He turned to look at me. His dirty face streaked with tear stains as his eyes watered. "Was that her name?" I nodded. "There was no way I couldn't help her." He shook his head, trembling. "I just couldn't." Tears fell, cushioning his lips. I reached out and took a tissue from my pocket. He nodded as he took it, blowing his nose and wiping his tears. I watched him, waiting for the right moment.

His head rose, and he straightened his back. I took out my notepad. "Did you see what happened, Jeff?" I asked.

He nodded. "The whole thing."

"Can you talk me through it?"

His face paled, and he lowered his head. "You can't say it was me. He'll come after me next."

I nodded, resting my hand on his arm. "We just want him behind bars, Jeff. You can help with that."

He looked up, fear cradling his sunken eyes. I looked him over. Scruffy jeans, a stained flannel jacket. "You're not his type, Jeff." He took a deep breath. "I promise I'll keep you anonymous. Remember, we protect our sources, you're safe with me." I smiled again as his gaze met my own. He still looked wary, but nodded anyway, recanting his story.

"It was a Friday night, and I was waiting for the baker to give me their old bread when they closed." I nodded, smiling. "Well, that's when that Philippa girl scream."

"What did you do?"

"I went into the alley and saw her shaking, then he punched her." I shuddered, remembering Eddy's fists. "He was shouting something, then he pulled out a needle and stabbed her neck."

The wind caught my breath. I gasped. "A needle?" I asked. "Are you sure?" It's got to be Eddy!

"Yeah, cos he threw it on the floor when he dragged

her body away."

"What did it look like?"

"I dunno, like a big silver needle. It was empty though."

"Where is it now?"

He shrugged. "It's gone. I left it there. When he came back... I ran away."

"Why did you run?"

"Because the guy saw me when he dumped her body in the back of the black car."

I winced. "What black car?"

"A Mercedes or something. It was big and black."

"Why did he take the girl?"

"I think because she was dead after that needle. He was angry about it, that's why he was punching her."

"Huh? So, he kept punching her after she died?"

"Yeah, it looked that way."

I stopped. Looked at him and he turned away, staring into the distance. It made little sense. Why would he punch her after she was dead? "Was he angry?" I asked. Jeff turned back to look at me.

"What? With her or me?"

"Philippa... Was he angry?"

"I dunno, why?"

"I'm trying to understand why he kept punching her after she died."

His lips pursed, and he turned away. "I dunno." He shrugged his shoulders. "Maybe the needle didn't work, so he got angry?"

My eyes widened. "He could have," I puzzled. "Maybe

that's why he was punching her, he blamed her for it?"

"Yeah. Still, doesn't make sense though," he said, staring into the distance.

I nodded. Jeff's body went rigid. His back straightened, breathing quickened, hands balled into fists. I sat back. "Are you okay?" I asked.

He shook his head, his face as pale as ice. "Look!" he said, nodding towards the railings by the gate.

Out behind the railings, across the road, was a black Mercedes, window down and engine roaring. Jeff stood up. "They've seen me. I'm a dead man!" He ran out of the bandstand to the other side of the park. I stood up, ran down the steps and towards the black Mercedes.

They couldn't get away with this! My heart raced, head pounded, fists balled as I reached the gate. It wasn't far away, and I could see the number plate, the same as before. The same damn car that was following me. That killed my mum! What the hell did they want?

The gate creaked as I yanked it open, slamming it shut behind me. I was ready. This time, I was ready.

Fists balled, spittle foaming, my eyes were wide, and I crossed the road. The offside back window rose as the face of an old man in sunglasses with a toothy grin stared back at me. Callous cackles shrieked through the air as the shrill of laughter screamed out at me. The sound of a female voice, her laughter familiar, stopped me dead in my tracks. The blacked-out window closed, and the Mercedes sped off before I could reach it.

I stood there in the middle of the road, dazed by what I'd seen. Who was the old man? And who was the voice I'd heard laughing? I know I've heard that laugh before, but who? My body stiffened as the sound of a car horn jumped me back to reality. I turned to see a blue Mini honking as it drove by. "Dick!" I shouted as I stepped onto the path.

Walking back home, my mind wandered off, caged by its own thoughts. So, if Eddy was locked up, then who drove that car? I scratched my head. The old man must be who Eddy works for. Jeff knew the car; he knew it was there the night they killed Philippa. He'd seen her broken body bundled into the boot and transported God knows where. The icy wind encased my body, encircling me as I carried on walking home. It was the same car that was parked beside the alleyway. The very car that would have had my bundled body inside if Nathaniel hadn't got there in time.

I shivered, my throat tightening. It'd all become too much. Too real. What had I gotten myself into? Tears welled in my eyes, cushioning my lips as icy winds pushed past me. I looked up the street, wiping my eyes. Not far and I'll be home safe and sound!

It was too damn cold to be out in this weather, and with the montage of murders that appeared to surround me, I wasn't feeling safe right now. I shuddered. What an idiot though. Why the hell did I think walking up to the car of a killer was a good idea? I shook my head. It was a stupid plan, a plan bore from anger. The anger of being watched and feeling so damn afraid of my own shadow. Shit, I mean they could watch me right now and I'd wouldn't know. I looked up from the pavement.

Two streets away. My steps quickened as the wind picked up its pace. Palpitations thumped through my chest. It ached as it pounded, my throat tightening. Fear constricting my airway. I ran. Had to get away. I couldn't stay here. Didn't feel safe and now I knew whoever that was in the car had made me their number one target. Eddy had known my name and ever since then, they'd followed me home.

Did they want to finish the job? Was I next on the old guy's hit list? Not that I feared him. I mean, what's an old-aged pensioner going to do to me? It's whoever else was in the car that scared me. I shivered as I arrived at my town house, unlocking the red door. I bounded through as quickly as I could. Taking off my sodden coat and hanging it up to dry. I was soaked, frozen to the bone and sick with nerves.

I grabbed a towel from the tumble dryer, switched on the kettle and made a coffee to warm myself up with. Snuggled in my chair by the fire, Maisy joined me. Her soft purrs soothed my nerve-wracked body as I took my notepad from my bag and jotted a few things down. I took a sip of coffee, placed it back on the side table and looked down at what I'd written. My eyes widened. I couldn't take it back now. I knew. I knew the Mercedes was the link between the Butcher, my attack, and the dead girls. But why?

Maisy snuggled down to sleep. Stroking her, I relaxed. What was I missing? I stared down at my tattered crime book resting on the arm of the chair. Then glanced across at the six unopened boxes. Could that be it? Could the black Mercedes be the same car that ran my mother down seven years ago? It was. Deep down, I knew it was.

A lump formed in the back of my throat. I remember that dreadful night. Mum was on her way home from work. It was cold and blustery, and there was a strong smell of smoke in the air from a fire at Joven's, the old bakery down on Daventry Road. We were going to Lydia's for dinner. She'd said she needed to talk to me. It wasn't strange. Mum always liked to talk. I'd often meet her after her shift for dinner. But this time, it felt different. Her tone of voice on the phone had shaken me. Her sentences felt urgent, her voice wavering, tapering off at the end. There was something wrong, and it wasn't just my mum's usual stress-head when she was working. No, something had scared her.

I'd met her early. She'd finished by six, as her friend had covered the rest of her shift. That alone screamed alarm bells. The night sky loomed overhead as Mum came out of the hospital and hugged me, holding me as tight as she could. Tears welled in her eyes as she kissed my forehead, pulling back and interlinking her arm in mine as we walked. I'd asked her if she was alright. I remember her tender voice answering as she feigned a smile. We crossed the road, and I guess Mum saw it coming before I did, as the next thing I knew she'd pushed me backwards. I tripped and heard the metallic crunch as it hit her body, followed by glass breaking and the animalistic shrill of my mother's screams as her body flew through the air.

Spectators had rushed to the scene as the car drove off. I still remember the squealing tyres as it hot-tailed out of there. The black Mercedes was forever imprinted in my mind, alongside my mother's bloodied face. She lay there still, eyes wide open, her chest unable to rise. She was dead. Killed instantly. If there was a blessing I could take from the horrific memory, it was that she never suffered.

I sighed, held Maisy close, and wiped my eyes. I would

figure all of this out if it was the last thing I did. But for now, I needed to attempt something I'd put off for far too long. I needed to face the boxes, unleashing the memories inside. Maybe there was something in there that brought everything together. I yawned, slipping back in the chair, closing my eyes. The day will come when I can open her boxes... just not now. I needed to rest, knowing full well that I'd need to be strong enough to unearth my past, and I certainly wasn't doing it feeling like this. The day had taken its toll. Hours of murderous torment filtered through my mind, engaging in a deadly battle between the past and the present. A quick snooze wouldn't hurt, and it was all I needed to recharge.

I stretched and groaned, body aching at the discomfort I felt from napping in a chair. Maisy was still snuggled on my lap. She purred, changed position, falling straight back to sleep. Lifting her, I gently placed her on the chair and walked over to turn up the fire. Yawning, I glanced out the window. By the looks of it, Mother Nature was still angry at the city of London. Haggard trees bowed through the shrill of December's almighty winds. It was nasty out there.

After making a drink, I knew what I had to do.

Lifting the first box down, and pulling off the aged parcel, I opened it. Inside there were a bunch of fusty old clothes, presumably mums. Although I couldn't remember her ever wearing a bright yellow jumper. That was more Aunt Clara's cup of tea. From what I remember, Mum was a lot less flamboyant. Black, white, and blue was her go to colour scheme. That and her uniform, which was also blue. My brow furrowed. I wonder why Aunt Clara's things were mixed up with Mum's. Then again, she stayed over a lot. It made sense that she had clothes stashed in the house somewhere. I sighed, looking over at the five remaining boxes. This was all I had left of my mother.

Biting my bottom lip, I opened the next box. It was full of old documents. I flicked through. Old bills, school reports, newspaper articles. Then there was a picture of my mum, me, and Clara. I smiled. We were standing in front of the entrance to London's cave system. I scratched my head; I can't remember that. But by the looks of it, I was only six, maybe seven. It must have been not long since Aunt Clara had walked back into our lives. Before that, I've no idea where she was. It was just Mum and me.

Placing down the photo, I picked up an old newspaper clipping. It was about a sixteen-year-old girl, murdered down a back alley. I shuddered. It sounded all too familiar. But why would Mum have this? Puzzled, I pulled out four more articles. Four more murders. All teenage girls with body parts scattered throughout London. What the heck?

The dates ranged over two years. The two years before they killed my mum. I shook my head; it made little sense! My mum was a nurse. Why on Earth would she be looking into a string of murders? Gripping the articles tighter, I took a deep breath. She was investigating him. The front page showed an old CCTV image of a dark hooded killer with a tendency to maim and torture. But why? What did she know that made her search for him like that? *Shit!* I bit my lip. *Is that what got her killed?*

Rummaging deeper into the box, I found an article I knew all too well, one Lydia must have added after my mother's death. It was my account of the night she was run down and left for dead. The camera from a nearby building had captured half a number plate. They detailed a description of the vehicle in the newspaper. *That confirms it. My memories are right.* As I sat staring at a picture of a dark Mercedes, I could see the last part of the number plate. It mocked me, as it spelt out L0L. Slumping into a heap on the floor, realisation sunk in. I now had the evidence needed to connect my mother's murder with the car at the crime scene of Philippa Langdale. I needed to tell Melissa. This could be the break they're after.

One issue concerned me, whoever killed my mum was now stalking me. Why did the elderly man in the back of the black Mercedes want me dead? He must have sent Eddy. But why? And who was he?

Picking up my drink, I gulped it down, wiping my mouth on my sleeve. My body shook. Was this getting too much for me? Shaking my head, I placed the cup down and rested for a moment. My brow furrowed; lips pursed. I recognised the voice from the car. The sadistic shrill of laughter. But who was it and why did they want to hurt me?

Drumming my fingers on the box, I thought for a moment. Perhaps they think my mother told me what she had found out. Maybe they think I know more than I actually do? I frowned. Then again, I do… don't I? After all, I'm the one investigating the same serial killer my mother once did? *I don't get it. Why did he start up again? Why dismember so many girls? What did they have in common? Shit.* I was drawing a blank. All I knew for sure was that Eddy Boland was the London Butcher, and now I had to prove it.

CHAPTER NINE

Later that afternoon, I compiled everything together and headed in to work. I knew I had a few articles to catch up on, and a piece one of the work experience students wrote to read.

Sitting at my desk, I kicked off my shoes and read through the article, wincing. It was bad. I mean, terrible. There was no structure, no supporting details, and the concluding statement was wishy-washy. Who wrote this? I looked at the by-line. Aimee Lowers. Ah, she was a first-year student. Damn, Gerrard must have been short-staffed last week. He should have rung. I shrugged, stretching out my shoulders. But then, he wouldn't have wanted to bother me after what happened.

Oh well. It looks like I'm going to be here for a few more hours yet.

I began with the opening statement:

The Butcher Strikes Again

By Julia Jones

The London Butcher has struck again. His latest victim, nineteen-year-old Phillipa Langdale, was a resident of Farrowday house at the University of Greater London. Authorities have reason to believe Philippa was the latest victim in a long string of crimes perpetrated by the London Butcher.

An eyewitness, who gave testimony to the murder, has contacted The London Chronicle. Our witness, Mr Jackson (name changed for safety reasons) saw the Butcher inject his victim with an unknown substance. This caused Phillipa's body to shut down. The Butcher used his famous Butcher's knife to slash open Phillipa's carotid artery, ending her life. Phillipa's body was found in several pieces, spread throughout the Thames Gate Park.

Phillipa was in her first year at university, studying English Literature. She was last seen leaving Bayonets Bar on the 19th of February, days before they found her body. Her mother Lisa Langdale told the police that Phillipa had phoned her from outside the club, drunk and upset as her boyfriend Mitchell Mackworth had ended their long-term relationship. This had caused Phillipa to be out in the alleyway alone that night, which led to her brutal murder. She has no known connections to the other victims, except that she was both blond haired, blue eyed with a slim build and pale skin.

With seven victims already. How safe are you in the city of London tonight? I urge you to lock your doors, close your windows and be home before dark. The London Butcher roams the streets, so until they catch him…

Stay safe, stay well, stay alive.

It's a tad on the gory side, but it gets the message across. I sent it off to Gerrard for checking, then closed the laptop.

Stretching, I gathered my things, turned around and looked outside the window. It was dark; the streetlights had already flickered on. *Shit. I really should take my own advice. Why the hell do I always stay late?* My breathing quickened, fists pummelled, chest palpating rapidly. Shaking off the fear, I took a few deep breaths. Stretching out my fingers, I groaned at the fresh set of nail marks imprinted on my palms. I took a deep breath. *It's okay, he's locked up, remember. It's only the night sky, everything else is the same as the daytime.*

I walked out, down the stairs and through the lobby, passing the reception desk as I buttoned up my coat, wrapped my arms around myself.

"See you later, Miss Jones," Dennis the security guard said, opening the door for me.

I smiled, gritted my teeth, and left the building. Huddled in my deep red coat, I rolled up my hood and stepped outside. The rain was hammering down, wind blasted along the street, darkness reigned. How did I forget? Storm Diane was on its way. It wasn't safe out here tonight. It was likely I'd be impaled by a Christmas decoration at this rate. Jeez, this time of year was tough. All the marvels, the sparkling lights, and excitable children. I missed those days. I missed being home with Mum, baking cookies for the carol singers. Aunt Clara stopping by for dinner. She always bought muffins just for me, caramel muffins with sprinkles, in fact. They're still my favourite to this day.

Sheets of soaked newspapers clung to the pavement. Yesterday's edition, I remember reading that story. It's sad that it ends up as trash on the floor. Don't people care anymore? I shivered as I took my hand out of my pocket, picked the paper up, walked over to the bin and deposited it in there. Pushing my hands as far into my pockets as possible, I looked up at the streetlight above. Night-time had crept in. Fumbling around, I found the alarm in my pocket, held it tight as my pulse quickened. Deep breath in. I looked across the road, past the parked cars. Deep breath out. Jeez, it was dark down there. Swallowing back the lump in my throat, I stepped off the curb.

"Wait!" Jimmy yelled, falling out of the exit. His blond hair and brown jacket already drenched from the rain.

A black Mercedes pulled out and sped past, missing me by mere inches. I fell backwards, tripping back up the curb. I caught my breath and groaned, cursing at the driver. But he'd already gone. What is with these cars! Turning, I could see Jimmy running to catch up with me. "Phew, that was close, Julia!" he said, looking up the road. The car had gone. I nodded, smiling. "I'm glad I saw you. How are you feeling?" he puffed.

"I'm okay," I said as I walked further up the street. He altered his pace to match my own.

"I'm glad you're okay, you had us all worried." He smiled. "I photographed where it happened for your article today. Want me to show you the images?"

Does he really think I want to see pictures of where it happened, right now, right here...in the darkness of the night?

"Oh, thank you. If you could email the photos, that would be great. I'm a little too tired to work tonight."

"Of course, Julia. I'm sorry, you must be exhausted!"

My lips creased at the sides. He was sweet; he meant well. "Thank you, Jimmy, I'm okay, really," I said, smiling.

"Good... they're a decent group on the fifth floor, aren't they?" I nodded. "Dylan told me there's a position opening up in the office beside yours… did you know?" I shook my head. "I'll apply for it. We'll be neighbours." He grinned, fumbling with his umbrella. "Here, let's both use it," he opened it, protecting us from the drizzle.

"Thanks Jimmy," I responded. "But I'm continuing this way," I added, pointing over the road.

"Oh, well, you have it," he said, offering me his umbrella.

"No thank you, my hood's fine." I smiled.

He smirked. "It looks good."

My brow wrinkled. "What?"

"Your hood."

"Oh, okay." I smiled, my eyes widened. *Strange!* "I have to go." I smirked.

"See you tomorrow, Julia." He waved as I turned and walked across the street.

"Thanks," I shouted. He was pleasant, but his attempts to charm me were obvious. I wasn't planning on a relationship anytime soon. I needed to get my own life in check first.

Heading up Farringdon Street, my shoulder ached. The damn laptop was heavy. I needed an upgrade. Why they're built like tanks, I'll never know. At least my bag was waterproof. I'd hate to tell Gerrard I lost my research… not that it was finished, anyway. I should ask Jimmy to give me a hand. He has a knack of worming his way into places, and I need all the information I could get about the Butcher.

Jimmy was the blond-haired, dorky geek with glasses. His average attire made him invisible to the rest of the world, but he used it to his advantage. He'd appear at the strangest of places, unheard, silent, and deadly. He reminded me of the photographer from the *Superman* books, sharing the same name, geekiness, and role. I felt sorry for him though; I suspected he'd never had a partner, unless you count Mary at the science fair in fifth grade. He'd mentioned her one lunchtime over coffee and cake. I had my usual caffeine hit, an espresso with a twist of lemon. I'd relaxed reading the latest Bella Day romance novel. He brought the cake, a caramel muffin, of course, then requested the chair beside mine. How could I say no? Since then, he's been appearing at the most random of places. Bella Day's book signing for one. Since when did he read any books by her? Apparently, he was passing by and saw me through the window. I would worry, but he's as skinny as a stick, five-foot nothing and has the clumsiness of a drunk on a merry-go-round. Jimmy, my favourite harmless stalker. My lips creased; dimples formed. He's not a stalker really, he's just lonely. I can relate.

London's a big city full of strangers. My mum used to say a stranger is a friend you haven't met yet. She was right, kind of. For me, a stranger is a source you haven't found yet. Everyone knows something, people have secrets. It's my job to expose them. That's why I have a small social circle. Not that I mind. Those that stick around, they're the ones that are worthwhile. Why bother with the rest of them? I shrugged.

Heading up the street I walked past the Italian Consulate and down Harp Alley. This was where it happened. *Jeez, it's dark down here.* My pace quickened, heart racing, my anxiety levels screamed out in fear. Why did I work late? Concentrating on my breathing, I continued forward. In and out, slowing my breaths down. That's what my Aunt Lydia said. It's the only way to stop a panic attack before it starts. The alley looked different. There was no blood, no primal urge to scream out and shout. He wasn't here. I gulped, walking past the spot of my attempted murder. *Keep going… I can do this.* It's one thing to tell yourself that, and entirely another thing to do it.

Being in my line of work, you see a lot happening at night. Heck, that was always the prime time, the perfect opportunity for the inside scoop. But three years ago, he happened, Dalen Frost, the local drug runner. I'd followed him for information on an article I was writing. He'd had a few too many to drink… and stupidly, I thought he'd be more pliable and give up what I wanted to know. Boy, was I wrong! He'd had me up against the wall and pushed his hands where they shouldn't be, leaving a nasty scar on my right thigh, courtesy of his flick knife. A single woman walking the streets of London alone is unadvisable. That's when the panic attacks started. Counselling helped, as did Tae Kwon Do. If only I'd had the chance to use it on Eddy!

Two attacks in the last three years. If I knew any better, I'd quit my day job and work from home. But why should I? Why should I let the bullies take me down? I couldn't stay cooped up. I'd end up an alcoholic couch potato.

Walking through the darkness, I breathed a sigh of relief as I reached the end of the alleyway. Light beamed above as streetlights twinkled under the night sky. Merging on to St Bride Street, there was more traffic. I stood at the zebra crossing until the traffic slowed to a stop. Headlights beamed, and I stepped down from the curb, crossing to the other side.

The grey buildings shrouded the skyline. Rubbish flew as the storm gained strength. I looked ahead. Lydia's coffee shop was closing. Heck, was it that time already? I looked at my watch, the sparkling gems discoloured by the moonlight. Eight in the evening. How on Earth did that happen? I remember sitting at the desk, head buried in my laptop with the side lamp on. I'd been attempting to write this damn story, but my mind wasn't having any of it. Who wants a job as a journalist? It isn't fun. It's hard work where I get to annoy people every day, trying not to lose my morality in the process. I yawned, my body heavy and tired.

I stopped outside Lydia's as she stacked chairs on tables; she waved when she saw me; her greying hair dangling down from a messy bun.

The bell chimed as I opened the door. "Julia, it's freezing out there. Come in, I'll get you a coffee."

"Ah thanks, but I've got to get home. Maisy will want feeding."

"I'm sure Maisy can wait while you warm yourself!"

I chuckled. "Well, if she claws me, I'll blame you."

Lydia laughed as she walked to the counter, filling up a takeaway cup. She smiled. "How about a coffee?"

"That sounds great, thank you," I exclaimed, taking the cup, and wrapping my gloved hands around it. The warmth made me shiver.

"How are you feeling, sweetie?"

"I'm okay… it hurts less," I said, bringing my hand up to my neck.

She smiled with sadness in her eyes. "Here look, I'm ready to close up, I'll give you a ride home."

"Aww thanks, Lydia, but I'm fine. I need to get back to reality again. The walk is doing me good."

She frowned. "Okay, just be safe, please."

"I will." I smiled, hugged her, and headed to the door.

"And next time wear more clothes." She smiled. "Your momma would turn in her grave if she saw you walking out in that."

I laughed. "Thanks, I'll remember to remind you of the same, when you're in one of your short skirts."

She grinned. "That skirt barely covers your womanhood, Julia. Is that what journalists wear nowadays?"

I laughed, looking down at the skirt. "Well, if your womanhood reaches your knees, I'd be concerned, Aunt Lydia." She laughed. "Plus, it's all I had that was clean at Lola's. I've been too busy to do the washing."

"Oh sweetie, next time tell me you're meeting some handsome young man or something." She grinned. "And bring the washing over mine."

"Ha, thanks, but I'm off men for a while."

"No, you need to get back in the saddle. What about that man you met online... what's his name?"

"Who? Malcolm?"

"Yeah, that's the one."

"We had one date a few weeks ago, and he had to rush off, a family emergency."

"Oh, that's not a good sign." She frowned.

"Yeah, he wasn't my type, anyway." She nodded.

"Is he male? Good looking?" I nodded. "Then he's my type. Send him my way."

I laughed. "Lydia, you're awful!"

"Sweetie, if you worry about that at my age, you'll find

no one." She winked.

I chuckled as I waved; the bell jingling when I walked through the door. "Be safe," she said.

The rain was bouncing off the cobblestones. I pulled my coat tight around myself, hiding under my hood. Maybe I should've accepted the lift, but I couldn't put Lydia out again. She'd already done too much for me. Heck, picking up the pieces after Mum died. If it weren't for her, I'd have been shipped off to Merseyside to live with a distant relative, Agatha, and her two spiteful children. She'd been there, standing in, when Mum couldn't. They'd been the closest of friends for years before she died. Mum was only fifty-two when she was hit by a car on Landon Road. They said she didn't suffer; it was instant. That was some comfort at least, but nothing can calm the hole she left in my heart. I was fifteen when she died, about to take my exams and living in a world of stress of my own.

Boyfriends, smoking, and fast cars were all I'd cared about. I'd been rebellious by nature. But after Mum died, and Aunt Lydia stepped up, I calmed down. The grief set me on the straight and narrow; I wanted to make her proud, be somebody, live my life with no regrets… and I did.

The night sky growled at me, brandishing its violent nature through the gloom. Like a predator to his prey, it howled again, threatening to pounce. I shivered. *Damn, it's freezing out here. The temperature's dropped since I left the office.* Pulling my coat tighter around my shoulders, I sped up, walking faster down St Andrews Street and onto Holborn. I know I should love winter, heck, who wouldn't enjoy snuggling under a blanket beside an open fire. But this was too cold even for me. Only three blocks left. It'd take no time at all. My tights were soaked, boots sodden… who wears suede boots in the winter. I cringed. If it weren't for my thick red coat, my chiffon blouse would be stuck to me by now.

CHAPTER TEN

Turning the corner, I walked towards Chancery Lane subway station. The road was deserted, all except a black Range Rover with blacked-out windows, parked outside the Grand Palace hotel. I looked over at the dilapidated building. The only thing grand about it was its name. The place was a dive, always had been. Heck, Matty said the last time he went in there, a rat ran out. Granted, I don't know why he was there. It's not like it was burning down, but who knows with Matty.

I'm surprised it hasn't been demolished by now, being derelict and detached from reality. Maybe that's a story I should investigate. Why hasn't it been? It must violate at least six building regulations, from what I could see. Where were the owners? I guess the whole place was left to wither and rot. It's a shame. It could have been stunning. I bet it was in its day. If I remember right, it dated back to the fifteenth century, once a prized place to be. I had seen no activity here in a while. Stepping back, I looked up. A light gleamed down from the penthouse. *Who is that? Is someone still running the place?*

I scratched at my temple, beating back the looming headache I had forming. *I thought this place was deserted. Maybe it's squatters?* My brow furrowed, hands clammy. Something's not right about this place. *Who's up there?* Stepping towards the door, I pushed it slightly; it moved. I stepped back, looking around at the dark, frosty night. *What am I doing?* I shook my head. Did I want to be attacked again? Fists balled, lips pursed, I pushed the door harder, walking inside. *I won't let them beat me!*

The lobby was silent, dark, and deadly. *I shouldn't be here.* What was I thinking? Shaking my head, I turned back for the door, taking the cool copper handle in my hand. "Grr!" I stomped my foot, letting go of the door handle. "Get a grip, Julia," I said, stiffening my stature. Gulping, I shouted, "Hello?" A pigeon fluttered in the back corner, making me jump, my heart pounding ten to the dozen.

Pulling out my phone, I turned on the torch function, severing the darkness. Blood red walls glared at me. Fleur de lis wallpaper with mahogany picture rails encased the entrance hall, holding it in place. Leaves crunched as I walked across the tiled floor. Footsteps echoed over the derelict surrounds, unravelling a picture of destruction before me. The homeless had dirtied the building, slept in it, leaving piles of rubbish in the corner. Youths had called this entrance a home, leaving their mark with spray cans over what once appeared to be a charming building to live in. *How long had the hotel been empty?*

I walked across the lobby, taking in its desolate nature.

The wind rustled decrepit leaves, swirling around me, chilling me to the bone. I shook my head as I looked over the tags a gang of kids had left. It was December now, time for fairy lights and tinsel, not the misgivings of an ill-spent youth. Why would someone destroy such a historical place?

I wandered over to the old mahogany reception desk, stood behind it and fumbled through the paperwork that had been left behind. "Overdue." Had they fallen so far behind that they upped and left, notifying no one? The rest of the papers were old customer receipts, wage slips and overdue letters threatening court action. So, if they had run off, where were the debt collectors? What happened to the court action? It made little sense. The debtors would pursue the owners, taking their assets–including this hotel.

A dusty black book sat beside a counter pen on a chain. Damp had gotten to its pages, seeping between the lines. I flicked to the last page, empty. Backing up a few pages and the last entry was dated September 23rd, 2018. According to the book, they had six clients that night, each staying on the second floor, rooms nine to fifteen. The third floor appeared unoccupied, and the penthouse above had a long-term owner, Jesus Mendel. I laughed. Who calls themselves Jesus? His parents were clearly the comical types. Smirking, I photographed the last few entries. I'd check the place out in daylight. It was too dark to see much of anything in here, and even with my instincts on high alert, I didn't fancy trekking through the halls, room by room in the darkness; trying to find a stray light left on.

I turned to leave. The streetlight outside flickered through the glass-panelled door. Shadows cast across the lobby, illuminating the Elizabethan decor of the deserted build. Closing my bag, I turned off the torch function and headed over to the front door. Reaching it, I pushed to leave, but something out of the corner of my eye stopped me. The streetlight glared through the glass panes as a car door closed outside. Someone stood there, looking in.

A tall man in a dark overcoat stood in darkness, silhouetted by the lamplight. *Who is he?* My chest tightened; hands clammed up. I should walk out, act as though it was normal to be in an abandoned building, alone in the darkness. I shuddered. Now wasn't the time to act brave. I didn't fancy meeting any man in a dark alley again. My body tensed as he walked towards the door. Heat rose, and I scarpered, hiding behind the reception desk.

The door creaked open, footsteps strode forward, and he disappeared up the staircase in the centre of the lobby to the first floor. *Should I follow him?* I gritted my teeth, fists balled. "Damn it!" Stepping out from behind the desk, I took a deep breath, walked over the tiled floor and eased myself onto the staircase, ascending the stairs one at a time. Reaching forward, I followed the handrail to the first floor, squinting to see ahead of me. *It's bloody dark in here. What am I doing? This is insane! I can hardly see a step in front of me, let alone defend myself should he jump out and grab me.* I bit my bottom lip. *I can't do this. It's too dark!* I shivered. *It's not safe!*

The blackened turmoil of a history past slivered into the hallway beside me. My mind conversed, encapsulating my fears, giving life to my nightmares. The dread of the darkness tightened my chest. Rapid breaths escaped me as I gripped the handrail, descending one step at a time. He could be anywhere by now... in front of me, beside me, behind me. The hairs on the back of my neck stood on end. I wasn't safe here. *Shit. What am I thinking?* A deafening thud sounded above; someone was upstairs. Footsteps pounded across the second floor. I stopped, frozen to the spot, mere inches from the lobby. Fear crept up my backbone as I gritted my teeth, balled my fists, bracing myself for a fight. It was that night all over again, the attack, the fear. Streaming through my mind, the blood of my attacker gushed over me. *It's not real. It's not real. Move, damn it, get out of here!*

Two or more voices boomed through the hotel, arguments, shouting, the scuffling of footsteps. *What's happening?* A door slammed; glass shattered. *Move, damn you, move!* I ran, hot-tailed it out of there, skipping the last stair as I jumped down, screaming my way through the front door. Escaping just in time for shards of glass to rain down beside me. I ducked, held my hands above my head. The roar of a broken man screeched past, slamming down from the sky above. Blood splattered from his body as he crashed onto the roof of the black Range Rover. In that minute, time stood still. Colours brightened; eyes widened. I was a face of fear, a body of fright. Crouched beside the Range Rover, I froze. The body above, motionless. All I could see was a hand silhouetted by starlight. With quickened breaths and bulging eyes, I didn't blink, didn't move. I was stuck in the moment. It felt like an eternity, yet mere seconds had all but passed. It was in that moment that I came to the realisation, the belief that my reality was one of poor judgement, bad luck, and fatal decisions. I realised the ultimate truth. I had witnessed the death of another; and I was cursed to walk the path of destruction.

To say I screamed would be an understatement. Mouth agape, eyes bulging, I brought my hand to my mouth to silence the overwhelming fear that escaped it. Any normal person would run in and help. Any sane person would call an ambulance. But at that moment, I was far from sane. I stood there, glued to the bloody pavement. *Dare I look?* I lifted my arm, steadying myself against the vehicle. I took a deep breath, calming my breathing. *Can I move forward, reach up high, check for a pulse?* There's no way anyone could survive that… could they? *I have to check.*

Forcing myself forwards I could see crimson blood flowing down the side of the vehicle. Raindrops bounced off, absorbing the fresh nature of death as they pooled down below. A pale hand lay draped over the edge. Still. Silent and broken. I stood upright, wiped the hair from my eyes, and stood up on the sill, climbing high. Blood splatter blended into my red coat as I leant over to check the victim for a pulse. Rich brown hair cradled his porcelain face as soft brown eyes stared dull into the night sky. I gasped. *It can't be him!* Nathaniel. The man that saved me. *Shit, he isn't moving!* His skin was ice cold, rubbery to the touch. I cried out, but he made no sound. Feeling for his carotid artery, no pulse. Nothing. He was silent, cold, broken, and dead. Tears welled in my eyes. How could this be happening? What happened up there? This wasn't the silhouette of the man I'd seen enter the hotel; this was the man that saved me.

I gulped as I looked around me. If Nathaniel wasn't the shadowed man, then where was he? Could he be the one responsible for throwing him out the window? Taking a deep breath in, I overlooked the vicinity. Fear crept up my backbone, holding my lungs tight. Panic engulfed me as my heart palpitated through my chest. I gasped, sucking back in the air. I was in danger. Again… and this time my saviour was dead. Tears escaped as the salty taste of tragedy caressed my lips. My heart pounded. Hands clammy. I stepped down, slipping on the mushed leaves over the sodden pavement.

Dimly lit streetlamps wavered in the darkness. Bustling leaves fled up the street, wind howled, rain pounded. The storm was getting worse. With senses amassed in a muddle of turmoil, something rattled from behind. Spinning around, I could see a man's shape clambering down the fire escape. Was that him?

Reaching in my bag, I gripped my phone. I needed help. Ice cold fingertips numb to the touch called for help. The police were on their way. Slippery hands juggled the phone as I lost my grip, plummeting it into a puddle. "Damn it," I yelled, picking it up. Silencing my voice as I bent down. The extremely dead Nathaniel twitched, then howled above me. In an instant, I was transformed into a moment of reflective horror. My mind was a mash of despair, body rigid like a deer in headlights. *Shit! What was that?*

The whites of my eyes bulged as I turned to face the vehicle. Nathaniel atop of the car. Brows raised, hands clammy. *Where is he?* His hand no longer dripped blood over the side of the roof. He'd gone. Wind crashed into my chest as a fist smashed into my breastbone. Slamming backwards, I hit the ground. Chest heavy, eyes watering, my face reddened as I choked out a spasm of splutters. A bulk of rubble crashed to the floor, missing me by mere inches.

Crushed like a vice, I gripped my chest, gasping for breath. Dazed and confused, my eyes strained to open. Thick muscular arms held me in place. Who was it? Head heavy, drooped down to the floor... I looked up. Black boots, jeans, a belt buckle shaped like a sideway number eight. As I lifted my head higher, he growled as he pushed me harder into the wall. The scent of leather caught my attention. I recognised him wearing the leather jacket that once wrapped itself over my shoulders. Nathaniel... but it couldn't be!

Raising higher, I caught up to his face. It wasn't him. I had to be dreaming, knocked out by the rubble perhaps, waiting for help to arrive. Nathaniel wasn't the dreamy eyed guy that kept me warm in the bar. What stood before me... what saved me from a certain death... wasn't quite human. He couldn't be. It's either that or he had a wicked sense of humour and wore masks for a living. But I could sense it on him, something unique, inhuman.

Thick, bristled hair pitted his skin, wired and matted with flecks of deep brown, black, and charcoaled grey. A muzzle of gnashing teeth salivated as he leant forward, moist breath caressing my neck. *What is he?* Curiosity overrode my fear. My hand raised, fingertips soothed against his heightened cheekbone, flowing over his bristled hairs. My hand dropped. This is insane! I should scream, run scared. But I knew this man. He'd saved me, and despite his appearance, he had made no move to cause me harm. Quite the opposite, saving me from the falling debris.

With my body at his mercy, I stiffened to his touch, intrigued but uncertain. He lent forward. I shuddered. Squeezing my eyes shut and holding my breath. His moistened breath caressed my ear lobes as he growled low but deep in my ear, pulling himself away. I exhaled, then sucked in the air. Oxygen rushed through me, and I opened my eyes, meeting his own. Even with his mask-like features, his soft brown eyes remained the same; it birthed a striking sense of familiarity deep within. Nathaniel studied me, watching me breathe. There was an innocence to the beast before me. Solemn eyes glazed as I opened my heart to his soul, untouched and unspoken. His heart yearned as it told the tale of destruction and dismay, loss, and despair.

"Nathaniel?" I whispered. He growled, pulled back and jumped, scaling the side of the building, clambering out of sight.

The night sky cried as a gruff male voice echoed behind me. "You need to go," it boomed, carrying across the darkness, piercing my eardrum. Spinning around to locate it, I wobbled. The permeating scent of sandalwood took my breath away. Dizziness took over as my heartbeat pulsed, pounding in my ear. A spasm of severe pain gripped me inside. Clinging to my abdomen, I fell to the ground. Bile retched; acid bubbled as a hot, warm liquid spewed from my throat. Sickness took over and my body constricted like a snake coiling its way around me. Body tense, clammy, and muscles rigid. I retched again.

A bulked figure stood tall, shadowing my body with a mass of muscle and madness. Silvered hair swirled through the wind as an aged face peered down. Clutching my arm, the man yanked me upright. He studied me, watching me wriggle away. "Let go of me!" I yelled. My hands heated, fire flowing through my body. He yelped and let go, looking down at his blistered hand.

He stopped, stared at me. "What are you?" he asked,

puzzled. Blood dripped from a gash on his neck. He stood silently, searching my face for recognition. *Who is he?* Something crashed in the alley behind, and he jolted round, revealing a tattoo of a falcon on the right side of his neck.

He looked over at the Range Rover and grimaced, cursing under his breath. "Go," he said, pushing me away.

"Who are you?" I asked, staring up into the face of Nathaniel's attacker.

"No one, now go!" he yelled, screeching at the top of his lungs.

Without hesitation, I jumped up, grabbed my bag, and ran. The cold shrill of winter's reign wrapped its claws around me. Something howled through the night sky as beads of rain turned to hail, pounding my sodden face; and I wept at the tragedy I'd witnessed.

Sirens blared. Red and blue lights flashed around me. Police cars screeched past. The cavalry had arrived. Sodden boots clashed with the pavement; puddles splashed up my ice-cold legs. Nothing prepared me for this. *What had I seen? How could a man survive such an epic fall? Was it Nathaniel in the mask?* I shook my head. *But it has to be! They shared the same eyes, the same leathery scent.*

Somehow, he'd battled against nature and won. I was sure he was dead. But no, he had risen and paraded his canines against my face. What was all that about? And why the mask? Did he have a hero complex? I scratched my head and entered the subway station. The mask he'd wore creeped me out. It was so real! I frowned… it had to be a mask. There's simply no other genuine explanation. It was like something out of a nightmare, a film set in the making.

What would make someone dress like that? He'd seemed so… human before. But now… what was he? I laughed to myself. Jeez, I'd be believing in vampires and werewolves soon. I smirked. It was just a scary mask and a guy with a bizarre fetish for the film *American Werewolf in London*. I laughed nervously, unsure of my humour as I headed through the tube station.

Boarding the subway carriage, an old woman gave me a toothless grin and continued knitting. I smiled, making my way to one of the empty seats. Two stops and I'd be home. I yawned, coming down from the surge of adrenaline from earlier. It'd all been too much. It felt like I was playing the role of a tragic character in a sad soap opera.

I grabbed my notebook out of my bag and made a few notes. I'll call the detective in the morning, see if she has any news. Perhaps I could question her about what happened tonight–without giving too much of my involvement away; at least until I know more about what I've gotten myself into this time. Who was the silver-haired shooter? I'd somehow become involved in a war I never knew was going on. But between what? The London gangs? Was Nathaniel a gang member? I shook my head. That was something I didn't fancy being a part of.

The train slowed. One more station to go. My body ached; stomach retched. My chest felt like someone had hit me with a barge pole. I yawned again, rubbing my eyes. I'll figure all this out in the morning. Packing my notebook away, I stood up and made my way to the carriage exit. The train slowed, the doors opened, and I walked out of the station and headed home.

When I arrived, my bright red front door gleamed under the streetlight. Silver handles turned under my grip as I unlocked and went inside. My safety net remained a den of open boxes, a mash of evidence from my previous life with my mother. Cream walls warmed as my chrome lampshade gave out a bright white light. Maisy jumped out, meowing for food. My lips creased as I bent down to pick her up, ruffling her tummy. Hangings of shaded art hung on the front wall, two pictures depicting the obscurity of mother nature. In the first piece, rampant reds seduced solemn blues, dancing into a symphony of dramatic desire. The second piece absorbed you into a cooler exterior, sunshine yellow with evergreen leaves.

A tangerine sunset blessed the sky, giving way to the silhouette of a couple embracing under the shade of a tree. The nectar of love was a piece I'd purchased from the All Saints gallery last August. Even though the colouring was different, the brush strokes matched the stars in my eyes that watered when I first saw it. It was the perfect piece alongside the battle of desire in a sea of seduction that took place in the first piece beside it. I sighed. The colours always calmed my mind. Getting lost in something so rich was worth every penny I'd spent for them.

My rigid body sank down into itself as I yawned. I fed Maisy, then headed up the stairs to the bathroom to clean myself up. My mind was a mess of death and destruction, but I'd never make sense of it alone. I needed contacts to form relationships in this city like never before. But first, before everything else, I needed sleep. Inhaling the world within me, I took myself to bed, sinking into the satin sheets of my luxurious ivory bed.

CHAPTER ELEVEN

The morning sun rose with the screeching of my alarm clock. Buried under a mountain of satin sheets and thick woollen blankets, I reached out, bashing the table to silence it. *Damn thing. It can't be morning already!* Maisy stretched, then curled back into a ball. "It's alright for you," I said, peeking out from undercover. Sliding out of bed, I fumbled about, searching for my dressing gown. Ah, there it was.

The warmth of thick cotton caressed my body. Snuggled in the scent of lavender, I headed over to the window, opening the curtains. The sun bloomed over the horizon, chasing the night away. Exotic shades of crimson swirled into husks of golden yellow, enriching the landscape before my eyes. Oceanic aquamarine enchanted the stage, creating an everlasting daylight to shine in. Sunrise was an art I could never miss, whereas sunset gave in to the darkness, the fear, and the blight.

Maisy meowed, padding at the blankets. "Okay, I know,

I'll feed you in a minute," I huffed, closing the curtains, so I could change and get ready for work.

Heading downstairs, I fed Maisy, grimaced at the boxes of my mums' things, and headed out into the world, ready for the cold winter walk to work.

I had a plan today, and nothing would stop me following it. Something went down last night, and I would be damn sure I'd find out the truth of it all. What had I walked into? Was it connected to the Butcher? To my attack? How was Nathaniel connected? Was Eddy a member of the same gang the silver-haired shooter was in? I had to find out.

Slipping and sliding across the icy walkway, I smiled. I had a purpose, something to fight for. Last night's storm had settled, leaving a parade of black ice over my journey to the office. Breathing heavily, I slowed down, taking my time. Hot breath exhaled from my mouth, leaving a trail of steam in the air, moisture on my lips.

Taking out my lip gloss, I topped up my lips with a touch of apple blossom. Vibrant lashings of long hair wiped across my face, strands stuck to the freshness of my lips, coating themselves in gloss. Releasing myself, I pulled my hair behind my ears and hunched my bag further up my shoulder, heading on, hopeful the subway wouldn't be heaving today. But then it was eerily quiet at this time of the morning. Was everyone still hiding away, scared for their lives? The carriage I boarded actually had empty seats. It amazed me as I took one. I don't think I'd ever found a seat at eight in the morning before. Rush hour used to be packed. Perhaps everyone was working from home… or maybe they had time off because of the forthcoming

Christmas celebrations?

When I arrived, I headed up the tiled white corridor and out into the open world. Walking up to the hotel, I could see bright yellow police tape cordoning the crime scene off. The Range Rover had gone, but the splattering of my masked hero was unmistakable. I know I should contact them, tell them what happened. A crime had been committed, and I was their number one witness; and we all know what happens to a witness if they have no protection. I shuddered. But who would believe Nathaniel was thrown out of the third-floor window and lived to tell the tale?

I kept on walking, hunched in my red coat, hood pulled high. It wasn't far to Lydia's. I could do with an espresso or two, anything to wake these tired eyes. Turning the corner, an old paper carrier bag swept across the road, wrapping itself around my legs. Damn thing, doesn't anyone use a bin nowadays? Picking it up, I noticed it too had been at the scene of the crime. A dried splattering of crimson blood decorated the side. I crunched it up, shook my head and crossed the street, placing it in the bin. Brushing my hands together to free the dirt and blood, I stopped before Lydia's coffee shop, as my hero, the masked man, opened the door.

"Coming in?" Nathaniel asked.

Mouth agape, I paused. How the heck was he still alive? Surely internal injuries would have claimed him by now, but he didn't have a graze on him.

"Are you coming in?" he asked again, smiling, holding the door open.

I blinked a few times, nodded and answered, "What? No mask this time?" I asked, standing in the doorway. He smirked. His soft brown eyes gazed into my own.

Smiling, he held out his hand.

I frowned, accepting his gesture. His gentle touch soothed me as he took my hand to his lips and kissed it softly. I pulled back, grinning. "What?" he asked.

"Oh," I smiled. "I still can't get used to that."

He laughed. "Now why wouldn't I want to kiss a hand as beautiful as that?"

I smiled. He had a way with words. "I saw you last night," I said, getting to the point.

"Did you? We appear to be bumping into each other quite a lot."

"Yes, well, I wasn't following you."

"Oh, I know." He grinned. Stepping back to let a customer pass by.

"Are you two going to take a seat or block my door all day long?" Lydia yelled, ushering us both in.

She startled me as I stepped back, almost tripping over a chair leg. "Careful," Nathaniel said as he reached out to stop me from falling.

"Err… thanks," I said, smiling, biting my lip. I stepped forward and took a seat. Nathaniel joined me.

Lydia smirked from behind the counter and brought two espressos over. "It looks like you both like the same coffee," she said, winking.

I smiled. "Thanks Lydia, this is Nathaniel," I said, introducing him.

"Oh my, it's lovely to meet you." She said, fluttering her eyelashes. I rolled my eyes.

"Nathaniel is the man that helped me in the alleyway."

Lydia's jaw dropped. Eyes wide. "Oh blimey! Really, thank you, thank you," she said, throwing her arms around Nathaniel. His face paled as shock reigned over him.

"Oh no, it was my pleasure," he said, patting Lydia's back.

"I'll bring you a cake as well, you look like a cake person... don't you think, Julia?"

"For breakfast?" I asked, confused.

She smiled. "It's cake Julia. You can eat it anytime of the day!"

I smiled, she had a point. We'd always had cake for breakfast when I lived there. Lydia walked off with a smile from ear to ear.

"I'm sorry, Lydia practically brought me up, she's very excitable." I smiled.

"Never apologise for the love of a wonderful family," he said.

I sipped my espresso. "So, tell me a little about yourself."

"There isn't much to tell, especially to a journalist," he smirked.

"Ah, so you know who I am," I smiled.

"I may have checked up on you. Did you receive the flowers?"

My eyes widened as I smiled. "They were from you?" He nodded. "They were beautiful, thank you, that was really nice of you."

"I thought you needed cheering up," he said, smiling.

I smiled. Silence executed the conversation, and I

looked down at my coffee cup, swirling the black liquid in the white porcelain cup. The door chimed as a customer left. I gazed over towards his hands, tough masculine hands cradling his espresso. Raising my gaze higher, I studied him, muscular arms encased in a black leather jacket. A buff chest covered by a blue V-neck, all the way up to his chiselled face, his delicate, smooth skin, and soft brown eyes; eyes that encapsulated the nature of burnt umber, dark sienna and a touch of supple hazel. A marvel of shades wrapped up in my desire to know more of him. Those delicate eyes softened my gaze. I could lose myself in them if I stared for any longer. His eyes met mine, and he sparkled through his smile. Nathanial, my sweet, sexy saviour.

"You're a quiet one, aren't you?" he asked.

I smiled. "Only when deep in thought."

"And what may I ask alludes you?"

"You"

He laughed.

"You're certainly the mysterious type."

I reached for the sugar; his hand brushed past mine as he passed it to me.

"And you the sweet type," he said, smiling. "So, what do you remember from last night?"

I smiled, unsure of how to respond.

"Hmm, that's a tough one…"

"Go on," he said, his hand reaching for his fork. "Would you like some?"

"I," I looked at the cake, "well okay then."

He passed me a fork and placed the cake in the centre of the table.

"Thank you," I said, smiled and broke off a piece of the cake.

The scent of luscious lemon caressed my senses as I brought the cake to my mouth, salivating as it entered. My tongue swirling it around as the sweet citrus nature encapsulated my mind. Nathaniel watched, taking a bite himself.

"So last night?" he asked.

"Well from what I saw you were thrown from three stories up, died, came back and wore a werewolf mask. Am I close?" I asked, as he choked on his cake.

"You're as close as you believe yourself to be."

"You're ever the riddler, aren't you?" I said, grinning.

"Indeed." He smirked.

"So, can you explain it to me?"

"I think I need to get to know you first." He smiled.

"Are you asking me on a date, Nathaniel?" I asked, smirking.

"Are you accepting Red?"

I smiled. "I might be."

"Well then, I might be asking."

Lydia walked over, smiling. So, you two, did you enjoy the cake?

"It was lovely Miss Lydia," Nathaniel said.

I laughed. "Yes thanks," I said.

Lydia picked up the empty plate. "So, Nathaniel, did you hear they still have that awful attacker in custody?"

"I did yes, it's a good job too. The streets are safer with him behind bars."

"My thoughts exactly," she said. I watched as she walked off back to the counter to serve another customer.

"Why do you think he attacked you?"

I turned back to Nathaniel. "That's the thing, I cannot find any connection…" I paused; brow furrowed. "Well, maybe one."

"What's that?"

"The London Butcher."

Nathaniel sat silent, then nodded. "I agree. He hasn't killed since the police arrested him. Eddy, isn't it?"

"Yes, how did you know?"

"I like to investigate what's going on in my city too," he said, smiling.

I smiled. "I believe he targeted me, as I had the testimony of an eyewitness. In fact, it will be out in *The London Chronicle* tomorrow."

"I look forward to reading about it." He swirled his cup of espresso. I smiled. He looked over at me and pursed his lips. "I have one question. Why were you at the Grand?"

"Call it my journalistic instinct." I laughed. "Actually, I just saw the light on and wondered who was in there… it's been derelict for years, you know."

"Yes, indeed." He smirked.

"So why were you there?"

"I was meeting someone, we… Well, we don't always see eye to eye." He smiled, looking up from his coffee. "We were investigating the Butcher and his connection to my colleague's endeavours."

"What endeavours?"

"Ah, that's something I cannot tell you. It would be for him to share that secret." He smiled. "But what I can say is that the three of us are all on the same page in believing that Mr. Boland is, in fact, the Butcher."

"Now we need the evidence to prove it."

"Indeed."

"But…" I paused; brow furrowed. "Why didn't whatever he injected me with kill me, like the other girls?"

"That I don't know. I will speak with an associate of mine and see if there is anything they know on the subject."

"Is that associate the guy that threw you out the window?"

He nodded. "Yes," he smirked. "Blake and I have our differences. But I'll contact him."

"Perhaps in more of a public place this time," I smiled. "Less chance of any… mishaps," I said, smirking.

He laughed.

"So, do you think he injected me with something, after all?" He nodded. I gulped. "But I don't feel any different?"

"I don't know why. But for now, you clearly need answers, and we need to provide the police with the evidence they need to keep Eddy behind bars for a very long time."

I took the last sip of my coffee. Lips pursed, brow furrowed. "I have one last question…"

"Yes?"

"Why do you want to be involved in all this?"

He smiled. "It's my job to protect humans from the monsters of the night."

Humans? Why did he say it like that? I frowned, then

shrugged. Well, he certainly looked the vigilante type with his mask and exceptional death-defying stunts.

He finished the last of his coffee. "It looks like it is time to go," he said, smiling, and stood up. I stood up with him. "Thank you for the coffee, and cake." I smiled and nodded. He took my hand and kissed it. I squirmed and smiled. "So, would tonight be too soon for that date?"

I smiled. "I believe I have a space in my calendar."

"Would seven be okay?"

"I think seven would be perfect. Where would you like to meet?"

"How about I bring Gladys and we pick you up?"

I laughed. "Gladys, really?"

"Well, you wanted to meet her one day."

I smirked. "Okay, well I'll make sure I'm dressed for the occasion."

He smiled, nodded and left.

I took a deep breath as Lydia rushed over. "So?"

"So, we may be going on a date tonight."

"Eek!" she yelped, hugging me.

I laughed, hugged her and left with the takeaway coffee and croissant she made for me to keep me warm.

CHAPTER TWELVE

I headed over the road and towards the *Chronicle*. "Thanks," I said as Dennis opened the door for me. The chrome stair rail glided through my hand as I felt my way upstairs, sipping coffee to enlighten my senses.

Reaching the second floor, it became harder to breathe. *Jeez, I'm unfit. I've got to get back to the gym.* I carried on up the stairs, panting into my coffee cup, slowing to a snail's pace as I reached the top of the tedious mountain. Five flights of stairs were enough to build up an appetite. Slipping into my office, I sat down on my thick leather chair, twirled around beside the enormous window behind me, and took a bite from a piping hot croissant. My favourite savoury for first thing in the morning. Hunger appeased, stomach at ease. I smiled, kicked off my boots, and opened the laptop. Now, where was I?

Flicking through the computer files, I grimaced. The London Butcher, could it be Eddy? Nathaniel seemed to think so. Was I almost nearly his next victim? I let out a deep sigh, swirling round and round in my chair. I came to a stop. Lips pursed, fingers tapping on the desk. Detective Monroe didn't think so. I wasn't his type. Maybe he changed his type? Maybe whatever he was injecting didn't work on the bottled blond university girls. Brow furrowed, I continued tapping at the desk. To be fair, though, I'd rather not be his type. After all, he dismembers his victims and hides them all over the city. I shuddered. It's horrible, but what a great start to my next article. The people of London need the truth. I was his latest victim, and now I needed to find the evidence to back up that theory.

The door opened and Jayden walked in, plonked himself down, and picked up the framed photo of Lola and me from my desk. "Mmm, nice," he said.

"Erm… thanks."

He sighed. Placed the photograph back and tapped his fingers on the arm of the chair.

"Can I help you?" I asked, my brow furrowed.

"Eddy Boland."

Ah yes, I'd asked him to ask about his contacts on the force.

"Yes, did you find anything?"

"Hmm, that's the thing. They have nothing. Absolutely no evidence whatsoever."

"Shit."

"Yeah."

"What about the samples they took from under my nails?"

"Inconclusive still. It's literally, like your word against his."

"So, do you think he'll get out?"

"Honestly... yeah, they have nothing to hold him on."

"Shit. Well, that's not what Detective Lee told me."

"She said your guy didn't come forward."

I pursed my lips. If Nathaniel came forward he wouldn't he be arrested too? After all, he did put the bastard in hospital. Taking a deep breath, I thought for a moment.

"What about the paramedics?"

"They were there to mop up, nothing more." Mop up! Is that really what he called it. I gritted my teeth. "Look your detective was trying to keep hopeful. Nothing more. There's no CCTV, no witnesses and zero DNA. Which is strange as even the smartest of criminals leave DNA somewhere."

My body slumped. Perhaps he was right. If they had nothing, then he'd be out in days. They could only hold him for so long. As soon as the preliminary hearing takes place, he'll be out on bail. "Thanks Jayden."

"Okay," he said as he stood up and walked away.

"Wait!" he turned around. "Did you find out about the number plate?"

"Ah yes, you'll never believe it..."

"What?" I frowned.

"It's owned by a guy named Jesus!" He laughed.

Wide eyed, I gulped, nodded and smiled as he walked out of the office, closing the door behind him.

I sat swinging around in my chair. Jesus? Jesus Mendel? The guy that rented the penthouse suite the night before the Grand shut down. Why's he following me? Did he drive the car that killed my mum? Damn. The clues just keep coming, but I still can't make head nor tail of them. I sighed. I can't worry about that now. I've got to take things one step at a time. First things first... the matter of last night. I noted down what happened, from the light on in the hotel, down to Nathaniel being thrown from the window. Why didn't I ask him more about the mask? Then there was the silver-haired shooter... I tapped my fingers on the desk again... What was his name? I'm sure Nathaniel mentioned it. Damn it! Huffing aloud, I racked my brain. Still nothing. That didn't surprise me. Oh well, I shrugged. Nathaniel said he was going to talk to him first, anyway.

Jeez, the whole thing sounded like a speech from a fairy tale, one by the Grimm brothers on rabid wolves and werewolf hunters. Shaking my head, I smirked. Those things were only myth and legend. But then, how else do I explain the average male surviving a fall from such a height? Could it be some kind of super body armour? I shook my head; no, I'd have seen it. What if... I grimaced. What if it wasn't a mask? Is that even possible? Could he change, like one of the characters in the books I'd read? All I needed now was blood-sucking vampires, and we'd have the makings of a sparkling love story. I smirked.

Memories syphoned to the forefront of my mind. I wondered what impact my appearance made last night. Had I wandered into a meeting gone wrong? Nathaniel had called him a colleague, but a colleague in what? They didn't seem like friends. Who was the other guy? What was his name? Damn it, I should have written it down.

Searching for news on the Grand Hotel told me that a company called Infinite Encounters had purchased it. That's the club... so does Nathaniel own the Grand, too? If so, what happened there? Why did it get shut down? And who was the mysterious Jesus Mendel that rented the penthouse out? As per usual, I had more questions than answers. What else could I remember?

The silver-haired shooter. What about him? He was tall, older than me... early fifties, at a guess. His face had searched mine, just as mine had searched his own. What had he seen in me? Did he know who I was? Where I worked? I gripped the edge of the desk. But Nathaniel said he'd contact him about my bloodwork. So, if he trusts him, should I? Heck no. He threw Nathaniel out of the window, and by some miracle, he survived that. I certainly wouldn't.

From what he'd said, the silver-haired shooter liked to hunt. He was hunting the London Butcher after all. But would he see me as a threat? What if he's on his way here now? Brows raised, I held my breath. Should I call the police? No... I couldn't. I exhaled, panting for air. How would I explain what I saw? It's okay though, at least no one was killed. Maybe he'd let me go. I won't say anything, well nothing I wouldn't print in the newspaper first. I sighed, grip lessening. I've got to get a handle on this, needed to swallow my fear and parade through this travesty.

"Julia!"

I jumped. "Shit!" I snapped, unaware of my surroundings.

My bouncy right-hand Selene bounded into the room. Her short blond hair curled around her earlobes. Placing a coffee on my desk, she smiled, looking at me. Her brows raised, "Did you hear about the Grand?"

I gulped, shaking my head.

"Someone vandalised it last night. My man Joe at the station said some woman phoned in, claiming they had a jumper."

"A jumper?"

"Well, they couldn't hear her well enough. The storm was wild last night."

I took a deep breath and smiled. "Did they?"

She nodded.

"Did they find him?"

"No, no one was there but Joe said a passerby saw a car smashed in and blood everywhere."

"Damn," I said.

She nodded. "Mmm hmm. Well, the strangest thing is when the police got there, the car had gone."

"What car was it?"

"Erm, a Range Rover I think."

I gulped. "Okay, I'll look into it."

"Thanks Julia, it weirded out the officers, you know."

"Perhaps it was just a prank?"

"No, couldn't be… there was glass everywhere."

"The jumper had leaped out of the window on the third floor."

"Strange, normally jumpers jump from the roof."

"Yeah, that's what I thought."

"Leave it with me," I said, smiling.

"Thanks." She waved her manicured hand as she left.

Damn. I can guarantee Gerrard would know about this 'jumper'. He'd be asking me about it if I didn't put something together. Little did he know I was prime suspect number one. How would I spin this one? The only thing I could do was phone this Joe at the station and write a puff piece for the morning edition. I nodded to myself, picking up the phone.

"Greater London police force."

"Can I speak to Joe please, Joe White?"

"Yes, hold." Music played in the background, then the phone crackled.

"Joe speaking."

"Hi Joe, my name's Julia Jones and I work with Selene at *The London Chronicle*."

"Yes, she said you'd be calling." He said, lowering his voice. "I told her all I can. Some lady rang about a jumper and there was no one there."

"Thank you, but did the witness get the number plate of the Range Rover?"

"No, ma'am, he didn't."

"Do you know the name of the witness?"

"I, well yes, but I can't tell you."

"I'm sure Selene would be more than grateful if you could tell us anything more."

"Yes, oh well, okay, but don't mention my name."

"Of course," I smiled.

"It's Ted Cooper on Langdale road."

"Okay, thank you Joe, you've been a great help." I put the phone down and searched the Internet for a Mr. Ted Cooper. Excellent, his social media presence was enormous. He was a thirty-two-year-old hockey player. His website even gave his contact details, including his number.

I picked up the phone again. "Hello, is that Mr. Ted Cooper?"

"Yeah, that's me."

"It's Julia Jones here from *The London Chronicle*. Do you have a few minutes?"

"Yeah, is it about that Range Rover?"

"Yes, it is. Do you remember the licence plate number at all?"

"No, I wasn't looking. I heard shouting, then a loud bang. It looked like someone had pushed some guy out the window. But he wasn't there, just blood and glass. Then there was a woman running off in a red coat, but that's all I saw."

"A red coat, you say?" Shit.

"Yeah, she must have been the one that rang the police as when I went to ring, but they were already on their way."

"What happened to the Range Rover?"

"Some old guy got in and drove off. I didn't see him well enough. The storm was severe last night."

"Oh, I see, so if the storm was bad, how did you see the red coat?"

"Well, I, well maybe I didn't. I don't know. It was late, and I just wanted to get home from training."

"Okay Mr. Cooper, thank you for your time." I put the phone down. I'd dodged a bullet there.

Time for a puff piece to keep Gerrard happy.

Murder at The Grand
By Julia Jones

We have reason to believe a man was pushed out of the third-story window late last night. An eyewitness told police he heard arguing as the man fell to his death, landing on top of a black Range Rover. Blood spatter analysis and the shards of glass confirm that a body should have been atop of the vehicle that night, however, there was none to be found!

What happened to the body and is there another killer in town? Stay safe Londoners, and lock your doors tonight.

Done. Jimmy can take a picture and I'm sure Gerrard will elaborate and sensationalise it more. Sorted. So, for now I had my investigation to complete, and that started with trying to remember who Mr. Silver Haired Shooter was.

What was it about him? The falcon tattoo strained my memory? I searched the Internet trying to find answers. There had to be something somewhere, image after image, search after search... I found nothing. Only a collection of falcons from past and present. There was something different about his tattoo. His falcon had wide eyes that glared at you through the depths of his soul. Maybe he was part of a group, part of a team. He couldn't have acted alone. The strength he showed when he climbed down the fire escape, even though his arm was gashed up, he must have been an assassin... or have I been watching too many films?

I searched for *falcon tattoo gang*, but nothing came up. Trying my luck with an array of search terms found a hit close by. A man by the name of Blake Huntsman, that was him! I remembered the name! He worked at a local University; he appeared to be a professor of antiquities.

Seriously, he wasn't an assassin at all. I was a little deterred by this. He liked old antiques and stamp collecting, according to his bio. Couldn't have been more boring! So how can this old guy be the same one that acted like a ninja at the Grand last night? I shrugged. Nothing made sense. This being the man that threw Nathaniel out the window, then let me go. Why did he let me go? I was a witness? He didn't seem to have a problem with ending the life of another. Why was I spared? I had to find out, so I packed up my things, locked my laptop in the draw and left the office.

Leaving the building, I saw Dennis standing guarding the front door.

"Bye Miss Jones," he said, smiling.

"Bye Dennis, have a lovely Christmas," I said. "Oh, and I hope I'll see you both tomorrow for dinner?"

"Of course, Miss Jones,"

I smiled. "You know me by now Dennis, it's Julia,"

He laughed, tipped his cap, and said, "Goodbye Julia, Lydia and I will see you Christmas Day."

I smiled, waved, and walked away, hailing a taxi. Harrington university wasn't far away, and I hoped I'd be able to get an appointment to see the professor soon. Then again, it was the holidays. There was a high possibility he wouldn't be there. After all, who works through Christmas except me.

As I sat in the back of the taxi, we drove through the streets of London city centre. Daylight caressed the rooftops, high-rise buildings loomed over, and pedestrians stepped out in front of us without a care in the world. I remember when my mother used to take me to the local market all those years ago. We had to dodge traffic and cyclists with suicidal intentions, but the worst of it all was the older folk barging in front, incapable of waiting in a queue. Some were nice, though. My grandparents were, well, what I could remember of them. I remember Grandma Josephine, always bright and bubbly, with her rounded belly. Her laugh sounded like a hyena high on sherry. Grandpa John was a grumpy old man, but he always made me laugh. His dry humour would get him into the most difficult of situations. They were made for each other like chalk and cheese, but somehow, they fit. They didn't last long after Mum died, heartbroken at the death of their first-born child. Mum's siblings weren't much use. Uncle Joe moved away when Grandma passed, then Aunt Clara disappeared after Mum died. If it weren't for Lydia, I'd have been alone.

The university appeared desolate and drained when I arrived. Where was everyone? I'd expected some last-minute Christmas shopping at least. The Lanes Shopping Centre was next door and even their car park appeared empty. Getting out of the taxi, I paid the driver and walked over to the entrance. Climbing the steps, I entered a tranquil reception area, established with plantings of miniature trees aligning across the walls. The roof was made of glass and marble pillars framed the entrance. A little old lady greeted me with a stern look.

"Can I help you?" she asked, staring at me over the top of her glasses.

"Hello, I'm looking for Mr. Huntsman, the Antiquities professor."

"He is in a meeting with the other faculty members."

"Oh, do you know when he will be out?"

"It could go on for some time."

"Okay... can I wait?"

"Yes," she sighed. "I suppose so." Her brow furrowed.

"Thank you, I don't suppose there is anywhere I could get a coffee from?"

"There's nowhere open today, it's Christmas Eve!"

"Great."

"Can I ask what you are here for?"

"It's a private matter."

"Okay, well, wait then," she frowned. "But... there is a coffee machine down the hall if you have the correct change."

"Thank you," I responded, heading down the hall.

The rest of the university wasn't so elegant. It appeared to comprise a mahogany finish, with panelled walls, and midnight blue tapestries, clearly in need of an update. The first tapestry beside the coffee machine displayed the artist's portrayal of A Winter's Night. A family of six were sitting on the top of a hill overlooking London city central, under the starry sky. It was beautiful and welcoming.

Inserting a pound coin, the coffee machine rumbled. It groaned as I pressed 6B, then groaned some more as I pressed enter. Nothing happened.

"Damn machine!" I said, annoyed.

"Here, give it a stern kick on the right," a gruff male voiced.

"Thank you," I responded, smiling, and turning to see who it was. My smile soon dropped, as I came face to face with the silver-haired shooter with the falcon tattoo. I gasped. Standing as still as a statue.

His eyes narrowed. "You shouldn't be here," he said, brows furrowed.

I took a deep breath and uncurled my fists. *Remain calm, Julia!* I picked up my coffee and put on my reporter's face. "What happened last night?" I asked.

"You need to leave."

"No, I need answers."

He looked around, checking no one was watching. His voice growled in the depths of his throat. "Leave!" he demanded, gripping my arm and pulling me along the corridor. What the heck?

"Let go! You don't need to hold me, I'm more than capable of walking on my own." I was getting quite fed up with being pulled about lately.

"Fine," he said, letting go. I walked away, rubbing my arm. Grimacing, I stopped, turned back, and shouted, "I'll be talking to the police instead then." His jaw clenched; anger penetrated his irises. Veins popped out of his temples. He stomped forward, fists clenched, spittle foaming. Shit. I backed away, turned, and ran. "Damn it!" I cursed. Why was I so stupid? Now it wasn't just Eddy Boland after me. Bloody Blake Huntsman was too. Clearly, I had a death wish.

****

The taxi journey back was a short one. The silence was a godsend; it gave me time to think, time to consider what I'd witnessed. Blake Huntsman scared me. But he didn't seem an evil man. I'd seen evil, came up close to it, looked it in the eye... It didn't look like him. He appeared angry, granted, but more threatened than anything else. Shit. I had really done it this time!

The bright sky faded as we pulled up outside my tiny town house. Grey clouds threatened overhead, the shrill of wind blasted across the sidewalk. The storm hadn't finished yet. Frosted flakes of snow sprinkled down, cocooning my body with an aura of triumphant tranquillity. My rose red coat faded in the sleet, darkened by mother nature's caress, dampened by her icy terrain. It didn't last very long, as when I exited the taxi, the snow ceased to fall. A parade of youths filtered past me, pushing and shoving one another as the city lights blinked. My stomach grumbled, groaning for nourishment. Was it that time already? Carrying my bag over my head, I shielded myself from the storm, fumbling for my keys as Maisy wrapped around my ankles.

Opening the door, I ushered her inside. "Come on Maisy, did you want your dinner?" I asked. She purred, wrapping around my ankles again. I pulled out her favourite meal, Felix Sensations, and plopped it on a plate. "Here you go, now be good while I get changed."

I ascended the staircase, jumped in the shower, and got ready for my date with Nathaniel.

CHAPTER THIRTEEN

Nathaniel smiled as I opened the front door.

"You look smart," he laughed.

"Hmm, I thought these were more motorbike worthy." I said, looking down at my black jeans and rose red blouse.

"I jest, you look beautiful," he said, bending down to kiss my hand.

"Nope…"

"What?"

"I still can't get used to that."

He laughed, handing me a bouquet of deep purple roses.

"Thank you." I smiled. "Come in while I put these in some water."

He nodded and followed me into my living room. "Moving so soon?" he asked, staring at the unopened boxes.

I smiled. "No, these have been here a while. Sorry for

the mess!"

"No, not at all. I'm intrigued to know what they hold."

"Ha, well so am I, but not yet." I feigned a smile.

He paused, looking at me. "I understand." He smiled.

I nodded, walked into the kitchen, and arranged the roses in a vase of water. "Thank you for these." I placed them on the mantel.

Maisy pondered in through the cat flap, leaving a trail of paw prints across the linoleum. "Maisy," I said and sighed, laughing. Picking her up, I tickled her tummy and placed her on the armchair. She slinked her way up and on to the top and settled down for a nap. Nathaniel walked over and stroked her. She purred at first, then opened her eyes, jumped down, hissed, and ran away. "Maisy?" I shouted. "I'm sorry, did she scratch you?"

"No, not at all," Nathaniel said, smiling. Walking over, I checked his hand. His warm touch soothed me as his fingertips caressed the back of my hand. I smiled. "All fine." He smiled warmly.

"I've no idea why she did that, she's usually friendly."

Nathaniel smiled, and I let go of his hand.

Nathaniel looked over at the fireplace and the painting above. "Your artwork is exquisite."

I smiled. He had a good eye. "I bought them from a gallery a while ago."

"They're certainly eye-catching."

I nodded. Heading towards the door, I grabbed my coat. "So, where are we off to?"

"Ah, you'll see." He grinned. "But you won't need that," he said, pointing at my coat.

"I'll freeze," I said. Brows raised.

He smiled. "Don't worry, I have you covered." I shrugged, left my coat, locked the door, and hesitated, then jumped on the back of Gladys.

"She's quite comfortable, isn't she?" he said, elated. I laughed. "Do you want a hand?" he asked, pointing at the helmet.

I smirked. "Whatever gave it away?"

"Is this your first time?" he asked as he turned to face me.

"Pardon?"

He smirked. "On a bike?"

"Yeah," I said, brow furrowed, nerves kicking in.

Nathaniel smiled. "Here." He took the helmet from my hands. His right hand moved up to my face, brushing my hair behind my ear, gently caressing my cheek. His eyes met mine as he paused for a moment, then lifted the helmet and placed it on me with ease. Fastening the strap and lifting the visor, he stopped and looked, "there, does that feel okay?" he asked, smiling.

I nodded. The helmet felt heavy on my head.

"I have something else for you too." He pulled out a leather jacket, similar to his own. I smiled. "You may need this; it can get quite cool on the back of Gladys."

I laughed. "Thank you," I said as I placed it over my blouse, the warmth cradling my chest.

I took a deep breath. "Where do I hold on?" I asked, unsure.

"There's a handle behind you, or you can hold on to me if you'd like."

I smiled. I knew what I'd be doing.

Nathaniel kick-started the engine and Gladys roared into action.

"Hold on tight," he said, laughing.

I grabbed him as he sped off into the cityscape, my hands wrapped around his muscular torso as the bright lights of London's city centre beamed, shining the path ahead of us.

Speeding through the outskirts of London, on the back of an old motorbike, with a man I hardly knew… I'd never felt so safe. He was, after all, my sexy saviour, as Lola called him. I smiled. It was true, though. Where would I be now without him? He made me feel safe, even at this speed. I smirked, holding tighter, breathing deeply.

The headlights of cars flashed by as the city sphere dimmed. Moonlight lit the way as we left the centre and settled uphill, looking down on the world before us. Nathaniel pulled to a stop, put the brake on and dismounted, lifting me off as though I held no weight at all. I smiled. "Where are we?" I asked as we removed our helmets.

He looked across at me, stepped forward, and held out his hand. "You'll see, it's not far." I smiled. Took a deep breath and placed my hand in his. The heat of his touch warmed my body as we walked up another short hill. When we reached our destination, I huffed a little, my breathing heightened from all the exercise he'd put me through. I smiled, wiping my brow.

I looked beyond the trees and saw a covering of sparkling stars brought down from the night sky. Hundreds of fairy lights twinkled above. The flow of warmth fled through me as Nathaniel put his arm around my waist, directing me under the blanket of starlight. I was in awe. I may have squeaked a little as I delighted at the beauty of my surroundings. He had done this. For me! A large red blanket lay atop of the grassy hill, with six, maybe seven cushions piled across it. I ran over, amazed. Nathaniel laughed as he watched. I sat down beside the fire pit, already lit and roaring away. Its warmth was a pleasure against the cool breeze of Winter's reign. Taking off my boots, I curled my feet under myself, sitting against the cushions, surrounded by comfort. Nathaniel sat beside me, kicked off his boots and reached across for the wicker picnic basket.

"How did you do all this?" I asked, struck by awe.

He smiled. "I had help."

"Kenny?"

He nodded. "And a few others." He grinned. "Care for a glass?" he asked, pulling the cork on a bottle of champagne. I nodded as the froth and bubbles exploded over the side. He held it off the blanket, poured two glasses, and placed it back in the ice bucket.

Handing me a glass, he said, "I would like to make a toast." I smiled. He could make any toast he liked after all the effort he'd put in. He raised his glass. "I would like to toast to new friendships, forthcoming adventures, and the love of good company."

I raised my glass to his. The crystal clinked, and we both took a sip.

"I like the sound of forthcoming adventures," I said, smirking.

He grinned. "I thought you would like that." He winked.

"You're full of mystery, Nathaniel," I said, looking into his eyes as they sparkled in the moonlight.

"Indeed." He said, grinning. I smiled. "Are you hungry?"

"Famished."

"Good. Let's eat." He pulled out plates of hors d'oeuvres, sandwiches, croissants, quiche, salad, sausage rolls and crisps. "Help yourself."

So I did. The hors d'oeuvres were nice, as were the soft cheese and ham croissants. "Did you make these yourself?"

He laughed. "I would love to say yes, but our chef at the club can take credit for that one."

"I might have to marry your chef," I said, laughing as I took another bite of a croissant. "These are delicious."

He laughed. "I shall tell him that."

After we finished, the conversation turned to the night sky. Lying back on the cushions staring up at the constellations, Nathaniel explained the nature of Orion and how it backs on to both Gemini and Taurus.

"Is Capricorn up there somewhere?" I asked. As I moved closer, laying against his arm for warmth. "Sorry, do you mind?"

"No, I welcome it." He pulled his arm out so I could snuggle into his chest, staring up at the stars. "So, Capricorn, you say, is that your star sign?"

"Yes."

"Ah, so you'll be reaching your birthday soon then?"

I laughed. "Yes, another year older."

He laughed. "You make yourself sound ancient when you say it like that."

I nudged him with my elbow. He laughed harder. "Well, I'll be twenty-three, so no, I'm not as old as some I suspect?"

He laughed. "Ah, is that your devilish way of asking a man his age?"

"Why ever not?"

He smirked. "Well, I'm twenty-eight."

"That is quite old." I said. Laughing.

"Oi." He grinned. "Well, let's see shall we." He pointed up at the stars as I followed his finger, tracing the lines of each of the constellations. "Capricornus is visible between nine and ten at night. So, we're in luck." He stopped, his finger hovering over a triangular shaped constellation. "There". I looked over at the faint shape. "It is made by forty-eight stars coming together to form a mythical creature."

"What creature?" I asked, gazing high at the night sky.

"A goat," he said. Then laughed.

"What? Really?"

He nodded.

"So I'm supposed to be part goat or something?"

He laughed harder. "Not quite. But I know that people of your nature are highly ambitious and adventurous, but just as stubborn."

I huffed, elbowing him again.

"Ow," he laughed, sitting up on his elbow, jabbing me in the ribs, tickling me.

I laughed. "Enough!"

"Demanding too," he said, tickling me more.

I laughed harder. He stopped so I could catch my breath, leaning down as his face met my own. Soft brown eyes sparkled with a smile. He paused, and I took in his features. My hand rose to caress the face above me. Smooth skin, a delicate trimmed beard, wavy curls that wrapped themselves around my fingertips.

Heat rose from my stomach. Butterflies fluttered through as I took a deep breath in, then out. Warmth cradled my chest, my cheeks blossomed. He smiled, swallowed hard, and moved in to kiss me.

I parted my lips as the soft touch of Nathaniel's caressed my own. Apple blossom lip balm intermingled between us as he delved deeper into me, his tongue conquering the depths of my mouth. Hungry. Consuming. His body arched above as he caressed my face. Soft strands of hair flowed through my fingertips as I pulled him in closer, aching for more.

Fervent kisses consumed me as my heart pounded faster, harder, deeper. I was lost in the moment, encapsulated by the beauty of his gaze, the warmth of his caress. The way his hand slipped over my cheekbone, my neckline, and down to the side of my breast. Tingles rushed over my body as we came up for air. Our eyes meeting, his oceanic gaze hypnotising me with the love of his touch.

Time stood still. I inhaled deeply, his leathery aroma hypnotic beyond reason. My lips creased, the smile contagious. I brought my hands up to his face, pulled him closer, demanding more. Passionate kisses were stolen in the moment. My hands raced down to his back, fingernails gripping, hungry for more. His chest lay above my own, his skin soothing, soft, and radiating heat. He pulled back, looked at me, pulling me in again, leaving me with a delicate sensual kiss as I relaxed into the moment, giving into my desire.

As he pulled back, he grinned. "Apple?"

I laughed. "It's my favourite."

He laughed. "It's something I'll have to remember."

I smiled, relaxing in his arms. I wanted more. Needed him close to me. I wanted this to last, and I knew we had all the time in the World to make it so.

Falling asleep under the stars, Nathaniel woke me. "It's two in the morning, Red. I'd better get you home. Maisy will wonder where you've got to."

I laughed, yawning and sitting upright.

"Thank you for tonight," I said, smiling. "It was perfect."

He smiled, lent forward, and kissed me softly. I sighed, lost in heaven. Tonight was a delight of everything I'd ever wanted on a first date. The perfect setting, the perfect guy, the perfect kiss. He didn't push for more, even if I wanted it. He was what my mum would have called a true gentleman, and I'm sure she would have loved to have met him. I smiled.

Nathaniel packed away the picnic basket, helped me out from under the blanket and into his leather jacket. I smiled, thanking him. It was still dark out, and after a ride on Gladys through the cityscape, we reached my front door.

"Home sweet home," he said, smiling as we walked up the pathway.

He cradled my face as I leaned in for a final kiss goodbye. Delicate, sweet, lustrous kisses swept over my lips as we parted ways. "Till tomorrow?" I asked.

"Till today, you mean," he said, smiling.

I laughed. "Happy Christmas, Nathaniel."

"Happy Christmas, Red." He smiled, turned, and walked back up the path, riding away into the night.

CHAPTER FOURTEEN

I yawned as I awoke, stretching out into my bed. Maisy padded the duvet beside me. Stroking her, I stared out of the opening in the curtains. Bright light streamed into the room. What time is it? I picked up my phone. 10:22. Shit! I had guests arriving at 12. It was Christmas Day and this year it was at my house.

The bedroom door creaked as Lola walked in. "Wake up sleepy head," she said laughing, handing me a coffee.

"What time did you arrive?" I asked, sitting upright in bed, taking a sip. "Mmm thanks!"

"Oh, about two hours ago," she said, laughing.

"What! Why didn't you wake me?"

"Ha, honey, after reading your text at nearly three in the morning, I was sure you would need your beauty sleep."

"Ouch, 3am?" She nodded. "That was when he dropped me home."

She sat on the bed, pounding her hands on the mattress. "So… tell me all about it! What was he like? Did you kiss?

Make out? Get boned?"

I laughed, spitting out my coffee.

"Burgh," she said as she chucked a towel at me.

"Who even says 'get boned?'"

"Oh honey, you don't know what the kids are calling things nowadays."

I threw the towel at her. "Kids! I'm twenty-three, not fifty-three!"

She smirked, throwing a dress at me. "Here, get changed. He's coming today, isn't he?"

I nodded. "Well, I think so. We didn't discuss times."

"How did you not tell him what time dinner was?"

"Oh, I dunno, I forgot!"

"More like, lost in the moment." She laughed. "Here, text him, but make it quick. We've got dinner to cook."

I typed out a text message.

Nathaniel, I really enjoyed last night. Do you fancy dinner with us today? Julia btw x

He replied almost immediately. *I guessed it was you, Red. I can't recall anyone else I kissed last night. Thank you, I would love dinner with you, as long as you can cook. x*

I laughed, showed Lola, she laughed. "Cheeky!" she said.

I replied, *Haha, well is 2pm ok? x*

Sounds like a plan. I'll see you later x

I smiled, fell back on the bed, and swooned.

Lola laughed, hit me with a cushion, "Come on, I've prepared most of it, but could do with a hand with the Yorkshire puddings."

I sat up and pulled my dress on. Lola zipped me up. "You've prepared it all already?"

She nodded, "I was bored waiting!"

I laughed. "Okay, give me ten minutes to sort my face out and I'll be right with you."

"You'll need thirty," she said, laughing and running out of the room as I threw a pillow at her.

I smiled. Last night was perfect. He really was a true gentleman, and today, shit. He'd be meeting my family! I gulped. But then again, he's already met them. It was only Aunt Lydia and Dennis, Lola, her parents and Nathaniel and me. So, he'd met most of them… and I'm sure Lydia will talk his head off throughout dinner, anyway.

After freshening up and applying make-up, I headed into the living room.

The table was already set, the Christmas tree was sparkling, and fairy lights twinkled across the ceiling overhead. "Lola, it's beautiful."

"Well, duh, you didn't even have a tree up!"

"I was… getting round to it."

She frowned, then laughed.

I noted how tidy the room was. "Where's all the boxes?"

"In the spare room, and jeez, they were heavy, Julia!"

I laughed. "Think of all the muscles you're building up."

She gave me a snide look. I laughed.

"So, what do I need to do?"

"Err, like, yorkies?"

I grinned. "I'm right there with you."

She handed me a glass of something bubbly and I began making Yorkshire puddings and stuffing, my mum's favourite. "What about the bread sauce?"

"The what now?"

I laughed. "You know the white stuff my mum used to make?"

"Burgh, that's only for you, honey."

I laughed and started peeling an onion. "I'll sort it."

"Now don't go crying now." She smirked.

I pretended to sniffle. "You know if you don't cut the root end, then you won't cry?"

"Err no. I always let someone else cut the onions, otherwise this face gets ruined." She said, blowing me a kiss.

I laughed, finishing up by adding the milk, bread, and black pepper. "Ten minutes on full power and we're all done."

Lola nodded. "What's the time?"

"12"

"Plenty of time for our Christmas tradition." She grinned, pulling out a party hat, party poppers, and topping up the bubbly. I groaned, already feeling lightheaded from the bubbly.

Washing my hands, I joined her in the living room. She turned on the music and out blasted our favourite Christmas tune by The Pogues, Fairytale in New York. I laughed as she took my hand and we danced around and around the table, just like we did when we were at university.

The doorbell chimed. Lola ran to answer it. Matty was at the door. "Room for one more?" he said, holding a bottle of bubbly.

"Always," I said as Lola pulled him into the living room. We danced and chatted until the first of our guests arrived. Lola's parents. Stiff upper lips, but always warming and welcoming. They had opened their home to me one summer when I was nineteen. The business of London had become too much, and I needed the break. Lydia took me to their country home, and I stayed throughout the summer break where Lola and I had so much fun.

Next, Aunt Lydia and Dennis arrived. Dennis was as courteous as ever, holding the door so Lydia could walk in. Finally, Nathaniel arrived, bang on time, with a giant bunch of flowers and a bottle of bubbly under his arm. "I wasn't sure which was your favourite flower, so I bought all of them." He smiled.

"Blimey Nathaniel, I may need more vases for this lot." I smiled, moving in to kiss him. He pulled me closer, his leathery aroma caressing my senses.

"You have a house full I see," he said as he peered behind me to Lola and Matty dancing away in the living room."

I laughed. "Yes, it's a little crowded, but you're more than welcome."

He nodded, "thank you… it will be good to get to know you some more."

"Oh, no! No asking for family pictures or anything, that topic's not allowed."

He laughed as he walked in and hung up his leather jacket. "Oh, I promise."

We walked into the living room as Lola stopped dancing and grinned. Matty stopped, turned around to see what she was looking at, and grinned too. "Nathaniel, my man!" he said as they fist bumped. Nathaniel nodded as Lydia walked over.

"Nathaniel, it's good to see you," Lydia said, smirking. Dennis walked over and shook his hand. "This is Dennis, my bit of stuff." She laughed.

Nathaniel laughed, nodded, and I held his hand, pulling him into the kitchen. "Now Maisy won't jump out and attack me, will she?"

I laughed as he looked around. "No, she's out, playing in the neighbour's garden. They have an aviary," I smiled. "Keeps her busy for hours."

He laughed. I introduced Nathaniel to Lola's parents, and we sat at the table. I had Lola at the head of the table on one side with me on the other. Nathaniel sat beside me, next to Matty, with Lola's dad at the other end with her mum, Aunt Lydia and Dennis.

The food was fantastic, all thanks to Lola and her early morning wake up. She'd saved me this morning. Even the turkey was spot on. The last time I tried cooking it, it ended up dry as a bone. I laughed under my breath.

Aunt Lydia found time to tell stories about me growing up. Nathaniel found the tale of the wrong toilets a hoot, as she told the tale of our trip to France and me using the urinal as a washing sink. I was only eight, but my mother was horrified, throwing me in the shower as soon as I was home. I laughed. The things we do as kids. I shrugged, sighing. Happy days.

Lola enquired about Kenny as Nathaniel told her Kenny was eager to see her again. The beam on her face said it all. I could see those two ending up as a couple, eventually. Matty's boyfriend, however, ended their relationship after he found Matty canoodling two girls in their bedroom. I laughed; I could imagine that was something Matty would do. Apparently, Jamie wasn't keen on joining in when he walked in. Lola's parents appeared horrified by the path the conversation had taken. Lola smirked.

After a long but beautiful day, everyone left. Lola stayed behind with Nathaniel to help me tidy away. But could clearly see she was the third person in a love triangle and soon made her excuses to go home.

I smiled, kissed her cheek, and wished her a Merry Christmas.

Nathaniel waltzed over, put on some music, and twirled me around the dance.

I laughed. "Isn't it a little late for dancing?"

"It's never too late for dancing, my Rose Red." He grinned, twirling me around to 'Oh what a night,' as it filled the airwaves.

"Did you enjoy today?" I asked.

"Yes, it was great to meet your loved ones. You really have a beautiful family."

I smiled. "Thank you… I wish you could have met my mother; she would have liked you."

"I'm sure she would have… after all, what's not to like?" He grinned, spinning me around and catching me in his arms.

I laughed as my hand caught his belt. "Is that the infinity symbol?"

"Yes." He smiled.

"For the club?"

He nodded.

I thought for a moment. "So, what does the falcon mean?"

He stopped. Smiled and pulled me over to the settee. "Falcon, how do you know about that?"

"The tattoo Blake had?"

"Ah," he said, and smiled.

I frowned. "What did you think I meant?"

"I, well, I guess you're going to work it out, eventually."

"What?"

"FALCON... it's an organisation that works behind the scenes, keeping people safe. Or so they say…"

"What do you mean?"

"Blake and I have known each other for a very long time. We understand each other."

I laughed. "You didn't seem to understand each other the other day."

Nathaniel smirked. "No, well, he was in a mood."

I laughed, "So…?"

"Okay, well, you know there are things in this world that you can't yet understand."

"Like what?" I asked, brow furrowed.

"Like Eddy's strength."

"Or the fact you fell three stories and survived without a cut or bruise on you?" I said, my eyes widening.

"Yes, well, that too."

"So, what does it all mean?"

"For you, it means you're safe and I won't let anything happen to you."

I smiled. "But that doesn't answer my question, Nathaniel."

"What was the question, Red?"

I stopped, looked down at my hands. Recalled the heat, the burning. The mega early menopausal moments. "What happened to me?"

He smiled, his eyes soothing. "For that, you need to speak to Blake."

"But why? Last time I saw him, he was angry."

"What? Well, I'll talk to him."

"Not like last time I hope."

He smirked. "No, not like last time."

I smiled, leaned into his arms, and stared at the roaring fire as the light dimmed, with daytime riding on its merry way.

"It's time I go," he said.

I sulked. He laughed, kissing me softly. "I've got to open up in the morning."

"In the morning?"

He nodded. I stared at him for answers. He laughed. "Okay, well, I'm meeting a few colleagues."

"And by colleagues, do you mean Blake Huntsman?"

He grinned, "Yes."

I frowned, my eyes narrowing.

"It'll be fine, I promise."

"Well, at least you're on the ground floor."

He laughed. "I'll call you after?"

I nodded, walking him to the door.

We kissed goodbye as I watched him walk up the garden path as his motorbike, Gladys, roared and he rode off into the distance.

CHAPTER FIFTEEN

The shrill ring of the home phone woke me. "Hello?"

"Look outside Julia, I'm by your door."

"Lola?"

"Yeah, who else would it be? Wait, you've not got a man in there, have you?"

I laughed. "No, Nathaniel went home last night. He had to open up this morning."

"This morning? It's a club? Why this morning?"

I laughed.

"Anyway, let me in, it's freezing?"

"Where's your key?"

"I don't know, thought I left it here."

"Maybe… one minute, I'll be right down."

I chucked on my dressing gown, and ran down the stairs, opening the front door.

As I opened it Lola's bright red face blossomed into view. "Your cheeks are all red," I said, laughing.

Her brow furrowed, and she walked in. Behind her, a black Mercedes with blacked-out windows sat parked. "Wait…"

"What?"

"How long's that been there?"

"I dunno. It was there when I left. Maybe someone's been having a party?"

"No, it's the same one that's been following me. Look…" The number plate was the same. "It's Jesus!"

She burst out laughing. "Honey, I know it was Jesus's birthday yesterday, but really."

I gave her a snide look. "I'm being serious Lola. That's the car that ran my mum down."

"What!"

"The plates are the same. It's got the same last part." Lola looked at me, her brow furrowed. "It's L0L, Lola! It's been showing up outside lately."

"That's some messed up kinda shit right there, Julia. You being serious?"

I nodded. Lola stormed out of the house and over to the Mercedes. As she closed in on it, the engine started, and they sped away. Lola walked back. "Assholes," she said, walking in. "Right, now sit down and tell me everything."

I told her about the attack and Eddy's unnatural strength. About the injection and how my hands heated, burning Eddy in the hospital. I sighed, took a deep breath, and continued to tell my story. Moving on, I went through what happened at the Grand with Nathaniel and Blake. The strange mask he wore and how he survived without a scratch on him. I described the professor, Blake Huntsman at Harington University and how in his spare time he works for an organisation called FALCON. How I remember my mum's murder, and that no one pursued it, and just like my attack there was no evidence, no way of keeping the perpetrator inside. It scared me, but it also intrigued me. I had never been this close to solving my mum's murder, but by doing so, I knew I'd made myself a target and everyone around me.

"I promise I'll be careful," I said, as Lola scolded me for going to the Grand on my own. "But I know they're all connected, somehow."

"Even Nathaniel?"

I shook my head. "He's... different, granted, but he feels safe to me. I don't know why, he just does."

"Honey, I feel like we're reliving an issue of *X-Men*."

I laughed. What the hell had my life turned out like!

The phone rang. Detective Melissa Lee wanted me in to identify Eddy. By the sounds of it, it was our last hope. I agreed. What else could I do?

"I'm coming too, you know."

"Lola, you don't have to."

"Honey, you have just told me some bizarre shit. You're either going nuts or there's a secret society of super people that are out to get you. Either way, I'm down for the adventure."

I laughed. "Fine, where do we start?"

"FALCON, duh, crank up the old laptop and we'll start hunting the old Huntsman down."

I smirked, wandered into the kitchen, made a couple of coffees, then sat down with Lola and the laptop.

"Okay," Lola said, taking a sip of the coffee. "Shit. Hot." She winced. I smirked. "We've either got falconry groups; Falcon Lovers United or Big Birds do Brighton," I laughed as she winced. "You don't wanna see those photos! Oh wait. There's a post about FALCON saving some boy from a hairy monster."

"Like, seriously?"

She nodded. "I shit you not. It's on this 'monsters are real' forum."

"Heck, we know monsters are real, but they're the human ones."

"No, this mum, named Debbie572, actually wrote about her eight-year-old son being attacked by a monster with a hairy face."

"Like Nathaniel's mask?" I asked.

She nodded. "Look, there's a sketch."

I looked over. The sketch was so similar to the mask Nathaniel wore.

"But why would Nathaniel hurt a kid?" I asked sceptically.

"Maybe it wasn't Nathaniel, maybe there are more people with those werewolf masks around."

I shrugged, "could be."

She paused, reading. "Okay, so this is scary. FALCON quoted they are humanity's protectors."

"That's like what Nathaniel said."

"The kid also said it wasn't a mask. Shit… did you try

to take it off, Julia?"

"What? The mask?"

She nodded.

"No, I was a little preoccupied with him falling to his death."

Lola's eyes widened. "Yeah, makes sense," she said, smiling.

"Okay, so I think you need to talk to this Blake guy again. Check out if he owns a Mercedes."

I laughed. "He doesn't. I'm pretty sure the Range Rover was his… He seemed pretty pissed when Nathaniel landed on top of it."

"Well, he shouldn't have pushed him then."

"That's what I said."

She laughed. "So… are you going to ring Nathaniel then? You said he's meeting with Blake this morning."

"Yes, but…"

"But what?"

"I didn't want to look too eager."

"Sod that, honey, you need answers before you burn the house down with impatience."

I laughed. "I'm sure you're being the impatient one right now."

She looked at me sternly.

"Okay, okay, I'll ring!"

"Hello Red," Nathaniel said, with hushed voices in the background. The nickname had clearly stuck.

"Are they still there?"

He laughed. "Yes… you can tell you're a reporter."

"Wannabe journalist, actually."

I could hear the smile in his voice. "Well, Red, what questions do you have for me today?"

"Thank you, Nathaniel. I would like to know what you've been talking about."

He laughed. "Well, if I told you that, I'd have to kill you."

"That's not very nice after only two dates." I laughed. "We need to make it to at least five."

"Ha, well how about we get together over the next few days, and we make date five a trip to my beach house?"

"You have a beach house?"

Lola piped up, "Can I come?"

Nathaniel laughed. "Is that Lola?"

"Yes," I smirked.

"Of course, she can come, and I'm sure Kenny would like to join us too."

I nodded to Lola. She squealed.

We laughed. "Did you talk to Blake?"

"Yes, he apologised for the other day. He's still nursing his blistered hand."

"Oh, yes, well…"

"It's okay. We'll talk more about it when we get together, don't worry!"

"Okay, tell him I didn't mean to. I'm not even sure it was me."

"It was, Red. But it was because of what happened to you. It has changed you somehow."

"What do you mean?"

"You're one of Eddy's girls. You may have seen, and well… written about the missing girls that reappear."

"Yes."

"That's all because of the doctor."

"The who?"

"We don't know for sure, but it's someone Eddy works for. FALCON has been trying to find him for quite some time."

I took a deep breath. "Thank you."

"For what?"

"For saving me from him."

"Anytime, you know that. I just wish I'd have gotten there before he injected you."

"What was it?"

"We don't know. But Blake wants you to come to the University on Tuesday for a blood test."

"Okay, I can do that."

"Good, I'll let him know."

"Thanks Nathaniel."

"It's okay. I'll see you soon and it'll be my turn to come up with an amazing date this time."

"I don't think you can top your first date."

"Oh, you've seen nothing yet."

I laughed, and we said our goodbyes.

Lola jumped up. "Beach house, like seriously?" I nodded, smirking. "I gotta go pack! When is it?"

I laughed. "Hold your horses. He says it's date five. We've only had two dates!"

"Well, hurry! Go see him now!"

I couldn't help but laugh at her impatience. "He said we'll meet up later. It's his turn to make the plans."

"Wait, but you haven't arranged anything yet either."

I nodded. "Apparently Christmas Day was a date."

"Oooh, clever!"

I smirked, she smiled. "So, how's he going to top a romantic picnic under the stars?"

My lips pursed, and I shrugged. "It was pretty spectacular!"

She nodded, plonking herself down on the sofa beside me. "So, what are we doing today, fire girl?"

"Fire girl?" I said, laughing.

"Okay, so lava lady?" she smirked. "Oooh, what about The Big Blaster?" A laugh escaped my lips, and I punched her in the arm. "Ow, you're hot headed!" She collapsed onto the sofa in stitches of laughter. I frowned, then burst into laughter.

Gathering ourselves into some sort of normality, she asked, "So, like really, what are we doing?" I shrugged. "Well, you need answers, don't you?"

"Yeah, but it's Boxing Day. Nowhere will be open."

"True," she thought for a moment. "But the Grand will be."

My eyes widened.

"How about we take a trip up to the penthouse and see what we can find on this Jesus fella."

"Good plan. Although," I shuddered, "it's kinda scary in there, you know."

She laughed. "Oh honey, I'll hold your hand." That was

it. We were both in fits of laughter again.

An hour later we were ready, with coats and scarves, gloves to fight off the bitter cold and an umbrella which Lola thought could double as a weapon should we need one. I didn't know whether to laugh or cry at that.

I fed Maisy, and we left, standing in the cold as I locked the front door. The afternoon sky was already dimming, and the storm had picked up its pace. Snow was falling through the greyness of the sky, weeping as it fell, puddling on the ground.

We began walking to the subway station. Both of us boarded, sitting in silence. Even Lola appeared nervous as she sat staring out of the dark windows. After ten minutes, we'd reached our stop. The carriage lit up with the white clinical surroundings of the station itself.

"Are you okay?" Lola asked, feigning a smile.

I nodded. She smiled again. "Let's visit Lydia and grab a bite to eat."

"She's not open, is she?"

"She is, I just texted her."

I smiled. "Okay." I felt a little hungry.

Leaving the station, Lola opened the umbrella, and we both shrouded underneath for cover. A mesmerising array of snowflakes protruded from the sky, settling their moist nature beside us. Lydia welcomed us with open arms when we reached her coffee shop.

Sitting beside the vintage window dressing, I gazed

out at the world outside. Men, women, and children were gathering on the street, flurrying through the snow, purchasing goodies in the Boxing Day sales. This time of year was always busy. I sat staring out of the window while Lola chatted to Lydia at the counter. Outside, a young family with a toddler and a baby in tow were rushing through the street. The toddler looked weary as his father opened the door, ushering the family inside. Shrieks of wailing cries escaped from the mouth of the newborn baby, deafening every customer in the coffee shop. A businessman from the next table got up and left, scowling at the young mother.

Lola sat down and Lydia rushed over to the family with a pot of coffee, trying to soothe the tears from the young mother's eyes. It must have been hard for her when she couldn't stop the baby from crying. Taking the child from its pram, she began to breastfeed. Her eyes searched for approval as she latched the child on. It was admirable to see. I smiled as Lydia walked over to us.

"Isn't it beautiful?" she said. I nodded. "It reminds me of when your mother used to sit there and feed you." I smiled as she fetched me an espresso with a hint of lemon. "What would you both like to eat?"

"Surprise us," Lola said, sipping her coffee. I smiled and nodded, continuing to watch the world go by. After she fed the newborn baby, the father left to take the other child to choose a cake. I smiled, and the young mother smiled back.

"She's beautiful," I said.

"Thank you," she replied, then looked over at her partner.

That could be me one day. A loving husband, a couple of children, and a daytime spent shopping in the sales with the family. One day. Lydia came over with two plates of fries and double cheeseburgers. "I held off on the garnish," she said, smiling and placing the plates down in front of us.

"Thank you, it looks delicious," I grinned, tucking in.

Lydia smiled and walked back to serve a new customer.

Lola devoured her food. I always wondered how she stayed so slim. "So honey, are you ready for our big adventure?"

"Err... no," I said, nervously smiling.

"Ha, it'll be fine. I've got the Big Blaster by my side."

"Seriously, choose a different name!" I smirked, rolling my eyes.

"I'm thinking, I'm thinking..." she said, putting her hand out to stop me from jabbing her. "So, what's that guy called in Fantastic Four?"

"Which one?"

"Really, Julia... the hot one," her face hit her palm.

"Oh yeah," jeez!

"Torch something?"

"Yeah, that's the one. You could be his Torchette?"

"Really..." I frowned. "There's got to be a better name... I don't know... how about... Julia? Now there's an idea!"

Her lips pursed as she frowned. "Oh, you spoil all the fun."

I laughed.

"Anyway, Torch lady, I want to see you flame on!"

"Flame on?"

"Yeah, you know, fly on fire."

"Wow, really…" My eyes widened. "No. That's never going to happen!"

"Oh, but!"

"Just no!" I laughed. "But really Lola, I don't even know if I can flame on."

"You've got to try!"

"I don't fancy being burned alive, short stack!"

She laughed. "Okay, so what can you do?"

Lydia walked over. "What are you two on about?"

I laughed. "Lola's trying to turn me into some superhero."

Lydia laughed. "Ah Julia, with great power comes great responsibility."

I smirked. Lola laughed. "That's Spiderman, Lydia, not the Fantastic Four."

"Oh," she huffed. "I didn't hear that part of your conversation," she said, taking the plates and walking away.

"Come on," Lola said, "we'd best get going." I nodded. We said our goodbyes, kissed Lydia on the cheek, and headed over to the Grand Palace Hotel.

The snow had stopped falling now, but the day was still grey and miserable. It was already three in the afternoon, the sun would set soon, we needed to get a move on. Standing before the Grand, I shuddered. If it was still dark in there, I might not stay too long. I gulped.

Lola stood staring out at me. "It'll be fine Julia; we've got my trusty sidekick Umber the Umbrella here and the

Big Blaster is ready to sizzle the skin off of any foe we come across."

I rolled my eyes. "Really... you won't drop the name, are you?"

"Not until you pick a name."

"I have a name."

"Not a super name."

"Fine, I'll think on it... not that I have any superhero powers, anyway."

"You can sizzle people's skin."

"It could have been a fluke. I don't even know how to do it."

"You will do. Superpowers always work when you need them to."

"You've been watching way too many movies."

She shrugged. "Let's go in." She walked up the steps and through the swing door.

I took a deep breath and looked up. No guy had better fall on me again. Hands clammy, body tense, I walked up the steps. Pausing for a moment, I inhaled, held my breath, exhaled, and walked in.

Lola was standing by the reception desk rummaging through the paperwork. "Come here," she said, waving me over. "Is this him? Jesus Mendel?" she asked, pointing at an entry in the hotel's diary.

"Yeah."

"There's a phone number," she said. I frowned. I couldn't remember that being there last time. Grabbing a scrap of paper, I wrote the number down, shoving it in my coat pocket.

"Okay, let's head up there," she looked over at me as I gulped. "You ready?" I nodded, feigning a smile.

Lola grabbed my hand, pulled me up the staircase and into the hallway, turning the corner towards the penthouse. What if Blake is here? What if someone else is there, all ready to jump out and grab us? Shit. We're alone in this dark, damp place. Shit. My mind is messed up. Do I really need to think like that right now? I felt around in my pocket for my phone. It was dark in there. Turning on the torch, we headed down the corridor. Graffiti scrawled over every wall, carpet trashed and burned; the place was a mess. Lola wielded the umbrella like a sword in-front of her. I whimpered as we walked forward; the heat rising in my body. Lola dropped my hand.

"You're getting hot," she said. I nodded. Somehow, my body sensed my fear and turned on its all-new microwave rays to protect me. As long as it didn't burn me to death, I didn't mind. I needed some sort of protection before we entered the Penthouse of carnage and crime.

Down the corridor, a set of double doors were open, welcoming us into its arms. Walking towards the entrance, I could see a smashed window at the far end. Is that where it happened? I gulped, my throat tight with fear. I had to be sure. Standing before the entrance, I stopped. Lola stopped with me. I composed myself, stepped forward, and broke the threshold of the room. The room was a tip. Trashed and broken up by squatters. There was nothing of value left. The remaining cream carpets were grey, burnt, and bloodied by last night's destruction. There were old clothes, ragged and torn, littering the floor, and a shabby old sleeping bag discarded in the corner. I walked over, gagging when I smelt the stench of stale urine. Backing away, I headed for the broken window. Beside it was a satchel, open to the elements. I peered inside. An old jumper, three cheap looking mobile phones, burners perhaps. A wallet with no ID and a business card, with the infinity symbol on it. Nathaniel's? It was the same symbol as his belt buckle and of his club, Infinite Encounters.

"Do you recognise anything?" Lola asked.

"It's Nathaniel's, it's the symbol for his club."

"So, the man in the mask was definitely him?" I nodded. "Okay, so now we need to find out what he's up to and if that mask is real or not."

"It's got to be real... hasn't it?"

"I dunno Julia, has he said anything to you?"

I shrugged, shaking my head. Lola frowned. "Then again, he said we were different."

"Okay, so what do you think he meant?"

"He said something in that injection had changed me. But... he also said the word we."

"Yeah. So, he isn't human then?" she asked.

"I don't know. But he must be. I'm human, yet he said I'm different somehow."

"Okay, so what is he?"

I shrugged. "I don't know. Originally, I thought he had a hero complex, but now, I'm not sure what he is."

Lola walked over to the broken window, looked down and stepped back wide-eyed. "Hell, have you seen how high up we are? No mere mortal could survive that."

I joined Lola, looking over the edge. "Shit."

"Exactly."

"Let's get out of here," she said, pulling me back. "I think the one person you need to talk to is the one person who survived that fall."

I nodded, taking her hand.

"Damn, you're still hot."

I pulled away.

She laughed. "No, you're fine," she grabbed my hand and pulled me out of the penthouse, down the stairs and out of the Grand into the snowy open air.

We headed back to my house, lost in thought on the way. Who was Nathaniel really? Was I safe with him? I felt safe… I sighed, reminding myself of his powerful arms as they held me close last night. Then the kiss, intense and seducing, his alluring brown eyes tempting me further. He was the picture of perfection, loving, carefree, devoted to his friends and family. So how did he fit into all this?

CHAPTER SIXTEEN

Boxing day came and went, and Sunday followed through with Lola's insistent need to phone her newest bit of stuff, Mr. Kenny the bulky bouncer. Nathaniel's visit had sparked her interest, especially when he said Kenny would like to see her again. The problem was… she never got his number. So, to ease her discomfort and need, I agreed to venture into the daylight and hunt down her man for her. This, of course, involved a tactical conversation on how we were going to 'accidentally' bump into him. Jeez, it was like we were sixteen, sweet on the boy next door, head over heels in love. Don't get me wrong… the idea of going to the club meant the possibility of bumping into my own sexy saviour himself, and I didn't mind missing that opportunity.

"Julia, are you ready?" Lola shouted from the bedroom.

"Yes, ready when you are." I'd been ready for over an hour now. A little lip gloss, concealer, and my job was done. Granted, it wasn't my best work, but I didn't fancy donning a full mask of makeup to nip to the club and get

Kenny's phone number. My brow furrowed; lips pouted. It was unlikely I'd meet him there anyway. I'm sure he said he was out on business tonight. I shrugged, then smiled. I was still hopeful.

Lola walked out. "Honey, what's with the pale, lethargic look?"

I laughed. "Perhaps if you hadn't kept me awake all night watching old movies, I wouldn't look so dire!"

She laughed. "Ok, well, at least put some mascara on. You never know who you might bat your eyelids at tonight."

I groaned. "Really… he's not even there tonight."

"He might be." She winked.

I smiled as we put on our coats and headed out the door.

The taxi journey to Infinite Encounters was quiet, as quiet as the evening sunset as the sky dimmed and the frozen landscape misted over. London was silent for a Sunday evening. Even the park had slipped into solitude. No mothers taking their children out to play. No boys kicking footballs or girls taking picnics. The world had changed, and I'd hazard a guess that the London Butcher had something to do with it. People were afraid. He'd already murdered over seven girls this season; and the police were no closer to catching him. Maybe the fact that Eddy is behind bars speaks a thousand silent words, considering that the Butcher hadn't taken its latest kill this week.

We arrived at Infinite Encounters, paid the driver, and stood outside as he left. My mobile phone rang. Lola went to try the door, but it appeared locked.

"Hello?"

"Hello Miss Jones, this is Detective Melissa Lee."

"Oh, hello Melissa," I said, hopeful for better news.

"Well, we have some news," her voice sounded strained. I winced. "Eddy Boland has lawyered up. They are pushing for his release."

"But why?"

"They say we don't have the evidence."

I scoffed, "But what about the lineup?"

"Yes, that still could help." Her voice crackled as I walked towards the club.

"So, is it my word against his?" I said, bile rushing in my throat. "He's not getting out, is he?"

Lola came over, placing her hand on my shoulder.

"No, no, don't worry," she said as her voice tapered over, replaced with crackling and interference. I checked the reception on my phone. Great. One bar! "—Still behind bars."

"I'm struggling to hear you. Melissa"

"He's still locked up, Julia!" she shouted.

"Good!"

"I just had to inform you—" more crackling.

"Oh, okay, I think I understood," I said, my panic settling down. "Thank you for letting me know, Melissa."

"No problem," crackling, "when we know more."

"Bye," I said, my gut slowly coming down from my mouth. The phone went silent.

"Are you okay?" Lola asked.

I feigned a slight smile. "I think so. The damn phone lost its signal."

"He's still in jail, isn't he?"

I nodded.

"Well then, you're okay. Remember… we'll take this one step at a time," she said, and smiled, hugging me.

Inhaling, I stood tall, stretching out my limbs. "Okay, so are we going inside, then?"

Lola frowned. "That would be nice, but…"

"But what?" I asked, looking over at the door.

"It's closed."

I stood back. "What, on a Sunday night?" She nodded. "I thought all bars were open till at least ten?"

Lola shrugged, looking dismal.

"Okay, well, we can come back. Maybe tomorrow?" I said, checking my phone. No reception. I shrugged.

"Sounds like a plan, honey." She smiled. "I'm sure he will call me, if he's interested."

I smiled, pushing her sideways. "How could he not be interested, short stack?" I said as we both laughed.

"Come on, it's not a terrible night, let's walk home."

"It's miles Julia! I'm wearing heels!"

I laughed. "Okay, so how about we walk a little until we get reception, then call an Uber?"

"Sounds better!" she said, holding her phone up as high as she could. "Still nothing."

As we started walking arm in arm, I smirked as Lola kept cursing her stilettos. She'd put on a full face of make-up, a sexy, sultry outfit, and stilettos to finish it. This girl meant business. It would have worked too if the club was open. But we now had to walk miles home with her cursing every crack in the pavement. Thank frick I'd kept my jeans and jumper on. My boots, however, had next to no grip and venturing out over the iced path was a delightful pain in my arse. But it was nice out; frosty and cold, but still nice. The sun had almost set as the streetlamps bellowed out their soothing nightlights.

"Are we there yet?" Lola asked as we reached the end of the Old Trent Road. I laughed.

"Not yet," I said, smirking, slipping on a cobblestone.

"Ha, caught you," she said, laughing. We both came to a standstill, checking our phones. Still nothing. "What's going on with the signal tonight?"

I shrugged. "It's weird."

She nodded, and we crossed over the road towards the park.

"This place is usually buzzing at night."

"No one dares come out here anymore," I said. "He's killed seven already this season."

"Great!" She shivered, looking around her.

"I wouldn't worry," I said. "It's got to be Eddy. The Butcher hasn't killed anyone since." She nodded. "And Jeff gave me a character description, too. It looked just like him."

"Yeah, true… Nevertheless, it's creepy out here," Lola said, nervously humming a random tune, while holding my arm tighter.

I nodded, entering the park.

The trees swished as the wind took flight. Leftover leaves broke free of their branches and the skeletal ferocity of Winter took over. Iced mist enveloped the grasslands, creeping away from the lake, as nightlights flickered and faltered, giving life to the shadows that spoke, forming the features of butch rabid men. A group of five, maybe six drunkards bellowed sleazy remarks from a distance. They stood, captured under the gaze of the moonlight, silhouetted by the lambent streetlight that shone overhead.

"Lola, look," I hushed, pointing over to the gang ahead.

She stopped humming. "Okay, so we go round them?"

"We can't, we need to cross over that bridge."

She sighed. Took out her phone. "Still no signal."

I held her arm tight, stood up tall and walked towards the gang, hoping to shimmy around them, continuing over the bridge to our safety net beyond.

Lola breathed deep as the wind gushed past us. I took a deep breath and approached. The men laughed, leering at us.

The front one whistled. "Ah, now what do we have here?" he said, walking towards us.

"Keep going," I said to Lola. She gulped, yet stood tall, biting her lip, and continuing to walk beside me.

"I'm counting on the Big Blaster to help here!"

"Shut it, short stack," I said, laughing nervously.

We walked past the front man as he whistled, staring at Lola's short dress. She tripped in her heels. I held her upright, pulling us both past the gang of men.

The one from the back, the taller, older one of the group, stepped forward. "Want a hand, lady?" he asked, walking to stand in front of us.

We stopped. "No, we're okay," I said, holding Lola's

arm tight.

"You shouldn't be alone at night."

"It's not safe, you know," the redhead said, laughing like a hyena. They circled us like predators to their prey.

"We can protect you," the first creep said, putting his arm around Lola's waist.

"Leave us alone," Lola shouted. Anger and fear welled in her eyes.

"Oh, come on, princess, show us your stuff," the blond in denim growled.

I pushed him back, yanked Lola towards me and punched the guy that had his hands on her. He yelped, staggering backwards. The taller man laughed.

"Get back now or I'll call the police," I shouted, my body temperature rising.

"And what do you think they'll do, little lady?" the taller man snickered. "They won't get here in time," he said, punching me in the chest. I fell to the ground, gasping for air. Lola screamed as the redhead pulled her away from me.

The heaviness of two men weighed me down, pulling at my clothes, hands groping my body. "Get off me!" I yelled, teeth gritted, face flushed with anger. Screams filled the air, both mine and Lola's. There was no way this could happen again!

In the distance, a ferocious roar impaled the air. Heavy footsteps pounded the ground. The man with the mask came into view. Snarling teeth shone in the moonlight as Nathaniel's mouth salivated. *It is a mask, isn't it?* Ferocious roars escaped him as he picked off the men one by one.

Their bodies flew through the night sky, screams entangling the airwaves. The battle was a work of art. Not one man had a chance against him. If I wasn't seeing it with my own eyes, I would never have believed Nathaniel to be so incredibly strong, protective, and just as horrific. The way he danced before my eyes, slicing, and dicing the men with his claws. It was magnificently frightful.

Lola's screams stopped. Mine too. We were both in a state of shock. The night was silent except for the bloody screams of men as something monstrous beat them to a bloody pulp. I sat upright; darkness consumed my gaze. Was it Nathaniel? It looked like him… moved like him… what was he? The streetlight no longer flickered. Lola crawled over to me, her dress ripped, makeup smudged across her face.

"Are you okay?" I asked.

She nodded, pulling her dress back down.

I took a deep breath, stood up, pulled my jeans up, and looked around. There was no sign of the men. No sign of the thing that used to be Nathaniel as he had pulled them away. Nothing except the light of a streetlight further in the distance, and under it was the shape of a man walking towards us. Lola grabbed my arm. I hushed her. It was okay. I knew this man; and as he stepped out from under the light, I recognised his shape.

He stopped two feet away, the moonlight bringing life to his face, his normal human face. "Nathaniel?"

"Yes, are you two okay?"

Lola broke down crying. I held her tight. "Yes, we will be," I said. "It was a group."

He nodded. "I know, I saw," he said, pulling us both in, holding us tight. "Come on, let's get you both home."

I nodded. Whatever he was, whatever mask he'd worn, he was still my saviour.

Nathaniel smiled. "Are you sure you're okay?"

I nodded. He looked at me, his brow furrowed. "I can't leave you alone for five minutes, can I?" He smirked. I laughed, wiping my own tears away. Taking my hand, he kissed it. I smiled. "My car is over this way."

Lola and I walked over with him; the group of men were nowhere to be seen.

"It's a good job I heard you," he said. "What were you doing out here anyway?" The driver got out of the car and held the door open for the three of us. "Thank you, Nigel," Nathaniel said.

I smiled. "Well," I said, taking a seat and smirking at Lola. Nathaniel sat in the front passenger seat, after he helped us both into the back.

Lola laughed, wiping her smudged tears, "I was coming to see Kenny,"

"Oh, well, I shall tell him you came by, Lola," Nathaniel said. The driver started the car.

"Where to?" Nigel asked.

Lola gave her address.

"I don't suppose you have his number, do you?" I asked. Smirking at Lola.

"Yes, of course, if it stops you walking the streets alone, then I'll happily pass it over."

He scribbled the number on a piece of paper and

passed it back to Lola. She smiled, cheeks reddening more by the minute.

He laughed, turning back to face me. "So, my Rose Red, I have our next date planned."

I smiled and bit my lower lip. "I'm listening," I said. Silently loving the nickname but wondering if he knew my name yet. I shrugged it off.

"It will be another spectacular surprise."

"Oooh," Lola said, grinning.

I laughed. "Tell me where and when and I'll be there."

We pulled up to a stop outside Lola's apartment. Nathaniel smiled and got out and opened the door for us.

Lola got out, thanking Nathaniel.

I got out. Turned back and kissed him quick, pulling away and smiling. As I went to walk off and catch Lola up, he grabbed my hand, pulled me back in, held me tight and kissed me hard.

"I'll see you soon, Julia Jones," he said, pulling back, kissing my hand, and disappearing, driving away into the night.

It looks like he does know my name. I grinned from ear to ear, skipping up the path towards my second home.

CHAPTER SEVENTEEN

Edging out of bed, I looked at the clock, six thirty. I had time to grab a bite to eat and wake sleeping beauty before she slept through the rest of the day. Jumping in the shower, I washed off their stench, remembering their thick hands grabbing at my clothes. My chest stung, aching from the punch. But no broken ribs, thankfully. I was sick of being the target of all the creeps in this city, the real lowlifes that prey on the innocent and weak. They saw us as weak last night, and we were. We were stupid to keep walking, thinking we were bigger and braver than we were. But what else could we have done? I shrugged, washing off the last of the soap.

Stepping out, I dried off, changing into jeans and a jumper. It was handy having a few clothes stashed here at Lola's.

Today was the day I faced up to The London Butcher. I

stopped, wiped the mist from the mirror and stared back at me. Could I do it? Shoulders straight. Head held high. I had to. I was tired of being afraid. Tired of the anxiety, panic, and tears. I needed to 'woman up' and sort myself out. The one thing I'd realised lately is that no one else could do it for me. Only I could.

Lola ran through the living room half dressed, grabbed her coffee with hair straighteners in one hand and a slice of toast in her mouth.

"Almost ready?" I asked, smiling.

She scowled, and I laughed.

Sitting down, I turned on the television to the news channel. Granted, I wrote the news, but it was always nice to hear someone else's take on it. Abbie Lloyd was on, with her bright smile and summery dress (in the middle of Winter). I yawned, taking a sip of my coffee.

"Another murder by Kings Cross station. So far, the police could not identify the Butcher's latest victim and are still looking for more body parts." I shuddered, listening. "If anyone sees a black bin liner wrapped in parcel tape, please call the crime number at the bottom of the screen immediately."

Lola walked in. "Shit, another one?"

I nodded, taking a deep breath. *How though? Eddy's locked up! Could it be the people in the black Mercedes?* I knew what case I'd be writing about later today.

"Come on, turn that off, you've your own problems to deal with right now."

She was right. I stood up, turned off the television, put

on my coat and we left the apartment, getting an Uber all the way to the police station.

Closing my eyes, I took a deep breath, counted to ten, and exhaled. My hands were shaking as I stood outside, looking up at the old grey brick building. I took a deep breath. This was it. This was the time I faced my attacker once again. *Can I do this?*

I took a moment and steadied myself. Lola turned to look at me, smiled and took my hand, squeezing it tight. Putting one foot forward, I walked up the steps to face my attacker. In the corner of my eye, a familiar face stood in the shadow, leather jacket and soft brown eyes staring back at me. I blinked, and he vanished. I shook my head. Great! I'm seeing things!

I sighed, entering the police station. A grimy old chap in a murky uniform greeted me. "Can I help you?"

"Yes, I'm Julia Jones. I'm here to see Detective Melissa Lee."

He nodded, picked up the phone and pointed over to the seating area.

Lola raised her eyebrows, turned, and pulled me towards two seats at the far end. There weren't many to choose from, and the characters that occupied the others looked like something out of a hillbilly horror movie. I caught Lola looking around, smirking. "What?" she asked, grinning.

I shrugged, smiling.

"What you in for?" a long-haired man covered in tattoos

asked. He swapped seats to sit beside Lola.

Lola sank down in her chair.

"Oi lady, I asked what you in for?"

Lola grimaced and remained silent. At a guess, I'd say she was hoping he'd vanish in mid-air.

"Rude," he said. Then sat forward and directed the conversation towards me. "What you in for?"

I gulped, staring into his tattooed face. "We're meeting a detective," I said, then released a deep breath.

"Yup, me too," he said. "I'm here for a line-up."

Lola sat up, turned, and looked him in the eye. "So are we," she said.

"Ah, she speaks." He grinned. She smirked. "I ain't nothing to be afraid of," he said, smiling. "The tats always put people off."

Lola took a deep breath. "They are actually quite beautiful," she said, studying his face. "Why the rose?"

"That's for me mam. She loved roses... Had a garden full of em."

Lola smiled.

"That's sweet," she said. "Where is she now?"

"She's dead."

I gulped, fidgeting in my seat.

"Shit," Lola said. I remained quiet.

"Yeah."

"What happened?"

"Mowed down by a black Merc last year."

I winced. Shit. Could it be the same Mercedes? "I'm sorry."

"Ain't nought to be sorry about. She had it coming anyway."

"Oh," I said, jaw dropped.

"Well, on that note, we'd better see where the detective is... Don't you think, Julia?"

Eyes wide, I nodded, standing up and walking after her.

"Bye," he said. "See you in the line-up." He grinned, waving.

At the reception desk, the officer was still on the phone. Lola stood, tapping her fingers. He put down the phone and stared up from under his glasses. "Yes?" he said sternly.

"Is the detective on her way yet?"

"No, she said to go in."

I frowned. "Don't you think you should have told us that?"

"Pardon?... Do I look like your slave?"

"Where do we go?" Lola asked.

"Right through those double doors, princess."

Lola smiled sarcastically, walked through the double doors, and cursed under her breath. I smirked, looking around, trying to take it all in.

The room was littered with lines of desks, cluttered with bodies trying to crack the next case. It was a mixture of emotion, turmoil, and hope. Who were they looking for? What had they witnessed? What lived in the night's darkness, corrupted by shadow, fearful of daylight.

Monroe caught sight of us, nodded and ushered us past the chaos towards Melissa, as he disappeared into another room. I glimpsed a photograph of the mutilated body of the sorority girl, the Butcher's latest victim. They'd been hot on his case for months now, but no new leads… Well, none except the witness Jeff Walters, and what he saw made no sense.

Walking further into the room, I could see Melissa's desk in the far corner. Monroe still wasn't back, of which I was thankful for. After all, he wasn't exactly the friendliest of people. Her head was down, buried in a case file as we walked over. I wondered if that would be me one day. If I'd be the victim in the file, my life laid bare on paper with bloodied photographs spelling a traumatic ending. *It nearly was me.* I shuddered. Taking a deep breath, I followed Lola over to the desk.

"Julia!" Melissa shouted, waving us over. I smiled. Under different circumstances, I could see we could have become quite good friends. Or at least she would have provided the perfect source in the department for me.

"Hello," I said, shaking her hand.

"Sit, please sit." She waved, pointing towards the chairs. "And who's this?"

"This is Lola," I said, then smiled.

"I'm here for moral support."

The detective smiled. "Would you like her in the room with you?"

"Yes, I don't want to do it alone."

"That's okay, just remember none of the men in the line-up will see you."

I sighed in relief. "That's good. I can't see him again."

"Ah yes, you saw him in the hospital, didn't you?"

"Err, yes."

"I heard he caught on fire," the detective said. I winced. "But how?"

"I've no idea."

"Yes, he didn't have a scratch on him. It's as though it never happened."

My brow furrowed. "That makes little sense."

She shook her head. "Not much of this case makes sense to be honest."

"That's comforting," Lola said, brows raised. I smiled, gripping her hand.

Detective Lee feigned a smile. "Come on, they should be ready for you now," she said, rising from her seat.

We followed her through the rest of the room, down the corridor and past a set of floor to ceiling windows. Outside, the dim light gave way to the sunshine as it broke its way through the cloud cover. Frost coated the greyed-out buildings, anxiously awaiting the warmth of the sun as it caressed the clouds, hiding its face from the dawn of night.

Before me, a door opened and Detective Monroe stepped out, waving me through.

"Now remember," Melissa said, "they can't see you."

I nodded, took a deep breath, and relaxed my body.

"Are you ready?"

"Yes," I gulped, facing the glass. On the other side, six men walked in. All similar stature, with an average build, dark-skinned and sunken eyes. I knew immediately who he was. The middleman, third from the right. He posed, watching me, appearing to stare straight down into my eyes.

She said he couldn't see me. It was one-way glass, mirrored on the other side. But he was staring directly at me, almost through me. He knew I was there.

"Take a minute," Melissa said. I turned, feigned a smile, and nodded.

Studying him, I could see the bristles of an unshaven beard, the dirt of an unclean face, and the worn, unironed clothes. He looked homeless, unwanted, and unkempt. I almost pitied him. Someone had to.

He stood staring right at me, licking his lips, like I was his next meal of the day. He took a step forward. "Step back number four," the guard said. I hadn't noticed him before; he'd been sitting in the corner, silently watching the men in the room.

Instead of listening, number four stepped forward again, grinning.

"Step back number four," the guard repeated, standing up from his chair.

But this time, he didn't move forward or back. Instead, he rammed his fingers into a fist, leapt forward, and punched at the glass. I jumped back, my heart racing. Lola screamed. Adrenaline surged as my body's fight-or-flight response kicked in. Holding my breath, my fingers pummelled into fists, I was ready to fight. Heat rose as my body sizzled and steamed. *What's happening to me?*

Lola grabbed my hand, dropping it just as quickly, yelping in pain.

He was there, inches away, punching the glass. Blooded fists sent a shimmer of cracks as the whole thing shattered and he stood staring straight into my eyes. He could see me.

I could see him. He paused as the guard tried to restrain him. The detectives had already left my side, running in to help. Besides Lola, I was alone.

Detective Lee jumped on my attacker, pushing him down to the floor. Face planted in the ground, wrists behind his back, they restrained him as the handcuffs went on. He turned his bloodied face as he lay in a pile of glass, grinning. "You will burn," he said, shrieking with laughter. "You will die," he screamed as the guards pulled him out of the room.

I fell to the floor, my body trembling, my mind a chaotic mess of reality. Lola sat down beside me, throwing her arms around me and holding me tight. I sobbed. What the hell just happened?

Detective Melissa Lee came into the room, her blouse covered in blood and glass. "Bloody hell!" she said, "I'm so sorry, that's never happened before." I continued to cry. "I didn't realise how strong he was!"

"Can we go to another room?" Lola asked as she pulled me upright, shards of glass sticking in the palms of my hands.

"Yes, of course, let's get you both cleaned up."

I nodded, swallowing back the tears, following her into the lady's bathroom. I shook off the glass from my clothing, picked out the pieces from my hand, then ran the cold tap. The small wounds in my right hand healed over quickly. Whatever was happening to me appeared to have its benefits!

Splashing water over my face helped, bringing me back to reality. Lola did the same, wincing in pain.

"What happened?" I asked, noticing the red mark on

her palm.

"It's nothing," she said, looking at me.

"Did I do that?" I asked, knowing full well that she'd yelped after she'd touched me.

"I shouldn't have grabbed you. It's fine, Julia, don't worry!" she said, feigning a smile.

My lips pursed.

Detective Lee came over. "Keep it under the cold water," she said. "It looks like a burn; I'll fetch a bandage."

"No, no need for that," Lola said. "It'll be fine." She smiled. "The water will help."

I frowned. "Are you sure?"

She nodded. I wasn't so sure; it looked blistered.

"Come on, let's get you home," she said, patting her hands dry.

"Bandage first, please," I said, looking at her blistered fingers.

She frowned. "Fine," she said as the detective disappeared and came back in with a first aid kit.

"There, all sorted," Melissa said, after bandaging Lola's hand. She looked up, puzzled, mulling something over. "How the heck did you burn yourself?"

I bit my lower lip, but Lola answered in time. "Probably the exposed wiring from the computer he smashed."

"Ah, okay, well, I'm sorry about that. If there's anything I can do, please let me know," Melissa said.

I nodded.

"Okay, well now you're both patched up, you're free to go. And again… I really am sorry for what happened. We will investigate, but for now, am I right in presuming that he was your attacker?"

"Yes," I responded.

"Then leave it with me. We will charge him later today."

I feigned a smile, exchanged pleasantries, and we left.

"My home or yours, honey?" Lola asked, nursing the burn on her hand.

I sighed. "Mine, I need sleep… Need to work a few things out."

"Anything I can help with?"

I smiled, turned, and hugged her. "No, you've done more than enough, Lola. You need to rest too. The last few days have bound to have taken their toll."

She nodded and asked the driver to drop me home first.

The journey back was a silent one. Sitting in the taxi, I stared out of the open window, cold air blasting over my pale face and rose red curls.

As I arrived home, I walked up the garden path, opened the red door and almost fell into my home. My body shook from the cold, iced hands had run their fingers up and over my spine. Fear crept over me. Eddy reached out, tried to take my life once again. I was a mess of emotion, a turmoil of pain, and my life had turned into a merry-go-round of death and darkness. I just didn't know how to get off. Eddy had so much anger inside of him. After all, I was the one that got away, the victim who survived, and because of that, he hated me, despised me in fact. I could see it in his eyes.

Pouring a glass of wine, I fed Maisy, then headed upstairs to bed. Sleep was what I needed. It was early evening, but the day had drained me. Tomorrow would be another day. A fresh day, one of hope, and one of new beginnings.

CHAPTER EIGHTEEN

The wind howled as I arrived at Harrington University. It was a cold, blustery day with no sunshine in sight. The clouds had overlaid the ground, as fog crept over the campus, shrouding it in a cloak of darkness.

Blake was waiting at the entrance when I arrived. He smiled and waved me over, which is rather strange.

I hurried over and smiled. "Hello," I said, still wary of his temper.

"Hello Miss Jones, it's nice to meet you."

"We've met before, Blake; don't you remember kicking me out last time?"

He stifled a laugh. "Ah, yes. I have the scars to prove it."

"Scars?"

He laughed. "Don't you remember blistering my skin?"

"I, well, yes," I said, looking down at my feet. "Anyway, it's Julia."

"What is?"

"My name. It's Julia."

"I know."

"Okay, so you can call me Julia, not Miss Jones." Wow, this was a hard conversation.

"Fine, Julia."

I smiled, unnaturally.

"So, Julia. You are here for a blood test, I presume?"

"Yes, but I was hoping you would answer a few questions first?"

He frowned, opened the door, and ushered me inside. "Perhaps a few." I followed as he made his way past reception, down to the left and along a long, narrowing corridor. "Keep up, Julia," he said as he walked faster.

I puffed as I followed, my stamina small compared to this old guy.

Blake turned the corner and disappeared. I stopped. Where's he gone? There was nothing but a narrow dark corridor, dusty books and an old typewriter stuffed in a display cabinet.

"This way," he said. I jumped as he appeared behind me.

Wide eyed, I followed him, always keeping him in my sight. He reached the end and walked straight through an old oak bookcase. What the heck? "Walk through, Miss Jones."

"It's bloody Julia!" I said as I stiffened up. Reaching forward. I touched the shelf, and it disappeared under my grasp. Shit! An optical illusion? Waving my hand through, something grabbed me and pulled me into it. It was Blake.

"You took your time."

I scowled. "It's not every day you walk through a wall, Blake!"

"Technically, you can't walk through a wall. That was an illusion."

"Obviously... So how did you create it?"

"I don't have the foggiest idea."

"Who does?"

"Ah, that would be Miranda, our resident Magi."

"Your what now?" He walked down another dark, dank corridor. I followed.

"Magi, magician, wizard, hocus pocus, that kind of thing," he said, rolling his eyes. "You're never going to survive this world if you don't pay attention, Julia!".

"Well, I plan to. As long as I know what world I'm walking into." We turned a corner and two guards with spears greeted me.

"Stand down," Blake said as I jumped backwards. I followed him past them, turning another corner.

"Welcome to FALCON!" he said, as I turned to see the wondrous world before me.

It was like a scene from *Charlie and the Chocolate Factory*. Every colour captured in spheres of light, hanging from a ceiling of darkness. The world above us did not exist down here. It was magic and marvel, all mixed in one obtuse setting of wonder. Before me lay a set of marble stairs, descending into the cobblestone streets below. The architecture mimicked that of Victorian England, slate roofs, stone buildings and lead beaded wooden windows.

A handful of shops paved the way before us. Blake stepped down, descending into the world below. I followed.

Blake stopped, turned, and smirked. "That's the look I love to see on the faces of the new ones."

I gasped as a three headed lady briskly walked by, muttering, "It's not time, it's not time."

"Dinsk, what's going on?" Blake asked, as the lady stopped. Each of her heads turned, with all eyes set on me.

"What's she doing here?" she said, her three noses smelling the surrounding air. "She's not fully formed yet." Blake laughed, she walked off. "Half baked, half-baked," she said as she wandered down the street.

"What is she?"

"Well, we're not sure. But a mutation of sorts."

"Clearly," I muttered under my breath. "Why have you brought me here, Blake?"

"Let's just say, I have a feeling you're more one of us than one of them."

"One of who?"

"The mortal world, Julia, you're changing. You belong to us now."

"I don't belong to anyone but myself, Blake."

He laughed. "Fair enough. Come on, let me show you around.

"Fallon's Forge is known for its exquisite weaponry," he said, pointing at an old shop with a hanging sign out front. Inside the crooked window, a young lady stood talking to a customer, whilst her hands sat inside a forge.

"Doesn't that hurt her?" I asked, eyes wide.

"No, she's made like that."

I frowned. Blake smirked. "We're all different here, Julia."

Next, we came to a butcher's, then a tailor's and finally an old Inn.

"What is this place?"

"It's our safe space. A world run by FALCON." He smiled.

"What do you mean… how is there a world beneath a world?"

"Magic is capable of many things, Julia; this is merely the tip of the iceberg."

The buildings disappeared into the abyss over the horizon. A never-ending cascade of marvel and wonder. Old creatures from every fairy tale my mother had ever read to me walked the streets of this land, mixed with a magnitude of humans in a world where no living mortal could ever lay their eyes. It was a land of spectacular delight with building after building, street after street disappearing into the abyss.

As we walked down another street, Drury Lane, a horde of wolves ran through, hurtling past me chasing an iridescent human. I darted to the side, startled by their snarls. Blake carried on walking. "Wait, shouldn't we help her?"

"Who?"

"The woman?"

Blake stopped, turned to face me, and smirked. "You mean Hilda?"

"I don't know. But those wolves looked pretty nasty."

He laughed. "Hilda loves to tease them. Did you not see how luminescent she was?"

"Yes, but…"

"She has no physical body, Julia." He laughed. "No one can hurt her."

"Oh, okay. It's just they looked hungry."

"Oh, they're always like that. But they'll be at the Witchers Inn tonight, filling their bellies with ale as usual. It's all just a game to them."

"How are they going to fill themselves with ale in a pub? They're wolves."

Blake laughed again. "I adore how simple-minded the new ones are." He carried on walking. I tutted and followed his footsteps. Two children with impish ears ran across the street chasing butterflies. *How the heck do butterflies survive down here? I have no idea!*

"We're here," he said, opening an old wooden door. The house smelt like a hovel, covered in pig shit and urine.

"Burgh, that's where I've got to have a blood test?" I was bound to catch something in there.

Blake smiled. "Beauty is in the eye of the beholder, Julia," he said as he pushed me through the door.

I stumbled forward into a bright white clinical laboratory. A normal-looking lady greeted me. "Hello Julia, I'm Joanna, I'm here to take your blood."

I smiled. This looked more like it. "So why the hovel house?" I asked, turning to Blake.

He smiled. "It stops anyone wanting to go inside,

doesn't it? We wouldn't want anyone interfering with our business, would we?"

I smiled. It made sense. Joanna got a few things together and ushered me over to a seat in the far corner.

"So how long has this other world been here?"

She laughed. "It's not another world, Julia, it's just our home."

"But how is it no one has ever found this place?"

"Only the GM's can."

"Gems?"

He laughed. "G. M's. That's the technical term for genetic mutation. We're basically just abnormal."

"So, I'm a GM?"

Blake walked over and nodded. "Yes, you wouldn't have been able to pass through the bookshelf if you weren't."

"But what about the guards? What are they for?"

"Not all the mutated are good, Julia. Many lose their humanity when they change. Their darker side comes out, and that's when FALCON steps in."

I nodded.

Joanna smiled and tied a tourniquet at the top of my arm. "Are you ready?"

I nodded. She pulled out a needle and syringe and pierced my skin. Blood flowed into the vial. Loosening the tourniquet, she pulled out the needle and held a piece of cotton wool over the injection site. "There, all done."

I smiled. "I hardly felt a thing. So, when will the results be back?"

"In a minute," Blake said.

My brow furrowed. "How can you analyse it so quickly?" All the blood tests I've had, have taken days.

"Just watch," he said, staring at Joanna.

Joanna stood up with the vial of blood, walked over to a whiteboard, and picked up a pen. Opening the vial of my blood she turned, smiled at me, and said, "bottoms up!", drinking the whole damn thing.

I gasped as blood trickled down the front of her chin.

"Shit. Why did she do that?"

"Watch," Blake said.

Eyes wide, I watched in awe. Joanna's eyes rolled inside their sockets. Her hand rose to the whiteboard, and she wrote in acronyms and numerical symbols.

"What is she doing?"

"Analysing your blood, Julia."

"But she looks so normal."

He laughed. "So do you, so do I… Just because we're different, doesn't mean we're going to grow two more heads like Miranda."

I smiled. He had a point.

"So how did Joanna know she could analyse blood?"

"She was a typical goth teenager; she didn't realise she was a born reader."

"I was adopted," Joanna shouted over, then continued to work.

I nodded, listening.

"When Joanna reached puberty, her thirst came in. She followed a couple of wannabe vampires around, then she ate them."

"Pardon?"

"She ate the wannabe vampires."

My jaw dropped just as Joanna walked over. "Technically, they tried to eat me first. I just protected myself."

"By eating them?"

She nodded.

My eyes widened. "Okay then."

She smiled. "So, Julia, you're no longer a simple-minded mortal. You appear to have been hiding your fiery nature for quite some time."

"What do you mean? I was only injected a few weeks ago."

"Oh, no, sweet thing. They changed you from a young age. That's why you're so powerful now."

"Powerful. I don't have any powers."

Blake smiled. "You do, Julia, you just haven't come into them yet."

Dansk's voice filtered through my mind, so that's what she meant by half-baked. I smiled.

Joanna walked off.

Blake put his hand on my back and gently ushered me out of the laboratory. "Joanna will need to rest now."

"Oh okay," I said, walking out. As we left, I puzzled over how I could have been different all these years and not know it.

"You have many questions," Blake said.

I nodded.

"Follow me." He led me over the cobblestone street and into an old broken house with mismatched brickwork, broken flooring, and a coat hook with a variety of luxurious velvet cloaks. "There's someone you should meet."

Darkness enveloped me as a shroud of velvet covered my shoulders. Blake had fastened a cloak over me. "You'll need this."

"Why?"

"Trust me." I shrugged my shoulders and walked through a red velvet curtain and into an arctic landscape. Damn, it was cold in here. Shuddering, I pulled the cloak around me. "It's over this way," he said as we trudged through the snow.

The air encapsulated my breath as my body's warmth escaped me. Over the horizon I could see an igloo, the kind an Inuit would live in. I only knew about Inuits from a recent episode on the Discovery Channel, that and Mrs. Brigham's fifth grade humanities class. For some reason, it always stuck in my head.

As we arrived, my feet had turned so cold they no longer resembled part of my body. I feared frostbite would take me and reminded me to wear better boots next time.

Ducking down, we entered the igloo. Blake shook hands with an older gentleman covered in animal furs. His face wore the scars of many battles and his wiry grey beard curled into the shape of a V.

"Julia, this is Pana."

I smiled and shook his hand. Pana sat down on a bed beside an open fire with a tripod cooking stand and an old pot brewing above. *How does that not melt the igloo?* I shrugged.

"Pana can see the souls of those that have passed."

"Oh, okay." I wasn't sure how this would help me.

"I know your mother died at the hands of what we believe was the doctor."

"Wait… do you mean Jesus Mendel? It was his car," I exclaimed. Finally, someone believes me!

"Yes, they are the same person."

Pana waved his hand forward, offering me a seat. "Thank you."

"So, what can contacting my mother help with?"

Pana growled under his breath; his head bowed low as his skin fogged over with a blanket of thick smoke. The veil before me shrouded his body as he tapped into the world of the deceased.

"Pana has a direct line with the underworld, Julia, he can find out what your mother knew."

Pana leapt up, making me jump. I scuttled back into the seat as he chanted and disappeared inside the veil.

Before my eyes, my mother's shape formed. Her hourglass figure, the black hair she always tied up in a bun. Even down to the two wrinkles by the sides of her right eye that she always hated when I pointed them out.

"Julia?" she said, her voice delicate. I gripped at my throat to stop the choking wail of shock that formed from the sound of her voice. Tears streamed down my face as I sat frozen on the spot. Tendrils of fear crept up my backbone. I coughed out a splutter of tears as fear gripped at my heart, pulling me down to Earth with a hard, fast thump. "Julia," she said, her eyes searching through the veil.

My voice ached for her, crackled, and broken, I replied. "Mum?"

"My Julia!" she exclaimed, reaching out in joy.

Blake stood up. "Mrs. Jones, I'm Blake Huntsman. I'm here with Julia and we need to know what happened to you."

"Blake… Do I know you?"

"No ma'am, I am working with your daughter. They attacked her."

"My Julia," she gasped, her hand raised up to her mouth. "Is she alright?"

"I am, Mum, I'm right here." I took a deep breath, calming my cries.

"Oh, Julia what happened?"

"I'm okay, Mum," I said. My eyes blurred from the tears.

"Ma'am, do you remember who killed you?"

"Yes, it was the doctor."

"Who?"

"She loved him. I couldn't stop them," she cried. "I'm so sorry they hurt you, Julia."

"Who Mum? Who was it?"

"It, I…" Her voice crackled and faded.

"No Mum, wait." The picture of life before me glittered and glimmered, luminescent beauty faded as the smoke swirled and twirled.

"It's time to say goodbye, Julia," Blake said, his hand placed on my shoulder.

"But I need more time."

"I'm sorry Julia, Pana's connection is growing weaker by the second."

"Julia, Julia, are you there?"

"Mum, I love you."

"I, I love you too Julia. I'm so sorry I couldn't stop them," she said as she faded from sight.

Wails of utter dismay took over as I screamed out in anguish. Blake pulled me up to stand, shaking the screams out of me. "Julia, she's gone."

"I know!" I cried. That's why I felt so broken. My heart palpitated as Pana came into view. His hand raised to my face, and he blew a green dust into my face.

"Sit her down," he said.

Blake pushed me down into the chair. The dust encircled me, entering my body as I inhaled the obnoxious scent. Instant relief and calming thoughts blessed my mind. Palpitations eased as the pain of grief no longer gripped my heart in horror.

"Is she okay?" Blake asked Pana.

"Yes, this is the usual reaction of one so young."

Blake nodded, standing tall, watching me. "When will she be back?"

"Five minutes, Blake. She will enter our reality in five minutes."

"And she won't be screaming anymore?"

"No."

"Good, I can't stand the screaming."

Pana smiled, sat down, and heated an old soapstone cooking pot on the fire. He stirred it and poured it into two cups. "Drink," he said, offering Blake a cup.

"No, thank you," Blake said, shaking his head.

"It will help the wallowing sadness deep in your heart," Pana said.

"No thanks. The sadness you speak of gets me up every day."

"That is no way to live, young one."

Blake smiled and my mind cleared as I awoke back to reality.

Pana smiled. "You will be fine now," he said.

I thanked him as Blake helped me up, searching my eyes for any sign of panic or fear.

"I'm fine, Blake."

"Good," he said, ushering me out of the igloo. "Let's go back, shall we?"

I smiled, nodded, and followed him through the snow, over the ice, and back into the wonder of the magical world before me.

CHAPTER NINETEEN

Entering the Witchers Inn, we took a seat and a voluptuous female bought over two pints of ale in pewter tankards. This establishment wasn't one of finer dining. It was more of a rough-cut old brewery with wooden tables and chairs, a cold stone floor and a roaring open fire. It was empty except for a young couple joined at the hip, head, and abdomen. Blake saw me staring. "I believe you know these as Siamese twins, Julia."

"I think conjoined twins is the more politically correct term nowadays Blake."

He laughed. "The old freak shows used a lot of our GMs back in the day. Before then, shameful mothers and embarrassed fathers killed most of the unusual mutations at birth."

"That's awful!"

"The human world is an awful place, Julia."

I nodded. "But what about the murders committed by the mutated monsters? It's not always the humans that hurt one another."

He shrugged. "True. I presume you mean Eddy?"

I nodded. "What type of monster is he?"

"That we do not know."

"Why? How can you not know what he is?"

"He is something we have never seen before."

"What do you mean?"

He sighed. Sat down in the chair and paused for a moment. "There has been an influx of new creatures lately."

"Huh?" My back straightened; eyes wide.

"Don't worry, they're not all the evil villains you think them to be." He smiled. "In fact, Eddy is the first we've had to consider eliminating."

"What do you mean?"

"Our foremost rule that we live by is that we must protect humanity at any cost."

I slinked down in my chair. "Okay, so what exactly does that mean?" I sat upright. "You kill people?"

"Not people, Julia, monsters."

My eyes widened. "But you said they're not monsters."

"They're not all monsters. Some are just newly turned, or recently come into their powers. Many don't even know they're not human." He smiled.

"So, what happens to the new ones?"

"They're bought here, like you."

"And do I have to stay here?"

He laughed. "No Julia, this isn't a prison. You can come and go as you please."

I sighed with relief. "So how do you know which ones are evil and which are the good?"

"We don't," he said. I sighed. "It's the same as the mortal world, Julia. We can only police the streets. FALCON does that. But we cannot act until we know a creature has succumbed to their darker side."

"And then what? You kill them?"

"The majority, yes, but it depends on the circumstances. The Elders decide their fate."

"Elders? Who are they?"

"They are a council made up of the oldest creatures. The first in their bloodlines." My brow furrowed. He smiled. "For example, Proteus was the leader of the shifters. He and his wife Torone birthed the race of the supernatural shapeshifters. To join them people are born into the life, or turned, but not all survive."

"Was?"

"We do not know if he survived the wolf wars. We are awaiting word."

"What about the other races who govern them?"

"Not all creatures follow a bloodline. Most are simply mutations from their own genetic code."

"Like me?"

He nodded. "Yes, over the last few years, we have seen an increase in those that have been genetically altered. You, for example, you appear to be one of his creations, from a very young age."

"That makes little sense. Surely I'd know if someone

injected me as a child?"

"Perhaps. Perhaps not," he said, shrugging.

I sighed. Took a sip of ale and sat back in my seat. "So, when will you take Eddy in?"

"When it's safe to do so."

"What do you mean? Haven't you got access to the police station?"

"Yes, but the prison itself won't hold him."

I sat upright, wide eyed. "So why haven't you taken him in then?"

"It's harder than you may think. We need to wait for him to come out, otherwise he'd take down half the precinct before we got to him."

"Jeez, what about all the people?"

"We're watching Julia; we'll take him down when we can get to him without injuring any innocent people."

"Okay."

I took a sip of ale. It was fruitier than lager, sweeter than what I was used to. I took another sip.

"So, what's stopping the likes of the doctor or one of his followers entering this world?"

"Nothing."

I looked around. "That's concerning."

"Not really. The hounds would sniff them out."

"Hounds?"

"Mutated dogs. Our resident taxidermist brings life to all of his creations."

I shuddered. "That's awful!"

"No, it's more the opposite. These creatures have died.

He gives them a chance to live again, and to live in a more unique way, one that brings them strength, putting them near enough at the top of the food chain."

I shuddered again. "But still… it is a little like Frankenstein's pet project."

"That's exactly it."

"What?"

"Frankenstein? Your mortals would've called him that. Whereas really, his name is Harold." He smirked. "You've got to stop seeing these creatures as monsters. They're simply humans that took a leap down the evolutionary path before humanity did."

I paused, looking out of the window. A young girl skipped down the street playing a flute, followed by a stream of rats. It seems fairy tales and folklore were created down here.

The door flung open and a pack of six wolves ran in, shifting into their muscular male human forms. Their commodities on display for every patron in the Inn. The young barmaid walked over. "Tolvar, put on some clothes, you'll scare the new girl." Tolvar grinned, staring at me. The barmaid cleared a table and ushered two of the men over. They were already clothed and slipping on a pair of boots.

An older man in jeans stepped toward Tolvar. "Mate, she's not in season," he said as he threw a pair of jeans and a top at Tolvar. Tolvar laughed as my face reddened, and walked butt naked to the table, pulling on the jeans on the way.

Blake smirked. "Never seen a shifter before, I take it?"

"Not quite."

"You sure about that?" he said, smiling.

"What's that supposed to mean?"

"What do you think Nathaniel is?"

"A guy with a hero complex?"

He laughed. "Spot on, but he's also not human."

"I gathered. So, what is he?"

"That's for Nathaniel to tell you."

"You don't like him very much, do you?"

"What makes you say that?"

"You threw him out the window."

"Well, yes, I guess you would see it like that. We were simply sparring, and it got out of hand."

"So that's what the Grand is to you? A boxing ring?"

He laughed. "No, Nathaniel keeps the Grand on to remind him that everything can change in a moment."

"What do you mean?"

"Nathaniel wasn't always a loner, he had friends. A pack, so to speak."

I leaned forward. "What happened?"

"The doctor happened. We didn't know the Doctor and Jesus were the same person until that night. Nathaniel was closing up as his pack ran through, bloodied and battered. The creature chasing them looked human, but with the strength of a band of gorillas, the wild speed of a coalition of cheetahs, and the innate ability to predict their next movement before they even thought it. The pack had no chance, and Nathaniel was the only one left standing. Many believe the Doctor left him alive, as he was his first. He wanted him to spread the message that there was a new King in town, and this King was called Doctor Jesus Mendel."

"What do you mean, he was his first?"

"Nathaniel was the first human the Doctor genetically modified."

"I guessed he was a wolf shifter, but he never changed into a wolf, not like these," I said, pointing over at the ruckus the group was causing.

"He's different, Julia. You need to speak to him about his time with the Doctor."

I nodded. "So, what is the Doctor and why is he doing this to people?"

"We don't know. There are fables that speak of a creature such as this. A creature stronger than anything we have ever seen before. But these monsters aged, and because of that they died out a millennia ago."

"What were they?"

"Blood drinkers."

"Like Joanna?" He shook his head. "Vampires?"

He laughed. "I enjoy your human connotations. Vampires are merely a term used for a variety of unique creatures. Like Joanna, for example, we call her a reader, but the world would deem her to be a vampire."

"So, are there any other vampire-like creatures?"

"Oh, there are many, but none with the strength, agility and wisdom of an original vampire."

"Like the Doctor?"

"Hopefully not like the Doctor, because if he is what we think he is, then we're in for a complete load of trouble!"

I nodded, pursing my lips. "So, what other vampires are

there?"

"Well, there are many wars going on in the supernatural world, Julia. In fact, the evil hybrid Queen that lives in her crystal palace causes most of them."

I coughed, choking on my drink. "You can't be serious!"

"Oh, so you believe in fortune telling men in igloos, ghosts and shifters, but not hybrid Queens?"

I shrugged. "Good point! So does that mean she's two creatures in one?"

"Yes. A wolf shifter and a vampire."

"But how?"

"That's another story, Julia, and a dark one."

I nodded, taking another sip of my drink ,I asked, "Fine, so what are you?"

"I'm something else."

"What's that supposed to mean?"

He laughed, nodded over to Tolvar and his pack, then brought his hand to my face, morphing it into the claw of a wolf.

I jumped back. "So, you're a wolf too?"

He nodded.

"How did you become one of those? Did the Doctor change you too or were you born that way?" I asked, nodding over at the wolves.

"It's a long story." He sat forward in the chair and gulped down his ale. His hands tense around the tankard.

I watched him for a moment, the silence between us echoing across our table.

"What happened?" I asked in a soft voice.

"It was many years ago." I nodded. He picked up the tankard, finished the drink, and slammed it down on the table. I jumped. "You will not let this lie, will you, Julia?"

I sat back. "I don't understand why you can't tell me, Blake."

"They killed my family, Julia," he said. I gasped. His head lifted as he searched my eyes for recognition.

"I'm so sorry, Blake, I really am." My head lowered as he told the tale of a frenzied wolf entering his home one twilight eve two decades ago.

"I tried to fend it off, but it was quick. Too quick for me as it went for young Timmy."

My eyes drooped. "Timmy?"

"My two-year-old boy, he'd not long started walking and was outside with my wife Helena picking wildflowers for the table." He shuddered, bringing his hands to his head. "I heard her scream, a god-awful cry. The wolf dragged Timmy into the woods. I ran out and saw it. Helena was bleeding out. I remember her vivid red blood flowing over her newly planted daisies. I packed her wound, got her to hold it and went after Timmy."

My jaw dropped. "What happened to him?" I asked.

"I could hear him crying. But a wolf leapt on top of me, gave me this scar right here." He pointed to his abdomen. "The next thing I knew, a human wolf jumped in, tackling the wolf. His pack joined him, growling, attacking the rogue wolves. I must have passed out from blood loss, as when I awoke, I was in St James hospital, near Leeds."

"Nathaniel?" He nodded. "What about Helena and Timmy?"

"Helena died right there on the daisies. Timmy..." he took a deep breath. "Timmy didn't make it."

I lowered my head. "I'm so sorry Blake."

He nodded. "It took a long time for me to accept there were 'good' monsters in this world." I smiled softly. "If it weren't for Nathaniel, I wouldn't be here today."

"What did he do?"

"He saved me from the wolves that night. Him and his pack. He pulled me free from the one that attacked me, just as FALCON turned up and electrocuted him." I gasped. "It took the reader to see the truth behind what happened."

"Like Joanna?"

"Yes, she is a reader."

"The *not vampire* type?"

He laughed. "We don't call them vampires, as they do not share the abilities an original *vampire* would have. These readers can see your memories when they drink your blood."

"What, like bite you?" He nodded. "But doesn't that turn a human into one of them?"

He laughed and shook his head. "You have a lot to learn, Julia Jones." He stood up from his chair and ushered me up and out of the Inn. "For now, you must speak with Nathaniel. Tell him there is always a place for him here, should he wish for one." He paused, stopped, and spoke. "And when you speak to him about what he is..." his brow furrowed, "be open-minded."

I nodded, followed him out into the streets, up the stairs, through the bookcase, and waved goodbye as I headed out into the darkness of the mortal world above.

CHAPTER TWENTY

What a peculiar day. If anyone asked me what I expected to happen today. That would not have been it.

I texted Lola, checking she was in. I really needed to run through the bizarreness of today with a sane person… if you could call Lola that! Standing in the cold, under a streetlight, I waited for my taxi.

Perusing the memories of the day gone by, I thought about Pana. Besides the ridiculous nature of the day, I was sure I hadn't banged my head and fell down a rabbit hole. I counted my fingers. Yep, I could clearly see straight. There were eleven. I smirked, laughing at my joke. No, but seriously. I knew I wasn't crazy. So, if the only explanation left was the unlikely explanation, then that's the only explanation it could be. I sighed, took a deep breath, and nodded. So, everything I saw today was real. I really walked into a fantasy world of epic proportions… and if that's the case, then I truly spoke to my dead mother. Shit.

My eyes widened.

I just spoke to my dead mother. I'm clearly insane.

Shaking my head, I recalled what she'd said. She'd called him a doctor. Blake verified that. So, the person who murdered Mum is the same person stalking and attempting to kill me. Great. I rolled my eyes.

The black cab turned up. I jumped in, giving Lola's address, and sat back, staring out into the snow filled night sky.

The streets were quiet, people still feared the butcher. Well, except the odd crowd of brightly coloured lunatics thinking it was Purge night and a free for all, as they battled the city cops. It wouldn't be long before riots started, like those back in 2011. People were scared, and when they feared for their lives, they acted out.

Driving past Big Ben, we continued through London central. Bright city lights bled into one another as we picked up speed, skipping a red light and slamming hard down over a speed bump.

"Hey!" I yelled, my hand on the roof. "Not so fast!"

The man chuckled. "Sorry miss. Didn't see that bump back there."

I sighed. "Okay." I shook my head. Everyone was always in such a rush in the city.

Pulling up, I paid and got out as quick as I could. Lola opened the door. "Shit. What happened to you?"

"Maniac driver!" I said, as she put her arm around me

and we walked in and up the stairs.

Lola laughed. "Well, he certainly sounds like he gave you a ride for your money."

I winced.

"Too soon?" she said.

I nodded. "Too soon."

"So, what brings you to this neighbourhood, Big Blaster? Did you have a villain to incinerate?"

"Ha, you're so funny! Like I said. I get hot, that's all."

"Oh, Hubba Hubba, you sure are hot, my little cupcake." She purred and laughed as I pushed her through the door. "Brew?"

"Yeah please."

I plonked myself down on her sofa as she made a cup of tea with custard cream biscuits, bringing them over.

"Why, thank you!" I said, smiling.

"So, you're clearly not in the mood for my excellent sense of humour, so what's turned you all dark and devastating this evening?"

I rolled my eyes and smirked. "You're an ass."

"I indeed have a fine ass… So, you were saying…"

"Ha… well, where do I start?"

"The beginning?"

With wide eyes, I recalled the day's events. She listened, then switched out the tea for vodka. Biting my lip, I finished, taking a shot to wash down the lunacy of it all.

"So, you really spoke to your mum?"

"Apparently so."

"Like... your dead mum?"

I nodded; her eyes widened.

"With, like, an old Inuit bloke in igloo that lives beneath our feet?"

I laughed. Then stopped, brow furrowed. "You're making fun of me!"

She laughed. "No, not at all. It's clearly believable."

"So, you don't believe me."

"Oh honey, I believe what you believe."

"That's not believing me."

She smirked. "Why don't you believe you?"

"Huh... of course I believe me. I was there."

"Then I believe you too."

Shit. My head hurt.

"So have you figured out more about this magic voodoo hoodoo you can do?"

My lips curled. "Well, I'm sure it's not called voodoo hoodoo, whatever it is."

She rolled her eyes. "So, show me something. I need more proof than an Inuit living in a world below our feet."

I play-punched her shoulder.

"Ow! What's that for?"

"You said you believe me."

"Oh, I do, but I need proof too."

"Why?"

"Err, because even you don't believe you."

"Oh my god, Lola, we're not going through this again!"

She laughed. "Fine... but wouldn't it be good to figure

out what superhero power you have?"

Laughing, I punched her in the arm again. She hit back, knocking me back on the sofa. I glared and stuck my finger up.

She laughed. "That would be more impressive if it had a flame coming out of it!"

I sat forward, took a custard cream, and bit into it. She did the same. Taking a few sips of tea, I sighed. She looked at me. "Have you been training?"

My brow furrowed. "Training for what?"

"The Olympics..." She rolled her eyes. "What do you think?"

Smiling, I sat back. "No. I don't know where to start."

"Well, from what you've said, the heat comes when you get angry."

I nodded. She had a point. "So, let's piss you off."

"Err, no thanks," I said, frowning.

"Okay, well you've got to recall that feeling."

I sighed. "How can I recall being angry, without being angry?"

She flung up her arms. "I don't bloody know. I'm not Professor X!"

"Who?"

"Jeez! You need to watch more films!"

My eyes widened. "Or you watch less!"

She flipped me a birdie. Jumped up and brought over an unlit candle, placing it on the coffee table before me. "Try concentrating on that."

"And what? Get angry at it?" I said, laughing.

"Oi lanky, I'm only trying to help here... humour me." She crossed her arms.

"Fine. Fine. I'll give it a go."

I sat forward; she did the same. Staring at the candle, I tried to get the image of her sniggering face out of view. My hands heated. She was quite annoying. "You know, the fact that you're sat there sniggering isn't really helping." I huffed.

Lola's eyes widened. She stopped sniggering. Her face filled with an expression of awe. Bright eyes lit as a candle flame reflected in them. "Look," she whispered, pointing.

Turning back, I saw the bright burning flame of a candle. My eyes widened. I couldn't have! Slithers of warmth crept over me. Breathing shallow, I stared in amazement. Raising my hand, I could feel the pull of the flame, its heat, warmth, and the safety of its nature. It called out to me. Moving my fingers up and down, I played with it. It danced away, mimicking my moves, swaying in sync, following my hand. Lola remained quiet; jaw wide open. I smiled, then grinned. It was the longest she'd ever been quiet; I laughed. With the sound of my laughter, the flame rose to the ceiling. Wax melting exponentially. In an instant, the candle turned into a puddle of melted wax; the flame dissipated in the air.

"Oh, my god, Julia!" Lola mouthed.

I sat there in shock.

"Julia!" Lola said, her brow creased.

I still sat motionless. "Erm, yes?" I replied.

"You're a superhero!" she said, shaking me, pulling me in for a mega tight hug.

The constant squeezing pulled me back to reality.

"Ouch!" I yelled, shaking her off.

She laughed. "See, I always knew you were special!"

"That's just the thing, Lola."

"What?"

"My mum apologised for letting them hurt me. But Eddy has only just attacked me. What did she mean?"

"Hmm, I don't know… Maybe they tried to hurt you when you were a child?"

My lips pursed. "Could be."

"That would explain why your mum was tracking the killer."

"What, do you think he targeted me as a child?"

"Makes sense," she said. Shrugging.

"But all his other victims were teenagers."

"Yeah, but you were fifteen when she died."

I sighed. "I'd remember something like that."

"But from what you said, it was an injection. He could have done that while you were sleeping."

"Hmm, I dunno, Lola. I think it's farfetched."

Her brow furrowed. "What and a supernatural world beneath our own isn't?"

My brows raised. "Fair enough."

She poured us another shot. We downed it. Wiping her mouth, she said, "So let's say someone injected you as a child. That could be why it worked this time he injected you?"

"Yeah, but I didn't light any candles as a child."

She laughed. "No, but what if he didn't give you the

full dose?"

I nodded. She had a point. I excused myself and headed to the bathroom. Splashing cold water on my face, it steamed. Well, that's one way to dry myself. Taking a minute, I stared at my reflection. I looked the same. Well, kind of.

Lips pursed, I checked every part of my body. It was puzzling, but; I had felt different since the attack. I'd thought it was PTSD. Maybe it wasn't? Maybe Lola was right. Blake had mentioned that others were different, too. Was there more like me? Were the ones he rehabilitated back into society genetically altered? Were we all superheroes? I laughed.

"Hey, what are you doing in there?" Lola yelled.

I walked out smirking. "Nothing, just thinking."

"What?"

"That there may be more like me. Blake mentioned he helped some women back into society. I wonder if they are like me and changed somehow too?"

"Oh, I like your thinking!" she smiled, stood up and swirled me around. "I may be the beauty, but you're now the brawn!"

I huffed. "Oh, shut it." She laughed.

"So, I take it you're staying over tonight honey?"

"Yeah, I don't fancy a maniac ride back to the house."

"That's all good. You know my home is your home."

I smiled and hugged her. "Anyway, it's late, I'm heading to bed."

She smiled, "yeah you've had quite the day."

Picking up my coat from the edge of the countertop, I

hung it up. As I did, a piece of paper fell out of my pocket. I picked it up, an old note with a phone number scrawled on it. One I'd found at the Grand when I went with Lola.

"What's that?"

Lola asked, taking the shot glasses back to the kitchen.

"Hmm, I think it's that number we found at the Grand."

"Let's ring it!"

"What, now? But it's nearly 11pm."

"Yeah, they'll definitely be in."

I smirked. "Fine. You ring it, but put it on speaker."

She grinned, grabbing the number out of my hand, dialling 141 before she entered the phone number. It rang once, twice, then three times. An old, croaky voice cleared her throat. "Hello?"

Lola said nothing.

"Hello?"

"Oh, hello there. Could I speak to Jacques Strap?" she said, sniggering. I rolled my eyes. Was she really quoting Bart Simpson right now? The only reason I knew this was because she made me sit and watch every episode of the damn show.

"Who?"

"Jacques Strap?"

"I think you have the wrong number! Do you know how late it is!" the lady groaned, then put the phone down.

I laughed, but something was bothering me. I recognised that voice. Remembered it well. *Do you know how late it is?* But it couldn't be. That's exactly what my Aunt Clara used to say to me when she let me stay a little longer past bedtime. She pretended to be annoyed, then would offer me a cupcake and read me another book. It couldn't be her... could it?

CHAPTER TWENTY-ONE

The morning light beamed through the window. Shit. I'd been that far gone I forgot to draw the curtains. My mind had been a mess of vodka, a fairytale land under our feet and superhero abilities. Not to mention Aunt Clara. How the hell that got thrown into the mix, I've no idea. It's like one of those bad bar jokes, and since when did I live the life of Harry Potter with the Izzy Whizzy let's get busy band? Wait. Or was that Sooty and Sweep?

Yawning, I stretched out, my body more relaxed than yesterday. Jeez, yesterday was an unrealistic montage of misshapen reality! *Did it really happen?*

I heard laughing coming from the living area. Leaving my bedroom, I wandered into the bathroom, rubbing my eyes. I could see Lola sat watching her all-time favourite show in the living room as I passed over the hallway. The theme tune was now effectively stuck in my head. But surely this is what Saturday mornings were made for? Pyjamas, all-time favourite shows, and a day of relaxing and doing nothing.

After my long needed wee, I washed my face, and brushed back my hair. Burgh. I needed a shower. Sod it. That could wait till tonight. I was still tired from the overuse of vodka our party of two drank.

After changing, I went to the kitchen and popped the kettle on. The phone rang. It was a delivery company. I had given them my number to call to arrange delivery of a package. Strange.

"Lola," I yelled as I walked over, "I've got to head home."

"What, already?"

"Yeah, some delivery company is trying to deliver something. It must be for my neighbour."

"Ah, a little late-night shopping on Amazon again?"

"Ha no, when have Amazon phoned me up to arrange a delivery?"

She raised her eyebrows. "Good point."

"Right short stack. Give me a hug."

She came over, hugged me and we kissed cheeks goodbye.

As I left, she shouted after me, "oh, and no superhero stuff without your sidekick!"

I laughed, closed the door and got a taxi home.

The ride was mostly uneventful. Thankfully. Although it was another taxi driver this time and I dreaded to think about when I would come across that maniac driver again!

Paying him, I walked down the path, unlocked the front door, and a delivery truck arrived. Well, what I presume was a delivery truck. It was a white transit van with no markings.

A guy in blue overalls got out. "Miss Jones?" I nodded. He shoved a large square package in my hands, turned, and left.

"Err, thanks," I said. Struggling to find my keys and open the front door.

Walking inside, I tripped over Maisy. The heavy box flew from my hands and landed upside down. She hissed and ran. "Shit! Sorry Maisy!"

Clambering up, I brushed myself down, inspected my sore knee, and walked over to the package. It was wet underneath. Pushing it over, I noticed a red patch of liquid on the floor where it had laid. Strange. I left it there while I grabbed my keys and used them to score open the parcel tape.

Pulling the corrugated cardboard back, I found square white coolbox inside. Brow furrowed, I unsealed the lid, lifting it up.

I yelped. Bile burned my throat as I retched to the side. Sweat beaded on my brow, all colour drained from me. Fear took over as my body overheated. The scent of burning caressed my nostrils. I heaved again, thick yellow vomit splattering over the floor. Maisy cowered in the corner. Wiping my mouth on my sleeve, I bit my lip.

My sleeves blackened, smoking and ashen. Every inch of my top was burning right off me. Patting myself down, I ran to the kitchen, turned on the cold tap and dowsed the flames. "Shit!" I groaned, looking down at the mess I'd made. What the actual fuck!

Why would anyone send me a bloody head in a box? This wasn't some kind of Stephen King novel, you know. Huffing, I walked back over. I needed to see who it was. The entire living room stunk of vomit and burnt fabric.

Standing far enough away, I took a deep breath. Shook my body out, relaxed myself, counting to five, and knelt down. *I can do this.* Stepping closer, I pulled back the flaps of the lid and peered inside.

Gagging, I jumped back. It was Jeff! A tortured, broken, bloodied Jeff! They'd only gone and offed the witness! SHIT!

My chest tightened; throat constricted. I grabbed the chair beside me and ushered myself down into it. Taking out my phone, I dialled Detective Melissa Lee. Each ring lasted forever, droning through my ears, piercing me with its annoyance.

"Hello Julia, it's good to hear from you."

"It's erm…" I stammered, gripping the phone, breathing heavy.

"Julia, what's wrong?"

"The box, it's his h-head,"

"What? Who's head? What's happened, Julia?" I overheard talking in the background. Detective Monroe was close by. I remained silent, swallowing hard to subdue the tears. "Julia, where are you?"

"At home, it's in my home."

"Okay Julia, we're coming now. Stay there." I nodded unbeknown to her, dropping the phone and sobbing my heart out.

Sitting there in my old armchair, I stared over at the bloodied box, tears streaming down my face. Staring up at the clock, I noted five minutes had passed. They would be here soon. Taking a deep breath, I tried to compose myself. Wiping my tears on the back of my hand, I lifted myself out of the armchair, staggered over to the kitchen, turned on the cold tap and dunked my face underneath it. Moments later, I grabbed a towel, cleaned myself up and took it into the living room. Squinting to hide Jeff's head from my vision as much as possible. I draped the towel over the box. Much better!

A few cleaning products, bin bags and air freshener and my surroundings were vomit free.

The problem was, even with air freshener, windows open and the front door ajar, I could still smell a mixture of vomit and rotten meat. It was enough to turn anyone's stomach. I'm no coroner, but judging by the rate of decay, I'd say Jeff had been dead for at least several days.

I looked up as Detective Lee and Detective Monroe knocked and walked in. Melissa walked over as Monroe checked the surroundings.

"What's happened?" she asked.

I stood up from cleaning the floor and backed over to the armchair, pointing at the box. "He's in there."

"He?" she asked, brow furrowed. I nodded.

Monroe walked over, pulled the towel off, and gagged. "Shit! Well, at least it isn't your head!" he said, getting his notepad out.

I glared at him. Melissa put on a pair of disposable gloves and walked over. Looking inside, she nodded. "It's the witness."

I nodded, biting my lip. "Do you think he's dead because he came forward?"

Monroe looked up, "Yes," he said. Melissa glared at him.

"What Monroe is trying to say is it isn't your fault. This was the work of Eddy Boland."

My eyes widened, and I took a sharp intake of breath. "What? He's in jail."

"That's what we were about to tell you…" I gasped. "We had to release him late last night. We didn't know till we came in this morning."

"Why was he released?"

Monroe put his notepad away and shrugged. "There was no evidence."

My nails dug into the palms of my hands; teeth gritted.

How could they release him? What absolute idiots! Jeff's dead because of this!

"Of course, there was evidence. Jeff was all the evidence you needed!" I yelled.

Melissa stood up, placed the towel back over the box and walked over, placing her hand on my shoulder. "Judging by the decay. This could not have been Eddy Boland."

"Then who the hell could it be?" I gritted my teeth. Was it the people in the car? The ones watching us in the park? But he was elderly... there was no way he could beat Jeff in a fight? Nothing made sense right now.

Taking a long, heavy breath, I pulled away, sitting in the armchair. I was so bloody angry at everything. A man had lost his life because of the stupidity of the legal system. That could just have easily been me, or any innocent girl, walking home late at night. He was out there and there was nothing anyone could do about it. No one except me! I recalled Lola's hero talk, our candle lighting session last night. There had to be something I could do. I just had to train, get stronger, quicker, better. If the police wouldn't do anything, then I would!

Melissa was on the phone, calling in her team to take away Jeff's bloodied head. Monroe sat on the bottom step of the stairs staring out the front door and me, well, I sat seething, pissed off with the world. I needed to bide my time. Today and right now wasn't the time to get all Big Blaster on their asses. *Shit. I hate that name!* I could feel my hands heating. Bile encircling my throat. I needed to get out of here, needed fresh air, a walk to clear my senses.

"Right, I need fresh air," I said, walking to the front door. "I've got my keys. Please pull the catch and lock up when you're done."

"We need a statement!" Monroe said. I glared at him.

Melissa nodded. "I think we have everything we need, Julia. Walk it off. We'll get everything cleaned up here and phone you with more information when we have it."

I nodded, grabbed my coat, and walked out into the world once more.

CHAPTER TWENTY-TWO

A long walk later and I found myself outside Harrington University. The noon sunshine waned as I looked at my watch, just after one in the afternoon. He'd be in, he had to be. Blake had been the only one that was entirely honest with me. His underworld of supernaturals was a haven of the bizarre, and I knew he had a team ready to take on any threat they posed to the world around them. Eddy was a threat. He was clearly something 'different'. Humanity couldn't hold him, so FALCON had to. They must have a prison or something down there.

I took a deep breath and walked in and up to the old lady at the reception desk. She looked up from her computer. "Yes?"

"I'm here to see Blake Huntsman."

"Do you mean Professor Blake Huntsman?"

I rolled my eyes. "Yes, the same."

She nodded her head to the right. "He is down in lecture

room seven."

"Thank you," I said, then feigned a smile. For a receptionist, she had no bloody manners.

Heading down the corridor, past the vending machine, I came across the wooden door for lecture room seven. The door opened and students filed out, chatting and laughing about the lecture they'd just had. Apparently, old Blake could be quite the comical type when teaching. I smirked, waiting for the last person to leave. Looking around, I slipped in and saw Blake at the pedestal, clearing away his papers. The screen behind him showed an old artifact, golden, circular, and inscribed with tiny pictures, in a language I clearly did not understand.

"It's hieroglyphics," Blake said, staring over at me.

My eyes widened, and I nodded. "It's beautiful."

"It is, but just as deadly."

"Why? What is it?"

"It's one of the Dropa stones."

"The what?"

He laughed. "The Dropa stones were found in China. Humanity believes they tell the story of another civilisation that crashed into the mountains. Each stone releases a vibration, similar to an electric charge." He smiled. "However, what they do not know is that these stones can heal those that hold them."

"Really?" I asked, frowning.

He laughed. "So, you've seen an underground world of shapeshifters, witches, and wizards, but healing stones is where you call it quits?"

I smirked. "Good point... continue."

"So have you heard of the fountain of youth?"

I nodded. "It's a myth," he said. "But based on where a group of archaeologists found these stones."

"Let me guess, under a waterfall?"

He nodded and smiled.

I pursed my lips. "Okay, so you're telling me that these stones are actually the physical form of the fountain of youth."

He thought for a moment and nodded. "Well yes, I guess so."

"Excellent," I said and smiled. "So where are they? They could help a lot of sick people."

"True, but in the wrong hands they can destroy life, just as easily as give it."

"What? So, these things kill people too?"

"Yes, they drain energy and also give energy, restoring the body like a battery, storing the energy until it's needed."

"The energy being someone's life force?"

He nodded.

"Well, that's scary!"

"Exactly, which is why we have them locked up in the vaults."

"What? So it's here?" I asked, looking down at the floor.

"Yes, but don't worry, several countermeasures protect the vaults; no one has ever penetrated them."

"There's always a first time."

He sighed and nodded. "We are perfectly safe."

I groaned.

"Anyway, why are you here?" he asked.

I stepped back and sighed. "Eddy Boland."

"Yes?"

"He killed a witness I had, left his head in a box for me."

"Ah, so that must have been before then?"

"Huh?"

"Well, Eddy has been dead for," he looked at his watch, "approximately four hours and thirty-two minutes now."

My eyes widened. "Dead?"

"Yes, he was a problem that needed handling."

"So where is he?"

"Probably incinerated by now."

"Really?"

"Yes, Julia. Really. We don't hang around, you know."

"But how did you capture him?"

"We have a specialist team for that."

I nodded and watched as Blake turned away and put his remaining papers into his briefcase, turned off the projector and walked past me to the door.

"Are you coming?" he asked, his fingers on the light switch.

"What? Err... yes."

"I would stand and chat, but I have another class in half an hour. Is there anything else you needed?"

"Err, no. Thank you, I think."

He smiled and nodded, walking away. I stood there dumfounded. They'd killed Eddy. It was all over! I didn't have to fear him anymore!

Blake stopped walking, turned back, and shouted. "Did you speak with Nathaniel yet?" he asked.

I sighed. Maybe it wasn't all over. "No."

"Then you should." He turned, before continuing to walk away.

I walked out, past the grumpy receptionist and into the icy winter wind, beginning my long walk home. I needed the fresh air to clear my thoughts. My mind was a mashed-up version of its former self. Not only had I learned that supernatural creatures existed, but I also learned I was one of them. There was so much more to this world that I ever came to realise. Walking home, I felt at ease, safe in the knowledge my attacker was dead. They had taken the London Butcher out and once and for all, the city of London could rest easy tonight.

I sighed and smiled. Blake was right though. I needed to talk to Nathaniel. None of this was over anyway, not until I figured out what the Doctor had done to me. I scratched my head, lips pursed. The afternoon sun was low as I left the University grounds. I carried on mulling things over. Also, why was Aunt Clara's number left out in the Grand Hotel? I'm sure it wasn't there the first time I went in. What did she have to do with Jesus Mendel and why did it impact on my mother, causing her death? Even with Eddy dead and buried, I still had a hundred and one questions.

Pulling out my phone, I dialled Nathaniel's number.

Two rings later, he picked up. "Afternoon Red, I've been meaning to call you." His voice was so smoky and delicious, I could almost taste his masculinity from here.

I smiled. "Oh, you have, have you?"

He laughed, a sound that sent butterflies floating through me. "Yes, now how would you like to meet Ritchie?"

"Oh dear, but won't Gladys be jealous?"

"Oh no, she is happy to share."

I laughed. "What do you have in mind?"

"Well, I believe it's my turn to cook, so how about a home cooked meal, wine and a night by candlelight?"

"That sounds perfect," I said, smiling.

"So, seven o'clock?"

"Seven it is." I smiled, we said our goodbyes and I couldn't stop grinning.

Pulling my coat tighter around me, I continued walking. I was hungry and needed a pick me up. Texting Lola, I arranged to meet her at Lydia's for a coffee, lunch, and a chat. It was only two blocks from here and I really needed to sit down and let off steam about the morning's disaster.

Turning the last corner, Lydia's coffee shop was in sight. She opened the door as I arrived and pulled me in, rubbing her hands up and down my arms. "Julia! You look like an icicle! What have you been doing?" I smiled, my nose aching from the cold. "Here, sit down, I'll bring you a large coffee!"

"Thank you, Lydia," I said, taking a seat.

Lola walked in. The chilly wind blasted through the door as she shivered, shaking herself off. She waved, walked past Lydia, kissed her on the cheek, and sat beside me.

"Jeez, Julia, you look like death!"

I laughed, holding my nose to warm it up.

"Be careful, it might fall off…" I rolled my eyes,

"Oooh, actually, why don't you turn on the heat! Bring the Big Blaster out in full force. You'll soon warm up."

I smirked and shook my head. "I'll soon warm up."

Lydia bought over two coffees and two plates of burgers and chips. As we delved in, she smiled and walked off to serve another customer. Whilst we ate, I described what my morning had turned into.

"Well, I wouldn't order from Amazon again," Lola said, wide-eyed.

I groaned at her humour.

"So, what did Blake say?"

"That's it, he said he's offed Eddy, and all is right with the world again."

"Thank fuck he's dead!" she said. "He was really creeping me out at the station!"

I smiled.

"So that's what this FALCON place does then? Get rid of the bad guys?"

I nodded and pursed my lips.

"What's wrong?"

"What if I can't control what's happening to me? What if I hurt people and turn evil?"

She laughed. "You can't just 'turn bad' Julia, it's something dark inside you that unravels itself throughout your lifetime."

I smirked. "That was quite profound for you."

She grinned. "Thanks, I've been working on that for quite some time."

Laughing, we both finished up our food and coffees,

then said our goodbyes. Tonight was date night, and I had to get ready for my date with Nathaniel. Like Lola said, everything else can wait. I needed to live in the moment, stop worrying about the what if or what could be? Smiling, I headed home.

CHAPTER TWENTY-THREE

On the subway journey home, I found a seat and thought about everything I'd seen. Something was nagging at me. Something was missing. A prime piece of the puzzle. But what?

Okay, so the silver-haired shooter was Blake Huntsman, a supernatural university professor with a shady side-line of work involving shotguns, shells and shape-shifting. What about Nathaniel... and who the hell was this Doctor? I frowned, picking up my pace, shivering. The night was drawing in as the evening sun set and an array of colours flowed over the skyline. What do I know about him? I scratched my head, then searched through the gallery on my phone. The images of the sign-in book showed the last few weeks of guests. Jesus Mendel, who was he? Was Blake right? Was it possible that these two mystery men were actually the same person? Was the Doctor in fact Jesus Mendel?

Nearing home, I turned the corner, and walked up my street. It was desolate, apart from Old lady Jean's dog barking next door. Down the street there was a jazzy pink smart car, a 4x4 behind and Paul's burgundy Fiesta down the street. Thank frick, there was no black Mercedes!

I walked up and noticed a gold package with a red ribbon outside my front door. My brow furrowed. *Who was that from?* I'm surprised it wasn't stolen! Picking up the package, I shuddered. This had better not be another bloody head! Taking a deep breath, I headed inside. Maisy came to greet me, wrapping herself around my legs.

I walked through into my lilac kitchen. White units gleamed as mucky paw prints covered the work surface. "Now why would you do that?" I tutted, stroking Maisy, and making her evening meal.

Heading upstairs, I picked up the golden present and went to get ready for the night ahead. Reminding myself that it may take a while… half my wardrobe was still in boxes; I made a mental note to sort them out at some point.

Placing the golden package down on the bed, I wandered over to the wardrobe and flicked through my outfits. The smell of lavender lightened my senses as one of my mother's old charms greeted me. My mother used to sew little bags of lavender that she had picked from the farmland where she grew up. It was a trait I'd learnt too, refilling the bags every so often, keeping my clothes fresh and aromatic. It also meant that every time I opened the wardrobe or chest of drawers, my mother sprung to mind, making me smile. She had been gone for so long now, yet sometimes it felt like it was only yesterday.

I always wondered what it would be like if she had never walked home that night. I remember my Uncle Joe getting a phone call in the middle of the night. He had to come and pick me up. I had sat alone with my dead mother by my side. A memory I wished I could forget.

Uncle Joe had been living with us back then, his third wife having thrown him out. He had been drinking that night, so he was late as usual. But Lydia turned up. She held me. Took me home and stayed all night. The next day when I finally saw Uncle Joe, he was a broken man, his face drained of all colour, his eyes narrow and bloodshot, skin sodden from the tears that fell. The booze had left his system, and reality sunk in. He'd lost his sister. I'd lost my mother. He held me tight; my body had shaken with grief. It was a long time ago, but the memory still haunts me. If she had lived, she would be sitting here choosing an outfit with me.

Brushing my hand over various fabrics, I picked out a golden knee-length tea dress with matching heels and bag. Then stopped, stared in the mirror, and realised. He had a motorbike. Was Ritchie a motorbike too? What the heck do I wear for that? Grabbing my phone, I messaged him.

Dare I ask who Ritchie is?

Seconds later, the it pinged: *You'll have to wait and see.*

I replied: *But… would Ritchie be ok with me in a dress?*

Oh, Ritchie would love you in a dress.

I smirked, a dress it was then. I placed the phone down and set it to play RnB right back from the early noughties, with Destiny's Child caressing the airwaves. Taking a minute, I poured myself a glass of Sauvignon Blanc. Taking a sip, the taste of peach, lime and passion fruit delighted me.

The next song began, 'Lose my Breath'. Singing aloud, I jumped in the shower, washed, and changed, then moved to the mirror to apply my makeup. I opted for a strong yet sexy look, finishing with my sultry lipstick, a deep crimson, complimenting my long red curls as I headed downstairs. A thought twinged in my mind. *Damn it! The golden present!*

Stopping myself, I ran back up, grabbed the present, and began to open it at the end of the bed. *Hmm, no card.* Pulling the ribbon, something clicked inside. *What was that?* Baffled, I continued to pull the gold wrapping backwards. There was a noise. I listened closer, putting the package to my ear. Ticking. Why would it be ticking? Versions of massacred movie stars sprung to mind. The only time a package ticked is if it held a bomb inside. No… it couldn't be. I gasped, placing the package on the bed. Standing silent for a few minutes, I stared at it. It continued to tick. *Why the heck is it ticking?* If it was a bomb, it would have gone off by now, and it would have blown me to smithereens for standing here like an absolute moron contemplating it!

Okay, so it's not a bomb, then what? A practical joke? I stretched out my neck, elongated my arms, exercising my fingers as I plucked up the courage to check out the ticking time bomb in front of me. I'd better be right about this. Stepping forward, I bent over the package, carefully peeling back the gold wrapping. A brown cardboard box sat there… ticking. Two flaps were intertwined. Taking my time, I lifted the first one, releasing the second. The box opened, displaying some kind of device with a glass tube that was spinning around in the centre. Inside the tube there appeared to be liquid at each end, separated by the velocity of the motor that span. *What is that?* I leant over, studying the liquid. One side was black, the other white and as it passed by a red dot, it ticked. I pulled the device out of the box, watching it closely. It was slowing down. *Have I broken it?* The two liquids journeyed towards the centre as the device stopped, merging with one another to form a darkness in the middle. As they merged, the red dot lit up, and the device sounded out a callous, high-pitched laughter.

"What the heck…" A flash of severe light bleached my retina.

Then nothing.

Screams engulfed my mind, an inferno of detonation charred at my skin. Lungs on fire, body broken and burned. *Where am I?* Gasping for breath, choking on the black smoke, I opened my eyes to darkness. All around me, the soot of my former life had been devoured by flame. Embers settled to the floor as I looked down to see I was sitting in a pile of ash. Stretching out, I appeared unharmed, naked skin dirtied but unscathed, luminescent in the fire's light that dwindled around me.

The stench of burning wood intruded my senses. *What happened?* Darkness surrounded me with the burden of my reality. Sat in a pile of ash, I felt the warmth of a fire within.

I'd like to say I felt fear. The natural response would be fight or flight, adrenaline pumping with my body alight. But I'm not sure what I felt. Ruin surrounded me, emotions encapsulated as my past life drained from reality. My body's response was to stay sane, to toughen up, muscles stiff, hands clammy. My eyes bulged as I searched the bedroom, trying to decipher any normality. But there was none. Everything was black. Somehow, I had cocooned myself, protecting my body and surviving the blast. It made little sense.

Outside, sirens blazed, neighbours yelled, and the front door burst open. A whirlpool of water streamed through the broken window, soaking every inch of blackness in its wake. Pounding footsteps shook the staircase as a hoard of firefighters trudged upwards, soothing the flames as they rose. "She's in here," a man yelled, blasting the flaming remains of my four-poster bed with water. "Ma'am, we need to get you out of here."

"Where? Where is she?" another firefighter yelled.

"Matty, she's here, she's okay!"

Matty rushed down to my side with full on firefighter gear. "Jeez Julia, you're naked. What the hell happened?"

I spluttered, trying to formulate words.

He stood up and took off his jacket, covering my ashen body. "Does it hurt anywhere?" he asked.

I shook my head. My ears were ringing, and my head pounded, but my body felt fine.

He helped me to stand. I wobbled like a baby trying to take its first step.

Grabbing my legs, he hoisted me up and into his arms. "We can't have you falling down the stairs now, can we?" His eyes sparkled as he smiled.

Taking his time, he stepped out of the room and around the corner. His fellow firefighter lit the floor with a torch, guiding us down the perilous path towards the stairs. Looking down the stairs, I could see smoke had damaged the staircase, threatening to travel downstairs and into the living room. *Where is Maisy?* I looked but couldn't see her.

"Mind your step," another firefighter said, as Matty carried me over the firehose. My body shook as we left the house. Cool icy winds from the North collided with my bare skin. Goosebumps protruded, and I shivered with the cold. Teeth chattering, he took me to the ambulance, wrapped me up in a foil sheet and two blankets. The last time I'd laid on one was when Eddy attacked me. As for this time, well, I didn't know what happened. How was it possible I survived without a mark on me?

A female paramedic with jet black hair strapped me in, ready for the journey to the hospital. "How are you doing, honey?" she asked. I mouthed I don't know, but no sound came out. "Don't worry, you're in shock, it can take time for your body to return to normal." She smiled. I wish she were right, but I had the feeling it was something more than that. She leaned over and placed a blood pressure cuff on my arm. "Normal. Hmm... let's check your temperature." Taking out a thermometer, she placed it in my ear and pressed the button. It beeped continuously. "That's strange," she said, tapping the thermometer on her hand. "Let's try again." Again, it beeped continuously. "It makes no sense," she said, scratching her head. "It's saying you're over 48 degrees Celsius. That can't be right," she puzzled. "We'll check on the machines at hospital." She smiled. I nodded.

I felt hot. But it wasn't an uncomfortable heat, it was soothing, warming inside... like sitting beside a roaring fire on a cold Winter's day.

"Strap in. We're ready to go," the driver said, closing the doors.

My pounding head soothed through the softness of the pillow. Mind haunted by the evening's events, eased by the silence of the journey to the hospital.

Sirens dimmed, lights faltered, and the paramedic strapped herself in, heading off into the night.

Coming to a stop, the wail of London's turmoil ceased to exist. *Where are we?* In my mind the silence screamed out, warning me, something wasn't right here. The paramedic looked confused.

"Hmm..." she voiced.

"What's wrong?" I said, my voice gravelled and dry.

"We've stopped beside the docks."

"Why?"

"Don't worry, I'll check," she said as she leant forward and banged on the hatch. It opened and a flash of air resonated from the driver's seat. "Wait!" she yelled; gunfire exploded in the air and the paramedics' brain matter decorated the inside of the ambulance. She collapsed in a heap on the floor.

Eyes wide, heart racing, I fumbled around for the seatbelt strap. Unhooking the belt, I bolted upright. Hands clammy, muscles tense, I span around too quick, dropping my legs over the side, trying to stand up. Dizziness took over as snippets of reality collided with the fuzziness of the future before me. Sliced shards of silver specks shot through my gaze, my body heated, heaviness took over. I wasn't ready to stand, wasn't ready to move. *What is happening?* I turned to face the hatch. Turned to check on the driver but it was too late. The hand of my attacker flailed through, needle in hand as he stabbed my arm. Falling to the floor, I saw his face, the face I'd once met, the face of Eddy Boland. *It can't be. He's dead!* I collapsed in a heap, paralysed and unconscious on the floor.

CHAPTER TWENTY-FOUR

The stench of dead fish swarmed around me. Darkness encased my vision as my eyelids fluttered. Breaking open, I could see a damp, cold mist surrounding me. *Where am I? What the heck happened?*

My brain fogged as I tried to recall my last moments. Nothing. Fumbling around, I could feel something sharp binding my wrists together. Pulling at it, I couldn't break free. Whatever it was, it felt too thin for handcuffs, too smooth for rope. It had to be a cable tie. If there's something sharp around here, I could cut myself free. I searched around in the darkness, blinking rapidly, trying to get my eyes to adjust to the lack of light.

Through the darkened fog, I could see a light shining through a barred window. *Am I in jail?* Cold, grey walls caged me. I looked down, well at least I wasn't naked anymore. Someone had clothed me in a tracksuit and a vest top. I was thankful, but it unnerved me.

The concrete floor below iced my body with its shrill

exterior. I was sitting on the floor, shivering for warmth. With the fog and the sound of rushing waves, I could only presume I was still at the docks. The vile aroma of dead fish gave it away.

Who brought me here? I remembered an explosion, my body unscathed by fire. I remember the firefighters freeing me from the blaze. But I couldn't remember how I got here. *Think dammit! I'm tied up for a reason. Someone did this to me. Who?* There was an ambulance. I remembered the lady taking my blood pressure. I grimaced and yelped. I remembered her blood, the brain matter. *But why?*

I edged forward, taking my time to reach the other side of the room. I appeared to be in a makeshift cell. There was an old bed on one side, but no sink or bathroom. Surely, this violated the Human Rights Act, even criminals deserved to be treated with respect. Except I wasn't a criminal, at least I didn't think I was.

I checked over my body, everything intact, nothing hurt. That's a good sign. I edged further forward.

Reaching what appeared to be a wooden door, I pushed up from the ground, straightening my legs to stand. Near the top of the door was another barred window. There was a room beyond it. In the distance, I could see a table with two men sat at it, playing cards. They both seemed familiar. The bulky guy was sat with his back to me, but his hair… I winced. That long brown mop looked just like Eddy's. It couldn't be? Could it? I shuddered; he was dead. But who was the other guy? Thin, brown-haired. His stature was familiar, too. But who? Beside them was an armoury of weapons and what appeared to be the silhouette of another two guys in the distance. I shook my head; it made no sense. Why was I here?

Listening in, I could hear snippets of their conversation. A voice grated on me. I know that voice. I've heard it before.

"Ah, so you're awake," he said as he screeched the chair legs out from the table and placed his hand of cards down. "Jimmy, go tell the doc she's ready to go."

Jimmy? Jimmy, my dorkish stalker? Why's he here?

Thick, brutish arms pushed down on the old wooden table as Eddy raised himself up. I took a step back. He paused, a callous cackle vibrating through his voice box.

"So, Julia, we meet again," he said, turning around, his dark brown eyes glared through the light. Thumping footsteps echoed towards me, and I backed into the darkest corner, sealed in shadow.

"There's no beast to save you now," he cackled.

The cell door opened; Eddy's bulky figure silhouetted before me. He reached down.

"Get off me, you monster!" I yelled. He laughed, pulled me up and slung me over his shoulder like I was nothing. Which I can assure you I'm not! Kicking and yelling, we walked past the table. I kicked out, knocking it, cards scattered everywhere. He growled, squeezing me tighter. My stomach hurt; chest wheezed for air. Kicking and punching, my movements slowed. Instead, I concentrated on taking in what little air I could. He was holding me tight. So tight my body couldn't fight anymore.

As we left, we walked past another room. This one was filled with metal beds, dirty mattresses with springs poking out, and an army of young girls all chained up, cowering as they saw Eddy's face. *Who are they?* One girl was playing with an electric blue light as it zapped out of her hands, twirling and swirling it around in a dance above her. Another one's face shifted into several other faces, her voice deepening and changing with each new persona. One girl waved her hands around and the tears from her friend danced around before them. She smiled, cheering her friend up.

Eddy stopped, lightening his grip on me. "Stop pissing around. The Doctor will hear of this." The girls cowered.

"I'll take it from here," another voice said as he barged past us holding a cattle prod. I looked to the side. It was Eddy. But it couldn't be. Eddy was holding me. My Eddy laughed at the other Eddy, and walked off, my body bouncing up and down on his shoulder as he went.

Entering the door to the right, Eddy threw me down on a surgical chair. Like the ones you get at the dentist, the thought of which made me want to cower and hide. I realised my fate and accepted that for now; I was their prisoner. The only comfort I had was the knowledge that if they wanted me dead, I'd be dead already. Eddy left, slamming the door behind him. It was just me and the doc now. The fact that I still hadn't seen him scared me more. He'd been out of sight this whole time. Who or what was he?

"Well, my Julia, it appears you found my present," he said, his voice croaky and old. He chuckled callously. Shit. Perhaps they wanted me dead after all. I shuddered, gulping back the bile that rushed to my throat.

"You're not an easy kill though, are you?" he said. "You can thank me for that."

What did he mean? I puzzled as the doctor continued

to crash and clank beakers and other scientific apparatus behind me.

Realisation hit as I remembered what Blake said. The doctor was recruiting people. He must have meant the injection. Whatever was in that thing made me survive the bomb from last night.

"Your aunt said you were made of something special." I gasped… my aunt? Clara? "It's a shame your mother did not share her view."

Fists balled; lips pursed. "What about my mum?"

"Clara knew she would never let you be tested on."

"Tested on? What the hell are you on about?"

The heeled footsteps of a female sounded beside me. The door opened and in walked an older but prettier version of my Aunt Clara. My eyes widened. "What the heck is going on?" I asked.

"Oh, Jesus baby, she doesn't need tying up, she'll cooperate… won't you, Julia?"

"What the hell Clara, what's going on, why are you with this guy?"

She laughed. "Jesus?" She frowned. "We're married, princess, have been for the last seven years."

"What? Why didn't you tell me? You vanished after Mum died."

"Yes, well, we had some important work that could not wait." She smiled.

I glared at her. She'd disappeared and never gave a shit what happened to me. If it weren't for Lydia, I'd have been homeless! "Why didn't you look after me?"

"I was busy, Julia. Plus, you weren't ready, you needed

to reach your potential on your own."

"What potential, Clara? I needed you back then! Why didn't you care?"

"Oh Julia, we had to let your body get used to the formula. We couldn't interfere."

My brow furrowed. "What formula?"

"We needed you to have the final dose before you'd understand your purpose."

"Final dose?"

"Don't you remember when I babysat you?"

I nodded. Brow furrowed.

"And the special cakes I always bought just for you?"

Lips pursed, I nodded again.

"They had the formula in them, princess. You were our first test subject." She smiled; her mouth as wide as a Cheshire cat. I grimaced. What had she done to me?

She laughed and walked behind me. The neck collar loosened. "There, that's better."

"What about the rest?" I asked, pulling on the leather straps. She smiled.

The doctor laughed. "Let's talk first, shall we?" He sat down on a wheeled chair and wheeled himself into my viewpoint. The image of a silver-haired frail, pale man sat before me. He looked about seventy-five, eighty. I smirked. He looked old enough to be Clara's father.

"Who is he to you?" I asked.

"I told you already. He's my husband, Julia, I'd have introduced you two under better circumstances but after he murdered your mum, I didn't think you'd be interested in playing happy families."

I gulped. My heart wrenched at the thought of it. "No, not really, Clara…" I frowned, hands balled into fists, heart palpating. "So, why'd you marry a man twice your age?" I asked, spitting out the question.

She huffed. "Jesus isn't twice my age, you spoilt little child. He's the same age."

"You need your eyesight checking, Clara!" I said, smirking. I'd had enough of this facade. They had better tell the truth or I'll blast my way out of here… if I could figure out how to!

"Be quiet, you rude girl!" she huffed, crossing her arms. The doctor laughed. "I'm sorry Jesus. Julia here clearly did not learn respect from her own mother."

"Jesus?" I questioned. "So, you are both the doctor and Jesus Mendel?"

He grinned. "One and the same."

I frowned, thinking. "So, you killed my mum and Nathaniel's pack?"

He smirked. "No girl. I did not kill them, but I did order it."

"Why?"

"Because they were an interference."

"So, you dispose of people that get in your way?" Was he really saying that?

"Yes."

"And Clara… you were fine with him murdering my mum, your sister?"

"Of course, princess, she always had to stick her nose in where it wasn't wanted. This was my life. Not hers."

"Actually, no. I am her daughter. You tried to take me from her when you kept poisoning me throughout my childhood."

They looked at each other and laughed. Clara grinned, staring at me. "Oh Julia, you've got it all wrong! Don't you remember how ill you were as a baby?"

I rolled my eyes. "No Clara, I was a baby, I can't quite recall that."

She gave me a snide look. "Well, you were. If it weren't for me meeting this handsome fella here, you would not have made it past your sixth birthday."

Is she really trying to tell me this psycho saved my life? I shook my head. "I don't believe you, Clara."

She huffed and Jesus stood up, put his hand on her shoulder, whispered into her ear and she nodded and walked out of the room, leaving the two of us alone.

"Now Julia, you are very lucky we could cure your insatiable hunger as a child."

"What?"

"Your blood lacked the enrichment it needed. I developed a serum to stabilise it, but it made you into so much more!"

"What do you mean?"

He grinned. Sat down on the chair before me and placed his wrinkled hands on my knees, stabbing me with another needle. "You're a phoenix, Julia Jones. You're a phoenix." My eyelids faltered, darkness rose, and off I went to live in dreamland once more.

CHAPTER TWENTY-FIVE

"Wakey wakey, eggs and bakey." A familiar screeching voice penetrated my eardrum. I kicked at the blanket as the blinding light of the sun bleached my retina. Ow, my head banged.

"Feeling a little under the weather, Julia?" I turned to see Aunt Clara sat on the end of my bed.

"What happened?" I asked, yawning, bringing my hand to my forehead. Damn, it hurt.

"Oh princess, don't you remember?"

I looked around. This wasn't my bedroom. Bared windows and concrete walls. This was a cell. My head pounded harder. Eyes watered as I struggled to comprehend the magnitude of the shit storm I'd got myself into.

"Well, let me enlighten you." She smirked, giggling profusely. "I'm your Aunt Clara." She grinned. I sat up. Nodded and feigned a smile. She was always a tad strange when I was growing up.

"I know that, Clara. Why are you here? Where am I?"

"Oooh, all the questions. Well Dorothy, you're not in Kansas anymore."

"Clearly," I growled.

Clara frowned. "Oh, lighten up, Julia, you're our star pupil." She smirked. "You've been such a good little girl now, haven't you?"

Little girl? I'm twenty-three. I frowned. "So, who's the husband?"

"Ah, so you remember him..." I nodded. "Jesus is the love of my life. You know him as the Doctor."

I slumped. Shit. He was the one in the black Mercedes. He murdered my mum and sent Eddy after me. I pulled the cover tighter over me. Eddy. He's still alive. No, wait. There's more than one of him. What did she do to me?

"Questions princess?"

"Eddy? What is he?"

"A clone, obviously," she slumped down, unimpressed.

"Why did you kill Mum?"

She laughed. "You know this. I told you!" she groaned. "Jesus must have upped the dose this time"

"What?"

"Don't you remember our conversation before?"

"Partly."

She sighed. "Okay. Well, your mum was always a busybody, even when growing up. She always had to stick her nose in where it wasn't needed."

"So, you killed her for that? She was protecting me!" I

yelled, straightening my back up. Fists clenched.

"Oooh Julia, don't you go getting yourself all worked up there, now."

"Why the hell not?"

She laughed, a snide cackle escaping her lips. "Don't you remember when you blew your own house up?"

"Huh?" Shit. I had, hadn't I... hey wait. That wasn't me. That was the present they'd sent me! I glared at her.

"You've always been our first-born monster, Julia. We tested serum after serum on you until we cured you. It made you into much more than we could have ever anticipated! You made all this possible."

I gagged. My head pulsating as the blood rushed to escape me. "You made me sick!"

She laughed. "Hardly, dear, you're the most powerful creature we've ever made."

I remembered. All those sick days while mum worked, and Aunt Clara looked after me. She'd made me sick by testing on me. I was never ill; she made me ill.

"You're disgusting," I said, pushing her off the bed.

She laughed, rolling around on the floor. She'd lost it, pure and simple. When she regained some inkling of normality, she stood up and sat, perching on the edge of my bed again.

"Is that how Mum found out?"

She nodded. "It ended up being too much of a coincidence, me visiting and you being sick."

Tears welled in my eyes again. Salt cushioned my lips. "So, you killed her..."

"Yes, we couldn't let her stop the experiment. It's bigger than any of us, Julia."

My head lowered. "Why is it? Why did she have to die?"

She edged closer; her hand reached out to comfort me. I glared, and she lowered it down to her side. "We need to destroy humanity before it destroys us, Julia," she said in a softer tone. "Humans are causing our world to die. Not us."

"So, you want to kill every person you can't turn into a monster?" I'd lost my mum for her suicidal war. Nothing was right about any of this.

"Yes, and you can be a part of it, Julia. I know you write about the disasters humans create. Surely you can see why we're doing it?"

"No." I shook my head. How could I ever? "You're talking about genocide!"

She laughed, her callous cackles screeching through the air.

"I'm talking about saving the world, Julia, or are you too stupid to see that!"

I sat up, wiped my eyes, and looked her straight in the eye. "Get the hell out!" I yelled.

She laughed harder.

Heat rose through me, my skin tingled as each nerve fired, blasting out flames from my skin. Every surface of me ignited. She stood up, laughing as the blanket turned to a cinder. The mattress was next. Full on flames blasting through every part.

"Oh, you get fiery when you're annoyed, Julia," she said, laughing.

I gripped harder, my hands already blazing. "Get out!" I yelled. Fire bolts shot out, blasting across the room.

Eddy ran to the door, opening it wide. "Clara, you'd better leave until she finishes her tantrum!"

Clara howled in laughter, backed away from me and escaped through the open door.

Fire consumed me; it covered every inch of the room in flames. Crimson red swirled into vibrant orange, chased over by the rays of sunshine yellow. It all intermingled. There was almost a beauty to the devastation I was causing, and with this devastation, no one would survive it but me.

Lying on the metal springs of the mattress, I chased the flames over my fingertips, dancing them across, back and forth. The rhythm of it helped ease me back down to reality. I sighed, the flames dissipating.

I closed my eyes, trying to relax myself more. It's strange really… I always felt cold as a child. Cold hands, warm heart, my mother used to say. I smiled, my eyelids still shrouding my view from the absurdity of it all. I'd open them in a minute. Maybe when I did, it would all be one huge messed up dream. Freud would say I'm insane, absolutely bonkers. Well, no, maybe he wouldn't. But I felt a little like Alice stepping through the tiny door into a big wide world.

My life has been a lie, corrupted by one disaster after another. I thought it was just bad luck. Negative karma. Perhaps I'd been an obnoxious devil in a previous life, and this time I was paying for my previous mistakes. It didn't make sense, though. I never hurt anyone. In fact, I'd tried to help people, show them the truth behind their actions. I took a deep breath in, exhaled, and opened my eyes a little.

It was dark, the only light that of the waning sun as it set over the horizon. I sighed, unburdening my grip on the bed frame... what was left of it.

I looked around, eyes wide, taking in the carnage I had subjected the cell to. It was black, ashen, and sooty. The mattress I lay on had no fabric left. Springs popped and burst. They must have cut into my skin. How come I didn't feel that? I sat upright; I hadn't got a mark on myself. Lips pursed, I shrugged. Someone how I'd ignited every flammable thing in the room. Granted, that was mainly the mattress and my clothes. I shuddered, naked and ashen again. But at least I hurt no one... this time.

What would happen if this power got into the wrong hands? If I got into the wrong hands. I winced. *Shit. That's already happened.* Clara and the Doctor clearly wanted to use me for their vengeance on the world. I looked over as the door opened and Jimmy threw in a bag. He closed it quickly. My brow furrowed. *Is he scared of me?* I wonder why he's here, though. *Could he be a monster too? Are we all monsters now?*

I grabbed the bag, pulled out a grey tracksuit and got changed, wrapped my arms around me, and sat on the cold concrete in the corner, contemplating my new life. If anyone told me that one day I would explode and destroy everything, I wouldn't have believed them. No sane person would. I mean, who would actually believe that there was a world beneath our own? That supernatural creatures existed?

Blake said to think back to every fairytale, that every whimsical writer with an imaginative view on the world had written. He said the stories were true. There's the supernatural and what he calls the GMs. The creatures that were made. Human at first, then changed into something else. It's not just injections. Nathaniel had said a simple bite from a wolf shifter would start the change in a human. Not all survive, and it can be a fate worse than death. Especially as ten years to us humans… well, to the actual humans, is one year to the wolves. I'm guessing a lot of monsters have a delayed ageing ability. Which is great, in some respects. But that's only if they're good. *Are there good monsters out there?* Nathaniel seemed to be on the lighter side of the abnormal. The Doctor had changed him, like me. I gripped myself harder, staring up at the last rays of light as they passed through the barred window.

But what was I? Would I be on the good side of history? And what was stopping FALCON from seeing me as a threat and ending my life as soon as I stepped outside the door? Especially as I was mutated to serve the Doctor. This wasn't exactly part of a 'woohoo I'm powerful and amazing; scenario. This was a 'oh shit I'm doomed' one.

What was stopping the Doctor from releasing me into a schoolyard, as hundreds of children play? What if I heated and combusted, exploding every innocent soul into another dimension… their tiny burning bodies littering the streets? I hugged myself as my eyes watered. *What does he have planned? I won't ever let him do that to me.* Taking a deep breath, I exhaled, digging my fingernails into my arms. I can't let him use me to murder the innocent. Taking another deep breath, I shook my head. I'd die first. I could never live with myself. Destroying the people I'd vowed to protect.

Telling the public the truth means so much to me. But

how can I do that now? My whole life has been a lie. I've not been human for years, according to Joanna, so how can anyone believe anything I ever say again? Tears welled in my eyes. Hands clammy as I hugged myself tighter. Just because I don't know who I am, it doesn't mean my intentions are bad. I never lied; I just never knew. But now, if I carry on writing, then everything I write will be a lie, because now I know. I know what really exists, what I really am and how much damage I can actually do. No one is safe around me anymore. No one.

Salty tears cushioned my lips, and my body shook in anguish. Taking a few choked up breaths, I bit down on my lower lip, trying to stop the tears. No matter what I was now, the people of London, heck of the entire world, needed to know what's been going on here. The lives of those girls in there meant something. They had families, loved ones. The Doctor has been taking innocent people and turning them into monsters. There had to be a way to cure this. Help these girls, help me even? But then, was I too far gone? If they have truly fed me poison all my life, then I was never human to begin with. For all I knew, Clara could have been feeding my mother with me in the womb.

I almost accepted the fact I was different, welcomed it, in fact. At least it meant I had the strength to take down the evil in this world. But knowing what I'd come from. Knowing that the very thing that has made me what I was is as evil as evil can be. How can I move on from that?

Then there's the injection. The army of women the Doctor collected. It doesn't always work on everyone; I thought back to the butchered girls. Salty tears threatening to spill again. What was stopping him from creating more? Murdering more? I wiped my eyes. FALCON… perhaps they would step in. But, if they do, then would the girls I saw in that torture chamber be annihilated? Like Eddy the first was? They have done nothing wrong. They were captured, changed, and made to fight each other for their own survival. Is that what I'll be subjected to? Death matches and tortured dreams?

I sighed. What could I do? Who can I trust? I couldn't sit here crying waiting for rescue. Who would even come? no one knows I'm here. What if they all thought I died in the fire? No, Matty would tell them. I gripped myself tighter again. What if they kill Matty to stop him from telling everyone I survived? What if Matty was told I'd died in the ambulance? After all, who could survive an inferno like that? Would Nathaniel come? Would he believe I survived?

I couldn't wait for help that may never come. It was down to me. I had to get out of this place, go straight to FALCON and plead my case. Maybe they can stop this latent ability. Maybe they can figure out how to reverse it. If not, they'd kill me. Now I knew what I was, it was clear I was a threat. But my death is a hundred times better than the death of all of humanity.

The door creaked open. Clara walked in, her hips swaying to a silent beat, back lit by the light from the other room. She whirled and twirled around the room, laughing as she danced. What's wrong with her? She closed the door, still inside, twirling around in a rhythmic dance. Darkness enveloped the room except for the rising of the moon as it blessed the night sky. Clara came into view, stopping still in the moon's light. Her hair continued to move, as though it was alive with its own desire. She was not human.

"What do you want, Clara?" I said, my voice shaky.

Her snake-like tongue flickered out of her mouth. She bent down and faced up to me. Hundreds of snakes caressed her head, her hair alive with black vipers, forming the face of the Medusa before me. "I wanted to show you my true form, princess," she hissed.

I backed further into the corner. *Thank frick she can't turn people into stone like the myth!* Taking a deep breath, I raised my hands in front of my face. Straightening up, she slinked over, bending down so her face was mere inches away from my own.

"What are you?"

"Oh Julia, I wanted to show you my true face." She grinned. "I'm a stunner, aren't I…" she cackled, hissing out each of the words.

"You're something all right!"

She laughed. "Each of my babies pack a powerful poison, Julia," she smirked, her tongue flickering in and out of her mouth. "I wouldn't upset them if I were you."

I feigned a smile.

"Much better!" She stood up, swirling and twirling around the cell. Her lips humming the tune of an old nursery rhyme she used to sing to me as a child.

Three blind mice, three blind mice,
See how they run, See how they run;
They all ran after the farmer's wife.

She cut off their tails with a carving knife,
Did you ever see such a sight in your life
As three blind mice?

I shuddered as she opened the door and left, humming the tune. My eyes widened. I should have realised she was nuts back then.

Picking myself up, I brushed myself off, walked over to the door and watched as she left, entering the room to the far right.

Outside the barred window, the sound of a vehicle pulled up. Rushing over, I peered out, standing on my tiptoes. The black Mercedes was there, but another car pulled up alongside. A navy-blue BMW. The engine turned off. I wobbled; my feet flat to the ground. Grabbing hold of the damp wall, I steadied myself and stood on my tiptoes again. The driver's side door opened, and a brown-haired man stepped out. Walking towards me I shouted, tried to gain his attention "Help! Help!"

He stopped, turned, and walked over to the barred window. "Julia Jones."

I nodded, staring at him. The face of Detective Monroe stared back. I breathed a sigh of relief. He held out his hand as I pushed mine through the bars. Taking mine, he grinned. Shook it and let go. "I'll see you in hell, Julia," he said as he stood up, chuckling while walking away from me.

"No!" It can't be! He is in on it too? Who else was? They'd penetrated the police force, the hospital. Where else? I always knew the police force was corrupt, but to this magnitude. How many more monsters roamed the streets at night? They were meant to protect and serve, not destroy, and decimate. Was Melissa Lee a monster too?

I yawned, too tired to comprehend much more. My body had been through the mill. Besides the fact that no one would normally survive the torment I'd gone through, the mental anguish alone was hard enough. But part of me found solace because I'd found my mother's killer. Even if I couldn't do anything about it right now. To know she was simply trying to protect me means the entire world right now. I pulled my arms tight over my body. She loved me. I'd known that before. But now I knew that her last act as a mother was to save her daughter, and for that I'd be forever grateful.

As I settled into the damp corner, the moonlight wavered, and shadows came to dance and play. My mind met the drowsy reality of fatigue. With heavy eyelids and a slowing heart rate, I struggled to keep my eyes open any longer. I fell asleep to the sound of the torture and dismay, as the girls entered another death match, one where only one would last through the night.

CHAPTER TWENTY-SIX

When I awoke, I found myself strapped into the chair again. How the heck did I get here? Eddy stood beside me, tightening my neck strap. I wheezed for air.

I heard tutting coming from the side of the room. "Oh, Eddy boy, that's too tight. Her neck is still a fragile part of her."

"Sorry Clara," he said, loosening the strap. He quickly left the room.

Clara came into view, tilting the chair more upright so I could see my surroundings. Yep, we were back in the Doctor's operating theatre… or dentist surgery. Or… well, I didn't know which I'd prefer!

"My my Julia, what big eyes you've got," Clara said.

"Huh?" I asked.

"No princess, you say… all the better to see you with."

I frowned. "Are we really rehearsing Little Red Riding Hood right now?"

Clara frowned, pouting. "But it's your favourite book!"

"When I was like five, Clara!"

"Well, I liked it too," she said, stomping her foot down. Damn, she was acting childish right now.

The Doctor walked over. "Now now, you two, no squabbling."

Clara grinned, kissed his cheek, and skipped over to a chair, plonking herself down on it, watching me.

"What happened to her?"

"Nothing Julia, she likes to taunt and play with her prey."

"Prey?"

He laughed. I glared at him. "So why do you look ancient compared to my childish aunt then?" Clara hissed at me from her chair. The Doctor took a deep breath in and growled, releasing spittle as he did so.

"It's a rare condition Julia, I age quicker than humans."

"So, you're not human then?" He shook his head. "What are you?"

"That will become clear, eventually."

"So why do you age so quick?"

"Genetics," he said, laughing.

I shrugged. He lost me there.

I turned to Clara. "So why do you need me and why the hell have you associated yourself with the London Butcher and the world's shittiest doctor Clara?"

Clara huffed, then her smile raised, lips taught. "Each

Eddy is in charge of lots of things. But you knew that already, didn't you Julia?" She cackled, standing up and walking over to me. "Until you killed him," she smirked. "Your murderous appetite is already apparent, Julia." She danced around the laboratory, her hair flipping around as she swirled.

"Murder? I didn't kill him!"

She stopped. Her face an inch away. "No?" She puzzled. "Then who did?"

"FALCON," I smiled.

The doctor and Aunt Clara screeched out in joy. "Those flappy little birds," she dropped to the floor and howled in laughter. I watched. She was never as fruit loopy as this growing up! Whatever that husband of hers gave her sent her insane. The doctor tutted, turning back to his work. "They're no match for us," she screeched, getting up off the floor.

I frowned. *Of course they were. They had to be.* She watched me eagle eyed.

Clara smiled. "Your favourite foe was is in charge of operations. He found our recruits." Her eyebrows furrowed. "You're not the only one you know."

"Only one of what? What the hell did you do to me?"

She laughed as Jesus drew up a syringe of purple liquid, his right hand shaking in the process.

"Just two more doses and you'll be one of us," she smirked, dancing around the room. "The world needs to change. Welcome to the top of the food chain, baby." She cackled, her hair swishing as she swirled, coiling herself around me. Her body imitated the dance of a viper before it crushed its prey. Her hair tangled and twisted as hundreds of strands of snakes took form. Medusa arose, dancing her callous body around the room, paying special attention to the Doctor, then slithering out of the room into the other door where explosions blasted, ice storms crafted, and magic encapsulated the soul of every recruit around.

Consciousness was something I missed out on in this place. If it weren't for my firestorm wiping out my energy and sending me into a mini coma, it was the hazy purple liquid the doctor injected into me, sending me off to La La Land to snooze my days away. I wasn't sure how long I'd been in this place, but it felt like a while. Clara has said it'd be the last dose. But the last dose for what? I didn't feel any different. I ran my hands over my body. Everything was intact. No snakes for hair. I shuddered, picturing Clara's Medusa style image.

Sighing, I sat upright, feeling below me at the soft comfort the mattress gave me. They'd replaced it. *Thank heavens,* I sighed. After blasting through the last one, I'd thought I'd be sleeping on the floor from now on. Control is something I needed to master. I didn't fancy burning this one to a cinder.

Looking down at my hands, they appeared the same. My skin felt 'normal', body intact. I didn't know what the Doctor injected me with this time, but it didn't seem to have changed a damn thing. I took a deep breath and relaxed, looking around the darkened cell. It was still cold, damp and stunk of fish.

Sighing, I hugged my legs to my chest and sunk my head into my knees. I thought back to my friends, Lola,

Matty and Fi. They'd know something was wrong. Lola wouldn't rest until she'd found me. But what if they think I'm dead? No. They wouldn't believe it until they saw my cold, dead corpse in the morgue. I may feel alone, but I'm not. Someone will come.

A soft whisper of a smile enlightened my soul. Nathaniel. He could be that someone. He was different, inhuman, like me. If only we'd had time to have that conversation. I was sure he was some kind of shifter like Blake, but I needed him to tell me, in fact, show me himself.

I smiled, remembering the sensual kiss we shared on our first date. I had a huge crush on him. If I couldn't get myself out of this mess, I hoped Nathaniel would find me. He always seemed to show up at the right time.

Taking a deep breath, I sat upright. Gripping the side of the bed, straightening up more. *I will survive this!* No matter what they do to me, I will keep going. I still have so much life to live; twenty-two was no age to die.

I have to get out of here and take those girls with me. Then I'll blow the lid on the whole thing. People will think I'm nuts, but if I spin the mad scientist theme, it might actually be believable.

What if they thought we were freaks? What if the government locked us away, fearing our abilities? Shaking my head, I bit my bottom lip. We're not freaks, not me anyway… Clara on the other hand. I smirked. But those girls in there, they're just like me. Tortured souls tied up, broken, and twisted. We're not monsters, we're not humans, we're something in between.

Lola would say we're superheroes, but I wasn't feeling

very super right now! Although one thing she got right is we are super, we're beyond human, bigger, brighter, and better. We just have to believe it. Believe we can be more than the monsters he made us to be.

I won't kill the innocent for them. They're the monsters. A monster isn't down to what you look like or what you are, it's down to your actions and the way you live your life. So, I'll be the hero Lola wants me to be, and somehow, someday, I'll break free of this place, taking every one of those girls with me. I will succeed. I took a deep breath; I have to.

Outside the cell door, I could hear scratching and scraping. My brow furrowed. Now what?

"Who is it? I'm tired of all the fun and games. Just show your bloody self!"

"Err, o-okay…"

Two hands appeared through the barred window in the door. A face peered through, showing a very saddened Jimmy stood there.

"What do you want, Jimmy?"

"I've been told to come and get you, Julia," he said, his voice sheepish and slow.

"Fine. Why?"

"You're mad at me, aren't you?"

I rolled my eyes. "Whatever gave you that idea?"

"You did." I smirked. *Idiot.* "Father told me you had to come now."

"Father?"

"Yes Julia, we're cousins."

"Wait what?"

"My mum is your Auntie." Shit. I had a messed-up family.

"So, are you a monstrosity like them?"

"No. But my father is dying. He needs your help."

"Dying? Look, I know he's old and crippled, but he doesn't look like he's on death's door." Not yet anyway.

"He has a disease, Julia."

"I know that."

"So will you help him?"

"Help him? You want me to help the crazed psychopath that had me blown up then abducted?"

"Err… yes?"

"Err… how about no!"

He gripped the cell bars tighter. "Please Julia. They're the only family I've got."

"Didn't you just say I was your family?"

"Well, yes, but…"

"But nothing Jimmy. You don't treat anyone like this, especially not family!"

He sighed, releasing the bars. The lock turned, and he pulled the door open. "I had no choice," he said, stepping into the cell. "Come on, get up, we have to go, or he will get mad at me."

I huffed, stood up and followed him, balling my hands into fists. I was ready to fight my way out of this place if it was the last damn thing I'd do.

Walking past the girls' room, I could see one of the Eddy clones holding a girl's face down to the floor. The other girls were shouting at him, pleading he let her go. I sighed. Just another day in fucking paradise.

CHAPTER TWENTY-SEVEN

"Ah Julia, come sit down," the Doctor said, patting the chair.

I shuddered. He creeped me out. "So, what disease do you have, Jesus?" He looked up and glared at Jimmy. Jimmy held up his hands and backed out of the room.

"I have lived for a long time Julia, when my body degrades it needs to be reborn."

"What do you mean?"

"Much like you were reborn through fire. You are a phoenix, one of the rarest of creatures. Your ability will help me be reborn once again."

"So, you changed me to bring yourself back to life?" He nodded. "Are you a phoenix too?" he laughed.

"No my child, I am much more than you give me credit for."

"So, what are you?"

His brow furrowed and he grinned, showing his

sharpened teeth. "Let's see, shall we." Wheeling his chair over to me, he pulled out a syringe from behind his back. "Is this the last one?" He nodded. "What will happen to me?" I asked, my hands shaking.

"You will be magnificent, Julia. Just as I envisioned you to be."

He steadied the needle in a tray and wheeled closer on his chair. I backed as deep into the chair as I could. Achieving absolutely nothing. I sighed. There was no way out of this. The door was locked. Window barred. The only strange thing in here was the huge mirror. I could break that, use it to slice and dice him? What am I thinking? Psycho over here may look old and weak, but he sure packed a punch.

"Are you ready?"

"I have one more question first."

He huffed. "You humans have too many questions."

"Why me?"

"Did Clara not tell you, child?" I shook my head and huffed *I'm not a child!* "Your bloodline stems from Mathilda, the original phoenix. Mathilda and I were well acquainted, she gave me life after life. But she did not agree with my vision going forward, so she had her powers removed. Her ability to be reborn died with her."

"But how have you remained alive without her?"

"The blood of my own kind sustains me. But it does not rectify the process of ageing."

"Shouldn't you have been six feet under years ago?"

"Centuries ago, my child. But with my scientific advances, I have been able to produce a serum to solidify my body into one time. Remaining the same age for quite some time."

"So, my aunt really did marry an old man?"

He stifled back a laugh. "In your terms, yes, she did. But Clara shares my vision."

"So why not change her? She wanted it after all."

"Because she was too old when I met her. The process of reversing your DNA has taken years. Mathilda did not just remove her powers, she ensured future generations could not use them."

"So why do you think you can use them?"

His brow furrowed. "Because I am the greatest doctor out there. My scientific methods are years beyond your own."

I laughed. "Let me guess. You tried it on Clara, and she ended up mutated just like the rest of the girls."

Clenching his fists, he slammed down the tray. "Too many questions, child. That is enough!"

I turned away, bracing myself for a beating. Taking a deep breath, I considered walloping him right there and then. But then I'd face the serpent lady and god knows how many clones. I'd be risking my life and putting the girls' lives in danger. I expect they would use them against me. After all, it's what I would do.

"This will show us your full potential, Julia," he said as he injected the needle into my neck. My body screamed, vision blurred, heat rising, as bile rushed up to my throat. Anger filtered through my veins. The room was alight as he clapped, taking hold of my hand. The leather seat below me turned to ash as my body released itself from its cage.

"What did you do to me?" I screamed. My body knew nothing but pain. Every nerve ignited, shocks of severity rushed through me. I contorted and convulsed. Seizing as my brain turned to fire. Nothing could have ever prepared me for the intensity of the shocks. The seizure itself screamed out at a whole new level. It was at that one moment, the purest instance of agony that I realised, today I would die.

The doctor held my hand tighter. Shouting through my screams. "The serum will finalise your change, Julia." I continued to scream, my throat pulling apart from the deafening reality of my situation. "Your phoenix will rise," he yelled. "We will be reborn, remade. We will never die again!" With the fire, my pain began to ease. He stood up, pulling me up and towards him. "We are connected, Julia. Throughout time, the future is ours." Gripping my burning hand tighter, he grinned. "We will reshape this world as our own!"

He absorbed the fire surrounding me. Jesus inhaled, his face a picture of ecstasy as he appeared to enjoy being burnt to death. I tried to pull away, but he gripped harder, laughing, cackling as his skin barbecued right before my eyes. What the actual hell was he doing?

Clara ran to the door. "Julia, look at yourself glow." She pulled open the door and ran in, shielding herself behind the mirror, one that reflected my true form. "You're a phoenix, Julia, you're beautiful!" she squealed.

My hair smouldered in the blaze, my body alight with life itself. Flaming wings bore life to the world behind me. I was the epiphany of rebirth, a phoenix in flame, consumed by the aura of an inferno of power. Jesus held onto my hand as the heat scorched his body, turning his skin to embers.

"It's working, baby, it's working," Clara yelled, peeking from around the back of the mirror. The doctor gave no answer. "Jesus?" Clara asked, looking around. "No!" she yelled as she flung the mirror to the side. "You're killing him!" she screamed. The mirror smashed against the wall, and an angered Clara transformed into Medusa before me. "Why Julia?" she hissed. "Why?"

I looked down at Jesus's body. He'd let go; his body charred down to the frail husk of what he once was. Whatever he was, he was no more. But why, why would he hold on like that, killing himself in the process?

The hissing of snakes sounded in my ear as Clara screamed, "No! He wasn't meant to die from this! You stupid, stupid girl!"

Kicking me sideways, I fell to the ground. Everything around me burst into flame. Laboratory chemicals ignited, fizzling, and popping from the heat of the inferno; I was the perfect incendiary device.

Clara twisted, rippled, and conformed. Underneath the coat of her skin, snakes burst out, fangs bared, poison coating them as she seethed, crazy from her broken heart.

Serpents fled her skin coat as she became a force of nature before me. Slinking forward, she hissed and spat. Individual snakes slithered towards me, aiming their bite at my bare skin. All but one burned before it bit down, the last larger than the others, lasting a millisecond longer, enough time to inject poison into my body, I yelped, but the fire burned out the poison as quick as it came.

Clara rushed forward, wrapping her scaly body around

mine. Screams agonised my eardrum as her skin blistered and boiled. Squeezing tighter, tighter still, my body convulsed, panicking for air. Flame dwindled around me as my phoenix figure fought to stay alive. She hissed, her body crushing my own. I gasped out for air. Ribs cracking, bones shattering, my lungs were squeezed tight. I screamed out in agony. Memories of my mother, family, and friends flashed before my eyes.

Was this the end? My last moments? Would I be reborn from the ash? It didn't matter, even with no breath in my lungs she could not hang on any longer. Clara's body was not made to withstand the heat of my skin, the fire alive within me. I burned, and she burned, and as any supernatural assailant would know, there was no escaping the fire of the phoenix.

Struggling to hold on, her reptilian skin burnt down to a crisp, nerve endings shot, fatty tissue bubbled and blistered. She wept as she smouldered; the stench of her burning body engulfing the air. Bit by bit she passed away. Taking her last breath, her body turned to ash, ignited by the hottest of flames and destroyed by the very creature she had made me to be.

With the release of my dead aunt's grip, my body soared, igniting to its full potential. Through my eyes, I could see the heat signatures of living bodies in the next room. Hear the high-pitched cries of torture and dismay. I had the power now. The ultimate strength, and with my newfound ability; I was going to bloody well use it for some good. I stepped over the Doctor's fallen body, bypassed my aunt's smoking corpse. The first thing on my agenda was to take down every bloody Eddy clone in this godforsaken place!

Gliding through the room, I left a trail of flames in my wake. I entered the girl's room. Over twenty girls screamed and cowered, not knowing whether to run, fight or hug me. None of which would have helped the situation. All the girls remained chained to their beds; ankles red raw from the endless friction caused. Three Eddy clones stood in the centre. One had his hands around the neck of a petite blond, raising her up in the air. The other two watched, jaw dropped as they turned and saw me enter.

The main Eddy sent the other two running straight for me as he squeezed every living breath out of the poor girl's lungs. Her comrades cried, screamed for their friend to be released. I stood blazing, the flames wrapping themselves around, protecting me. The two Eddy's didn't stand a chance. The first Eddy grabbed my wrist. I turned to face him, concentrating on his arm as my flames slinked their way up and over his skin, dashing up to his shoulder, absorbing the fabrics on his chest and gripping his body through the inferno they thrived in. It wasn't long before his screams diminished, his vocal chords melting away with the heat.

The other Eddy stood motionless, watching his brother wither away. His eyes were wide, face withdrawn. He looked up at me as his brother's ashen corpse fell to the ground. Eyes pleading, he backed away. I was mesmerised. I had never seen Eddy Boland like this; he was the spitting image. Yet undeniable fear wreaked out of him. He turned and ran, bolting past me as I stepped towards him. I must have been a magnificent monstrosity if I sent an Eddy clone running. Unsure whether to grin or cry at the fear my body caused,

I stepped forward.

Raising my head, I saw the petite blond girl's body had slowed and stilled. Her breathing faltered. She no longer had the will to carry on. I remember that feeling. The moment every cell within me roared out in pain. She would not become his next victim! Standing tall, I held out my arms. Flames encircled as the phoenix inside let itself be known. Wings grew from flame, strength came from within, and I ran as fast as I could towards them.

My fists pummelled, body determined. I punched out, my hand connecting with Eddy's chest. He hurdled backwards, dropping the girl into the process. Her limp body slid across the floor, slamming against the metal bars of one of the girl's legs. The young ginger haired girl leapt off her bed, picked the petite blond's head up, placed it on her lap and laid her hands on her chest. A bright white light encircled her hands. The petite body convulsed and shook. Ginger hummed, louder and louder, her voice vibrating throughout the room. Finally, she pushed down hard, pulled back, and the petite blond opened her eyes. Even after all the malice and murder, the doctor had created something wondrous in this ginger-haired girl. He'd created a healer, and blondie lived because of it.

Eddy stirred, shook his head, and jumped up. His bulky legs ran as his thick, brutish figure sprinted towards me.

"Back the fuck off, Eddy!" I yelled. He roared as he ran, harder, faster. His thick hand connected with my head, punching me with all his might. There were two problems with this moment, and to slow it down, you would see why. The impact of said punch plainly knocked me off my feet, flying up and out of the door, landing smack bang down on the cold hard concrete. He'd knocked me out cold, as dead as a doornail.

The second particular problem was now that I was out cold, there was nothing protecting the girls from Eddy. In my comatose state, I never realised that the petite blond was already up and melting the chains, releasing every girl. Nor did I see that twenty-seven girls rose, joined hands and turned on Eddy; beating the living shit out of him. I should have seen that coming. Except I didn't. I was still unconscious, dying in a slobbering pile of damp, on the hard ashen floor.

As my flames dwindled, the final view I had was of one girl in particular. She walked over to me, her dark blue hair swishing over her shoulders. Bending down her silver streak fell forward, and she wrapped it around her ear. "Thank you," she said. Leaning down, she brushed her hand over my cool face and covered my body with a blanket. Ginger ran over, and that's all I remember of that life.

CHAPTER TWENTY-EIGHT

Rebirth is a thing. Yet not a thing I'd needed to use. Ginger had healed me, brought me back to the land of the living.

"JULIA!" a male voice yelled. He used my name. He only uses my name when shit's going down! A hoard of men thumped and fisted their way into the room. I jumped up, panic-stricken. Dazed and confused, I could see Ginger and the blue haired girl staring at me. Stumbling to stand, the blanket fell off me. I looked down at my naked body and yelped. Flames ignited, covering my modesty as the phoenix within protected me. The girls backed off, wary of what I could do.

Running towards me was the familiar face of another monster, but not a monster to fear or run from. This supernatural's face was the face of my very own sexy saviour. The man that had been there from the very start. The one and only Nathaniel Night.

Nathaniel's morphed face gave promise to the notion of Vampires and Werewolves, like those depicted in the story books. I watched him as he jumped through the air, over Eddy's ashen body, and it hit me as it confirmed it, he too was a creature of this war. Were we both destined to meet and destroy humanity once and for all? Was Clara, right? If the war was coming, had she changed me to protect me all this time?

No, fuck that. I shuddered. Who stabs a child and injects them with something that could kill them? Mum had found out, and they'd killed her to keep her quiet. None of this was right. They'd been covering up the murdering of innocent people for far too long. No matter how you look at it. They're the unnatural ones and now I'm part of this shitty army, too.

Another clone bounded his way after Blake, who shot his grappling hook up to clamber the walls, perching above him. He shot down, straight through Eddy's hulked body. Jimmy ran through screaming as Eddy lay in a bloody mess on the floor.

"Julia?" Nathaniel said, stepping towards me; his face full of concern. His clawed hand reached out through the flames, touching my emblazoned cheekbone. Pain and anguish soothed my heart. He had the face of a wolf, and I the face of fire, yet somehow, I felt, we were meant to be.

Blake barged over. Men in black suits, all adorned with the symbol of the falcon, stood behind him. He stopped and stared at the girls, some hiding behind their bed covers. Blake walked over as his men began to enter their room. "Julia? Julia Jones?" he asked.

I backed away. "Yes?" Blake lifted his weapon.

"Don't you dare hurt her!" Nathaniel yelled, standing in front of me.

"Okay, okay," he said. Placing his weapon on the floor. "But Nathaniel, your hair is smoking," he said. I backed away as Nathaniel hopped forward, away from me. Blake laughed. "It's okay Julia, I won't hurt you." He smiled. Was he being sincere? "We tested your blood, remember; you've been different for quite some time." I shuddered at the thought of it, the memories of the FALCON underworld flooding back.

Nathaniel's hand reached out for my hand; singed hair took over my senses. I pulled back, looking into Nathaniel's eyes. I couldn't hurt him. "It's okay Julia, look," he said, showing me his hand. Burnt skin healed as he stepped forward again.

"No wait," I said. Afraid I'd hurt him even more.

"It's okay," he said as he stepped forward to hold me tight. His body stiffened as he set ablaze with my flames. His hold on me was strong. He soothed my hair, kissed my face, and as the pain and anguish from my heart softened, I felt it. My grip on reality wavered. Fingernails unclasped my palms. Tears welled in my smouldering eye sockets, steaming themselves away one drop at a time. My bodily inferno dissipated, sitting beneath my skin, shielding me from harm.

I looked around at all the devastation. Was this me? Had I caused this? "I'm sorry," I said, looking down at the Eddy clone's body. "I didn't mean to kill them."

Blake nodded, and said, "Technically Julia, he wasn't a

he. By all accounts these beings were a clone of the original we had already disposed of."

Nathaniel pulled back, his body naked of hair, skin stitching back together. "He means you did nothing wrong."

"But," I said as Nathaniel pulled a blanket from one of the empty beds and covered me over, "my Aunt and the doctor."

Nathaniel's brow furrowed.

Blake stepped forward. "What about them?"

I pointed into the other room and Blake walked over; we followed.

Blake stood in the doorway. "He wouldn't let go, then my aunt tried to crush me, and the flames took over."

"I see," he said. I stepped back and Nathaniel stepped in front of me. "Back off Nathaniel, I will not hurt her." He turned and looked over my shoulder. "Soldier," he shouted, ordering one of the suited men over.

The soldier walked over, watching me, giving me space as he walked past me. He reached the doctor, touched the corpse, and jumped backwards. "What?" Nathaniel said, pulling the blanket tighter around me, covering my ashen body.

"It moved," the soldier said.

"Don't be stupid," Blake said, "he's dead, take him away."

The soldier moved in closer. Nathaniel watched as the doctor's body twitched. He jumped back, pushing me behind him. "He's alive," Nathaniel said.

"What! He can't be," I said, with fear in my voice.

Blake moved in, kicking the corpse. Jesus twitched, his body spasmed and seized as every ounce of molten skin fell away from him. He shed like a snake, swirling and twirling into a creature of venomous beauty.

Jesus rose from the ashes as a vibrant young man. A toned pale body and venomous fangs brought life to a vampire. His arm crushed the neck of the soldier in an instant, speeding past Blake and his army of men, gone in a flash of sanity.

How? How did he shed his skin like that? Had he wanted me to burn his old body to begin the shedding of his withering skin? But why didn't Clara know that? Surely she knew he'd come back to her, but as a fresher, younger, more vibrant man than he used to be.

"Shit." Nathaniel said. "Did that just happen?"

Blake nodded. He looked at me. "Now that, Julia, was an original Vampire."

Nathaniel nodded. "I thought they'd been wiped out years ago."

"Apparently not."

I shuddered. "But aren't vampires supposed to drink blood to stay young?"

Blake laughed. "Oh, they do, and as you know, they use it to read people's memories. But the Doctor still ages like us, all the originals did. They could only ever be reborn through the flames of another's soul."

I winced. Had I just birthed the world a new vampire? "Is that why they were wiped out?"

"What do you mean?"

"Because there weren't any fire types like me?"

Nathaniel nodded. "Yes, it looks like the doctor has been seeking to cure his own illness by working to create a phoenix for many years now."

"Great," I said, lips pursed.

"Oh well, it looks like you're part of the club now."

Blake laughed. "As long as you're on the good side, you'll remain on my better side."

I shuddered. "Yeah, I don't exactly want to be thrown from any windows any time soon."

Nathaniel laughed.

"Err, sir," a young recruit shouted from the other room. "SIR!"

"WHAT, PRIVATE?" Blake shouted.

"Sir, you best come here."

We entered the main room where Jimmy lay on the floor in handcuffs, playing cards littering the floor.

An army of young women hobbled from the other room. The girls that were chained up. They looked more like mismatched runaways than civilised ladies, all mixed up with magical powers and monstrous appetites. Shit. They took form, lining up, ready to do battle. This was what they'd trained for. Did they see FALCON as a threat? Blake and his men took form, both sides eyeing up for a battle. It'd be carnage. There was no way this could happen. Those women, some of them, were mere girls. I recognised three of them as the Sweet Beta sorority sisters. I'd written a piece on their disappearance a few years back.

I stepped forward, stood before the girls, in between

them and Blake's team of hunters. Nathaniel nodded, took my hand, and stood beside me.

"Blake, tell your men to stand down. There's no fight here," he said.

I turned to face the head girl, the larger, taller one with red hair. "We mean you no harm," I said. She stomped forward; her face full of ice with ice shaped swords in either hand.

"Please," I said. "We don't want to hurt you." Heck, who was I kidding? I couldn't fight to save my life. I was screwed, hiding behind a wolf and a team of god knows what creatures. That army of sorority girls would win hands down.

Nathaniel stepped backwards. "We'll go, we won't cause you any trouble." Blake and his men stepped backwards. There was no way any of FALCON would win this battle.

I looked up at the icy girl and smiled. "Stay safe," I said, as we all turned to leave the room.

"Wait," the head girl with rose red hair said. I stopped and turned back around. "But what do we do now?"

"What do you mean?"

"The war?" she asked. "What do we do now?"

"You live your lives," I said, stepping towards her. "There doesn't need to be a war. We can live in peace, we have to. Too many have died for nothing." She nodded. I reached out and took her hand. Water dripped from our palms as fire and ice eased the panic in the room. "Who were you before?"

"I, I think my name was Rose."

"Rose Livingston?"

She nodded.

"You've been missing for over a year now; your parents have been frantically trying to find you."

"My mum?"

I nodded. I wrote an article on her last year. Met her mum, too. Rose's ice melted as she flung herself forward and held me tight. Tears fell from both of us as the rest of the women stepped forward.

"I was training to be a lawyer," the blue haired woman said, falling to her knees. I remembered her as the one that was playing with electric blue light, dancing it around her hands. "My name was Devan, Devan Midnight. I had a daughter," she cried. "Please tell me she's alive." I let go of Rose and knelt down with Devan.

"I'm not sure, but I promise I'll find out for you."

The petite blond walked over hand in hand with the ginger haired girl that saved her. "Thank you for helping me," the blond said. "I'm Clemmie, from Massachusetts."

"You're a long way from home Clemmie, how did you end up in the UK?"

"University. I was at Oxford University when he came. He took me, Roxy and Stacey in the night." The ginger-haired girl holding her hand smiled and nodded. "Stacey didn't make it."

My face softened as I nodded and stood up. "When were you taken?"

"I don't know, we lost count after six hundred and seventy-two days."

"Oh honey," I said, shaking my head. "What year was it?"

"November 2017."

I sighed, placed my hand on Clemmie's shoulder and spoke, "That was five years ago, Clemmie." Roxy gasped. "It's a miracle you both survived as long as you did."

"We're not the ones that have been here the longest."

"Who has?"

Clemmie pointed to Devan, who was now sitting with a grey blanket wrapped around her shoulders, talking to a female soldier. I nodded. It was going to be hard to bring back every one of these poor girls. The trauma alone would take years to overcome, let alone the physical modifications he had made to all of us.

Out of the darkened room, twenty-seven voices sounded out into the light. Women from every walk of life. Some had been beaten, battered, and burned. Test subjects and broken bodies. Nathaniel, Blake, and I walked through the chaos, taking hand by hand of the forgotten souls. Some had been here for seven years, seven whole years, right after they killed my mum. There were many amongst them that had already withered and died. Starvation for some, incarnation of powers destroying the others. It had been a prison and only the fittest had survived.

From all accounts, I'd been the first test subject. The first that had survived, anyway. Looking at the doctor's files, they'd watched me throughout my life, injecting me when I was three years old. From that day on, I had no longer been human. Blake said the reason I hadn't shown powers was because I hadn't had a large enough dose in my system.

That final dose that Eddy gave me had awoken the power from within and, like a phoenix, I had risen from the ashes, ready to live again.

Blake collected all the girls together, arranged for transport, and we left the hellhole that had been in their lives for the first time in a very long time.

As we were walking out, Devan came over and took my hand. I remembered her face as the one who soothed me as I fell into an unconscious state. "I would rather we walk," she said. Nathaniel stepped forward and nodded. He saw the relief on her face, on all their faces, and he understood. They had been trapped in darkness for far too long. The last thing any of them wanted was to step into another dark place, in the back of a truck.

Nathaniel let go of my other hand and walked over to Blake. A few raised voices, a heated debate later, and we were walking through the main street in London city central.

FALCON protected us from all sides. Crowds of people embarked; camera phones and social media at the ready. I wasn't sure if FALCON was protecting us or protecting the mortal kind from us. After all, my hands kept igniting. I was semi-naked with a blanket wrapped around me and Nathaniel's leather jacket for extra warmth… not that I needed it. But it wasn't just me the public were wide-eyed and open-mouthed about, it was the fact that twenty-seven dirtied, bare-foot women were walking down the cold wet road of Main Street, brandishing a variety of magical powers.

Devan delighted in showing hordes of people her dance of electric delight. Roxy enjoyed placing her hands on the public, healing their woes, and walking amongst them like a goddess in her very own kingdom. Rose iced the park we passed by so the children could skate and play with the sculptures she created, and Heather shapeshifted, changed the shape of her face, as she mimicked the faces of her onlookers, both scaring and enchanting their minds.

Out of the darkness came an array of other magical creatures. They followed suit, walking behind us in peace, parading through the centre of London.

We were the eye-opening display of a new reality, a new dawn, and a new hope. We were the mutated, and for now we were only the beginning.

TO BE CONTINUED IN:
THE RISE OF THE VAMPIRE KING.

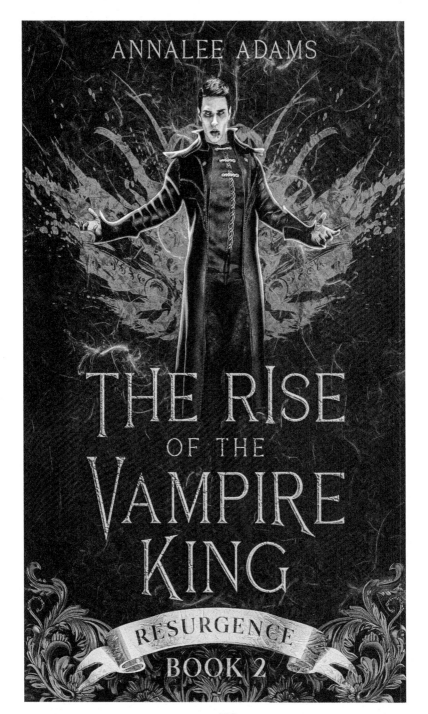

Other books by Annalee Adams

In this universe:
The Resurgence series:
The Heart of the Phoenix
The Rise of the Vampire King (out October 2022)
The Fall of the Immortals (out November 2022)

The Fire Wolf Prophecies:
Crimson Bride (out December 2022)
Crimson Army (out 2023)

The Shop Series:
Stake Sandwich
The Devil Made Me Do It
Strawberry Daiquiri Desire (out December 2022)

Other books not in this universe:
The Celestial Rose Series:
Eternal Entity
Eternal Creation
Eternal Devastation
Eternal Ending

Gruesome Fairy Tales:
Gretel
Hansel

ABOUT ANNALEE

Annalee Adams lives in England with her Husband, two children and a zoo worth of animals. She loves a good strong cup of tea or coffee, plenty of chocolate and binge watching her shows on Netflix.

Annalee began her career with the Celestial Rose series while at University. She spent much of her childhood engrossed in fictional stories, starting with teenage point horror books and moving up to the works of Stephen King and Dean Koontz. However, her all-time favourite book is Lewis Carroll's, Alice in Wonderland -which explains her mindset quite well.

CONNECT WITH ANNALEE

Join Annalee on social media. She is regularly posting videos and updates for her next books on TikTok and Facebook.

Join Annalee in her Facebook group:
Annalee Adams Bookworms & Bibliophiles.

Also, subscribe to Annalees newsletter through her website - for free books, sales, sneak previews and much more.
Subscribe at www.AnnaleeAdams.biz

TikTok: @author_annaleeadams

Website: www.AnnaleeAdams.biz

Email: AuthorAnnaleeAdams@gmail.com

Twitter: https://twitter.com/AuthorAnnalee

Facebook:
https://www.facebook.com/authorannaleeadams/

Printed in Great Britain
by Amazon